Maggie Gibson lives in the west of Ireland with her dog.

Also by Maggie Gibson

Deadly Serious
The Longest Fraud
Grace, the Hooker, the Hardman and the Kid
Alice Little and the Big Girl's Blouse
First Holy Chameleon

The Flight
of Lucy Spoon

Maggie Gibson

ORION

An Orion paperback

First published in Great Britain in 1999
by Victor Gollancz
This paperback edition published in 2001
by Orion Books Ltd,
Orion House, 5 Upper St Martin's Lane,
London WC2H 9EA

A CIP catalogue record for this book is available
from the British Library.

ISBN 0 57540 331 4

Printed and bound in Great Britain by
Clays Ltd, St Ives plc

For Auntie Mary

Acknowledgements

With thanks to Katy Egan, George Capel, Christine Kidney, Selina Walker and Rosie de Courcy. Also thanks to the late Kate Cruise O'Brien for giving me my first break.

Glossary

Culchie: Derogatory term used by city dwellers when referring to rural folk.

ESB: Electricity Supply Board.

Garda Siochana: Irish police.

Gardai: Collective term for the Irish Police.

Gurriers: Young delinquents.

Holliers: Holidays.

Knackers: Derogatory term for a gypsy or member of the underclass.

Left footer: More usually used by Northern Protestants to describe Catholics, but also used by Catholics in the South to describe Protestants.

Mauldy: Mouldy.

Chapter One

Lucy Spoon lay on her back and watched a penguin, wearing a sun hat, marching across the ceiling towards the window. The hat was new. It had appeared after a storm lifted a slate and the rain got in again. She turned on to her side and squinted at the damp patch. He was carrying a suitcase now. Maybe it was a sign.

Her ears were wet. Tears in my ears, she thought, and an ironic snigger escaped. Normal folk had tears in their eyes. Only she cried silently in the dark, lying on her back, staring at the ceiling, dreaming of escape.

A sudden draft flared the curtains and the bedroom door rattled. He stirred next to her, rolled on to his back and, after a certain amount of snuffling, continued to snore. Loud, epiglottal, slobbery, porcine snorts. In the dimness, she watched his chest rise and fall. He stirred again and smacked his lips, then took a rumbling breath and stopped, his chest fully expanded. Lucy waited. Hoped. How long before his brain would be starved of oxygen causing immediate brain damage and ultimately death? After ten seconds or so he exhaled like a Harley Davidson, and yanked the duvet off her as he rolled over on to his side again.

Rain lashed against the window and the wind battered the frame. It was cold. She shivered and tugged at the edge of the bedclothes, trying to reclaim a few inches. More slurping sounds from his side, then the cover slid back over her. She snuggled under it, holding it up around her ears. Her nose was freezing.

Wide awake now, she gave up and slid out of bed, grabbing her dressing-gown from the chair and wrapping it around her against the numbing cold. It felt damp. The mist on the Wicklow mountains left everything damp. At the bottom of the stairs she picked her sheepskin coat off the newel post and put it over the dressing-gown. Cold radiated up from the flagged floor through the soles of her thick woollen socks.

The kitchen was warm, though, and the old iron range still lit. She opened the door, threw on a shovel of fuel. Sparks flew as the coal hit the hot embers. She sat in front of the open door with her feet on the fender and warmed her hands and knees. Fionn, still drowsy, stretched herself and yawned. Lucy leaned over and scratched her behind the ear. The dog licked her hand, wagged her tail and went back to sleep. Too early. Too cold even to think of going outside for a pee.

After a while Lucy stood up and peeled off the sheepskin, dressing-gown, old shrunken cardie and flannel night-dress. The heat from the range hit her skin and she felt a wave of pleasure at the comfort of it. She dressed quickly in the layers of clothing she always wore. Knickers, leggings, two pairs of woollen tights with thick socks over the top, long-sleeved vest, deliciously warm from where she had hung it on the rack above the stove the night before, denim shirt, long heavy cotton skirt, hand-knit thick stripy jumper, ancient Timberland boots and fingerless gloves.

She heard a distant rumble of thunder, then the light dimmed and recovered. She pulled back the curtain and peered out into the darkness, hoping for lightning, but saw only her reflection in the glass. She ran her fingers through her hair, raking out the tangles. Warm now. Time for tea.

She filled the electric kettle and plugged it in.

Zzzapp! Two hundred and fifty volts shot up her arm, throwing her back against the dresser. Wallop! Dishes crashed to the floor and the milk jug shattered, splattering its contents up the walls and everywhere. The kettle bounced across the room. Fionn barked furiously in fright, hackles up.

Lucy sat dazed in a heap. Her left hand was numb and her arm still tingled.

Footsteps from the room above. Thump, thump, thump down the stairs, roaring, 'What the fuckin' hell's happening?' No, 'Are you OK?' No, 'Are you hurt, pet?'

She did hurt. Her back hurt where she'd collided with the sharp corner of the dresser, her ears were ringing and her head ached. She looked up at him. Then at the kettle, then hesitated.

'Em . . . nothing . . . I just slipped,' she said. 'Could you – could you put the kettle on?'

The dog padded over looking concerned. Lucy grabbed her collar.

His eyes were bloodshot from the night before and his hair was standing on end. A vision in off-white saggy long-johns. White flabby flesh. Angry with her for snatching him from sleep. Angry at the world for spoiling his life. Angry about everything.

He scratched his armpit. He scratched his beard and shook his head. 'Dozy stupid bitch,' he muttered as he bent to pick up the kettle and refilled it. Water gushed from the tap and splashed him, soaking the front of his vest.

'Clumsy fucking cretin. Now look what you made me fucking do.'

She flinched back as he reached towards the socket. She closed her eyes as he hit the switch. Then . . . nothing. He clicked the switch on, off. On, off. Nothing. That's when she knew that the bastard was fucking immortal.

At thirty-nine and three-quarters, Lucy Spoon was a little the worse for wear. Hippiedom doesn't sit well on the over thirties. A long road of too many drugs absorbed through the system, too much drink. Somewhere around the middle of the eighties, hippies metamorphosed into new-age travellers, and Lucy didn't travel. That was the trouble. She wanted

3

to get away. She wished with all her heart to be somewhere else, but she didn't know where. She had no idea how. Years of living with Marcus had drained her brain of rational constructive thought. Marcus had been a dreamer once. Now he lived his life in a state of disappointment and he was very, very angry.

They had met when she was nineteen. She was an art student in her second year at Hornsey College. She was good. Had talent. He was Irish. Ten years older. Had dropped out. They had met at the top of Glastonbury Tor. The Spring Solstice. Dawn. The sun rising, crimson and gold behind the ruins of the tower. She had followed him back to Ireland and they moved into a stone cottage an old uncle had left him in the Wicklow Hills. Very romantic. He'd been sexy then. Tall, slim and tanned. Had travelled the world, or so he said. Now she doubted that. Marcus only ever made grand plans. Impossible schemes to make his fortune. Their fortune. The trouble with Marcus was, he never had a realistic, achievable goal. Thus his disappointment.

There had been many projects through the years. There was the great candle scheme, for one. She was quite content making enough coloured carved candles to sell at the local market. But that wouldn't do. Painstakingly, Marcus had worked out how many candles she could produce in a given time, making moulds from her original carvings. He worked out to the penny how much profit they could make per candle. How rich they would be when he got the export market going. What grants they could get from the government. By the end of the day he was close to his second million. That was as far as it went. The plan had become so big and complicated it was impossible for him to settle for less. To do so would mean failure.

Another brainwave was the amazing foolproof individual ready-made trifle plan. One day Marcus found a case of small plastic beakers which had fallen off the back of a lorry (*really* fallen off the back of a lorry) and, for no apparent reason, decided that they should make individual trifles for sale to the catering trade. He dragged Lucy round the Cash & Carry, and they stocked up on jelly and catering tins of custard powder and UHT cream. Marcus was full of enthusiasm as usual, though by this time Lucy, knowing his track record, had her doubts. She tried to reason with him, but he accused her of not having faith in him. Of being disloyal. Consumed with guilt, she helped him. He wasn't too happy when she suggested that maybe he was adding too much water to the jelly, or perhaps they should make smaller batches of custard. This time he played the 'I know what I'm doing, you're always criticising' card. The jelly wouldn't set. The cream wouldn't whip. The custard was lumpy. And she hadn't the heart or the courage to say I told you so. He sank into a deep depression and blamed her for the failure.

If Lucy looked back she would have had to agree that, although all of Marcus's other get-rich-quick schemes had come to nothing, the failure of the great foolproof ready-made individual trifle plan was the turning point. Marcus got angry. With her. With the world. With life in general. After that, everyone was thick/stupid/moronic. The world, including Lucy, was conspiring against him. Trying to ruin his life. He was the only sane and sensible person alive. She was the butt of his frustration. It was left to her to put a crust on the table and this she managed quite well. There were the candles. She sold eggs from her flock of chickens, all of whom had names. She grew organic vegetables on a little plot behind the house, and a small quantity of cannabis for their own consumption in pots on the living-room window-sill. She drew charcoal portraits for tourists in the summer and between times sold the odd canvas. He would sit outside the market and wait for her. He was jealous if she talked to anyone. Watched her like a hawk. Alienated all her friends. He was envious of her talent and belittled her work. Because of that, she lost confidence and stopped painting. He had her total attention. He made himself the centre of her universe, believing that this state of affairs was normal and acceptable.

The truth was that Marcus wasn't the centre of Lucy's

universe, at least not in the way he believed. Lucy was afraid of him. Terrified of his temper and his mood swings. Not that he ever raised a hand against her, but there was always that threat in the black screaming rages that consumed him without warning. They sapped her energy. Drained her emotions. Lucy would have been quite content with her lot if only Marcus had been nice to her. Even though she didn't love him any more; didn't even like him any more. But he couldn't be nice because he depended on her. He needed her to look after him. He required someone around whom he could blame. He couldn't do without her, and he hated and punished her for it.

Maybe it was the electric shock. Perhaps that was the straw that broke the camel's back. But, on Monday, 4 November, at six forty-five a.m., Lucy Spoon knew that she had to get away.

Chapter Two

Jodie McDeal rattled the key in the front door. The lock didn't budge. Puzzled, she checked to make sure she had the right key and tried again. Same result, or rather lack of a result. The door stayed firmly locked. She heard movement inside. The thought crossed her mind briefly that maybe it was a burglar, but she dismissed the idea immediately. No one in their right mind would dare to rob Rogan Hogan's woman. Not if they valued their lives. Not if they wanted to hold on to all their limbs and avoid brain damage. He wasn't called the Grim Reaper for nothing.

She peered at the lock, checking to see if there was an obstruction. Maybe the kids she'd told to sod off on Hallowe'en night had squirted superglue in it to get even. As she was poking at the lock, Gnasher Gill, Hogan's minder, general assassin and handyman opened the door. All six foot odd and twenty-nine million stone of him.

'What the hell are you doing in my house?' she demanded as she tried to push past him.

He stood four-square, filling the doorway. 'Sorry,' he said, sounding far from it. 'More'n my job's worth.'

'Piss off, you pig-thick eejit.' She shoved him in the chest, but he didn't budge. He stood there with his arms folded across his chest. He had a smug smirk on his face, and his lizardy eyes gave him a look of a python who'd just swallowed a goat. Any minute she expected a forked tongue to flick out between his podgy lips.

Two can play at that game, she thought. She delved into

her bag and rooted out her phone. But he didn't react. Just stood there sneering at her. Was he tired of living? Had the last atom of grey matter in what passed as his brain given up the ghost? She glared at him, and started to dial Hogan's number.

Gnasher swiped the phone from her hand. 'You don't geddit, do yeh? Yer out.'

'What?' She was angry with him now. You can only make so many excuses for the brain dead. 'Give me back my frigging phone, you moron!' She thumped his chest as hard as she could. He didn't notice. He held the phone up in the air, way out of her reach. She resisted the urge to jump up and down in a vain attempt to grab it.

'Yeh won't be needin' it. Misther Hogan's got a young wan, an' you're history. He's taken her on the holliers.' In the telling she felt he exhibited more glee than was kind in the circumstances.

It stopped her in her tracks.

'What are you talking about? What d'you mean, a young wan – one? What do you mean history?' As she spoke, the truth dawned. If what Rogan's ape was saying was for real, she had just been dumped. Unceremoniously, cruelly, without any warning, dumped. He must have planned it. The locks changed and her only out of the house for an hour? The bastard! The unspeakable bastard.

Realising brute force wouldn't get her past Gnasher, she decided to try charm. 'OK, Gnasher,' she said calmly. 'I get the message. Just let me go inside and pack my things.'

Gnasher looked uncertain. He hadn't expected this. He'd been looking forward to having an excuse to give her a good smack. 'Sorry. No can do,' he said.

'But it's my stuff, Gnasher' – still trying to be reasonable. 'I need my clothes. My bits and pieces.'

He ignored that. 'An' I'll need the keys fer the Merc.'

To hell with charm. She exploded. 'The Merc? Are you out of your tiny mind? I'm not giving you the keys of my fucking car!'

8

'It's Misther Hogan's car, s'not yours.'

'It is mine!' – indignant.

'S'not.'

This was getting her nowhere. She spun on her heel and fled down the path. Possession is nine-tenths of the law, she thought, leaping into her car and speeding away. Gnasher made a token gesture of chasing her, but she saw he was laughing when she looked in the rear-view mirror. He was standing in the road, looking after her, helpless with mirth. Maybe it was all a joke? Naaaah. Not even Gnasher would be that stupid. OK, granted she and Rogan had had a few rows lately, but no more than usual.

As she always did, Jodie rationalised. It was all a big misunderstanding. She would go and see Rogan and sort it out. She might have to humour him, but so be it. If that was what it took, she'd humour him. Even apologise – maybe. A bit of wheedling would bring him round, as it always did. Pander to one of his favourite fantasies. He was putty in her hands when it came to her creative and unusual sex games.

Then she had second thoughts. Perhaps it would be better to talk to him on the phone first. If Gnasher was right, and he did have a young one . . . What did he mean, *Young One*? She was young. She was only twenty-six. That was young – wasn't it? She pulled the car in to the kerb and looked at her reflection in the vanity mirror. I am young, she thought. I am beautiful. Everyone says so. Why would he want someone else? She wanted to cry. *Get a grip*! Rogan was playing games. He didn't have another woman.

She had been Rogan's woman for six years. OK, so he had a wife, but *she* was his woman. *She* was the one he loved, inasmuch as Rogan could love anyone.

Rogan – aka Rogue, tee-hee, his little joke – Hogan was the Godfather of South Dublin crime. Nothing happened that he didn't know about. Apart from his drugs empire, protection racket and prostitution network, all criminals working within his domain paid their dues. Every robbery, burglary, bank or post office job on his turf was within his gift, and heaven help anyone who ignored that not insubstantial fact. There was guarded talk of people being nailed to floors and skinned alive.

They remember the pain.

They had met in one of his clubs. Always a party animal, she knew how to have a good time and wasn't about to let the small detail of no money affect her social life. She had run away from home when she was seventeen after her father caught her in bed with – whatever his name was. She couldn't remember. She never got on with her father. He hated her. She looked too much like her mother. Her mother, who ran off with the neighbour's husband when she was ten.

'Like mother, like daughter,' he had said, as he stood in the doorway of her room. He wasn't even angry. She was mortified. Not because he had caught her *in flagrante*. It was the look of total distaste and disgust on his face. After what's-'is-name had legged it, she packed her things, took her Post Office Savings book and thumbed a lift to Dublin.

She had seen him eyeing her up as she stood at the bar. Her original intention had been to bum a night's drinking out of him and maybe a bite to eat, but he overwhelmed her with his charm and generosity. He was a good fifteen years older than any man she had been involved with previously, and she loved the way he treated her, opening doors, pulling out her chair for her, holding her coat. She wasn't slow to observe the way other people's attitudes changed towards her when it was realised that she was his woman. An apartment, an allowance, credit cards, a decent car soon followed. She had a good idea how he earned a crust but didn't ask questions. She enjoyed the reflected glory and it beat the hell out of life in a small country town. And it was fun. No more Miss Selfridge. No more Penny's. No more Dunnes Stores. He only wanted to see her in designer labels. Brown Thomas charge card. Three holidays a year.

Then he got her to mule for him. She had been afraid at first. Bags of drugs taped to her body. Only three or four times a year, but she always travelled first class. Always with the Louis Vuitton. Flashing the Cartier watch. Sashaying along on the Gucci four-inch heels. And she got away with it. It was exciting. It turned her on. Rogan had the added bonus that she was so turned on by the danger that she was always gagging for sex when she got back from a trip. One time he suggested that she pose as a pregnant mother. She sailed through customs with four kilos of one-hundred-per-cent-pure, best Colombian Smack cunningly concealed in her bump. She felt her masterstroke was packing her case full of Baby Gap and declaring it in the red channel.

Now that really turned her on. Rogan thought all his birthdays had come at once.

Then one very close shave brought her back down to earth with a terrifying thump. It started when a butch-looking female customs officer, who resembled someone who would probably be involved in ethnic cleansing given half the chance, took, in Jodie's view, an irrational dislike to her. OK, so maybe she shouldn't have clicked her heels and given the Nazi salute, and it probably would have been wiser not to have made the comment about superfluous facial hair. Later, Jodie put it down to an adrenalin overload, extreme turbulence over the Atlantic and too much free champagne quaffed on the flight from Acapulco. Only fast talking and a certain amount of humble grovelling prevented a body search and a full rubber gloves job. It took Jodie past the point of turn-on, to cold, spine-numbing, knickers-wetting fear.

When she got through to Arrivals, she raced to the Ladies and threw up. Rogan thought she was over-reacting, but she refused to mule again. He tried to talk her round, but she refused. The honeymoon was over. He gave her a beating. Humiliated and mortified that anyone would see her with a black eye and bruising to the body, she ran away to a luxury health spa, pretending to the other guests that she was recovering from a road traffic accident. He, by this time was missing her, or rather her creative carnal arts. When he tracked her down, he begged her to come home. He promised he'd never touch her again, but something in her had died.

She had grown up, and fast. She had learned what her assets were and how to use them. How to keep him where she wanted him. Or so she had thought until now.

This was a whole new ball game.

She drove on a little way and stopped at a call box. She tried all his numbers but got no reply.

Humph, she thought. So he thinks he can dump me, does he? Wait till he comes crawling back, begging for it. I'll show him.

She put the car in gear and drove to the Shelbourne, where she booked a suite. After a long hot bath and room service she went shopping. Well, all her clothes were being held hostage by Gnasher Gill. What else could she do?

One hour and forty minutes' retail therapy in BT's designer department, trying on Donna Karan and Louise Kennedy, improved her mood no end. She picked out a forest-green Louise Kennedy suit, with trade mark scarf, a bitter-chocolate six-piece capsule wardrobe from DKNY (she felt obliged, what with brown being the new black) a charcoal-grey John Rocha trouser-suit, and a couple of pairs of obscenely expensive Manolo Blahnik shoes, just for spite. She had the saleslady bring up four sets of her favourite La Perla undies and half a dozen pairs of tights at twenty-five quid a shot. That'll show the bastard not to mess with me.

She handed over the BT Privileged Customer card. Better than sex, she thought. Well, better than sex with Rogan Hogan anyway!

That was when she discovered that she was in trouble. Real trouble.

'I'm sorry, madam,' the saleslady said, with a certain amount of embarrassment. 'But I'm afraid this card is no longer valid.'

'What do you mean, no longer valid?'

'Erm . . . It's been cancelled. Look.' The saleslady pointed at the VDU on top of the discreet cash desk. 'Sorry . . .'

Jodie didn't need to look. It was obvious what had happened. Rogan bloody Hogan had cancelled her Privileged

Customer card. Her stomach tied itself into a knot. She feigned surprise.

'I'm sure it's just an oversight,' the saleslady fluttered. 'How about a credit card?'

Jodie didn't want to chance having her gold card confiscated. She rummaged in her wallet, then shook her head. 'Don't seem to have it with me. Tell you what, you keep my parcels here at the till, and I'll pop home and get it.' She was burning with embarrassment. How could he?

It was a sure bet that if the rat had cancelled one card, he'd have cancelled them all. She ran up Grafton Street to the nearest ATM and stuffed her bank card in the slot. Her worst fears were realised. Her account held the princely sum of three pounds fifty. He'd stopped her allowance too.

She retrieved her bank card, stuffed her gold card into the wall and punched in her pin number. Maybe she'd be lucky and the machine would spit out some cash. No such luck. It swallowed the plastic whole and refused to give it back.

Jodie McDeal retreated to her suite to lick her wounds and draw up a battle plan.

Chapter Three

Monday, 4 November, one thirty p.m.

God was not smiling on her today.

The plan was that Lucy Spoon would head into town in the van, ostensibly to buy a few groceries, and then just keep driving. Why, today of all days, did Marcus have to change the habit of a lifetime and announce that *he* felt like going into town? Fancied a change. Felt like a couple of jars in Hartigan's and maybe a bet on the gee-gees. It was Monday, for God's sake. Marcus never went into town on a Monday. Tuesday was dole day. But what could she say? She couldn't face another confrontation.

She knew, from previous experience, the cycle of events when she tried to leave. First the shouting. He could keep it up for hours, and she couldn't handle it. It was a throwback from her childhood. Sitting on the top step of the stairs, listening to her parents yelling at each other. Her hands clamped over her ears, trying to block out the huge dramatic rows. Threats of divorce. Objects thrown. She had made devout and extravagant promises to God, begging him to make them stop. Fortunately, in that matter, God had remained resolutely deaf so she had never felt obliged to join the Carmelites. Her parents continued to go at one another hammer and tongs, and in the end she prayed that they would just get it over with and separate. That prayer had been answered.

After the shouting and yelling, Marcus used threats and recriminations, just as her parents had. And if that didn't work, he'd revert to plan C and go for pathetic, working on her conscience, loading her with guilt. She couldn't face pathetic. Couldn't hack it. Crying followed by hollow promises. It was all just manipulation. He didn't mean a word. Well, maybe he did at the time, but he had a short memory. She was perfectly aware that it was the sucker punch, but he caught her every time. She lapped up any few crumbs of kindness he threw in her direction, however insincere. Predictable or what?

She watched him drive off. Think positive. Make the best of the situation. She packed most of her clothes and a few mementoes in a couple of bags and hid them in the outhouse, along with two sleeping bags and the camping stuff. Better get something to eat. Better not to leave on an empty stomach. She was a bag of nerves. She fried some bacon and wrapped it between two pieces of bread. After one bite it stuck in her throat, so she gave the rest to Fionn, who wolfed it down in one gulp and was gratuitously appreciative. A mauldy rasher sandwich, and she was in doggy heaven. That was unconditional love for you. She stroked the dog's head and hugged her. They were two of a kind.

Lucy hadn't thought further than keep driving. She had no idea where she would go. But that seemed to be the least of her problems. Just get away, that was the important thing. Once she made the break, fate would take care of the details.

She argued with herself about the money. Should she? Shouldn't she? In the end, it was yes. She'd need money. He still had the house. A roof over his head. Legally, half of it was hers anyway. She'd take the money in lieu. Feeling very guilty, she raided the cash-stash. Two hundred and eighty-nine quid. She took two hundred and fifty, and put thirty-nine back. Then changed her mind and took another twenty. The freezer was half full. He wouldn't starve. He had his dole. What the hell was she worrying about? He was a grown-up. Time he took responsibility. Yeah? Yeah! Long past time. Fighting talk.

She stuffed the used notes down her vest, replaced the loose floorboard and pulled the mat back into place. She was ready. All she needed now was transport.

By nine that evening he still wasn't back. It was dark outside and the wind was howling. What now? She couldn't chance it on foot. It was too far to anywhere. It was too cold. Too wet. Her heart sank. Was this going to end up as just another fiasco? Better the devil you know? Safety in the familiar? It was still raining outside. Maybe in the spring? Her resolve was fading fast.

The dog whimpered and stirred in her sleep, then was suddenly awake. She pricked her ears and barked. Moments afterwards Lucy heard the familiar sound of the Hiace pulling up in the yard. A short time later Marcus wandered in, slightly unsteady on his feet. He was in good humour. Did God really feel it necessary to test her like this? He gave her a beaming smile and for an instant looked almost handsome. He had a wad of money in his fist. 'Won a hundred and sixty quid,' he said before he collapsed on to the sofa. He held it out to her. 'Here. Get yourself something nice.' Then he lay back and closed his eyes. Gimme a break, God!

She bent down and pulled off his boots. He was snoring softly now. Why didn't you drive into a bloody tree, she thought, then immediately felt guilty. The bunch of fivers had fallen to the floor. She picked it up, counted out fifty, which she stuffed down her vest with the rest, then left what remained on the table. She threw a couple of shovels of fuel on the fire and covered Marcus with the rug from the back of the sofa.

Now or never.

She hesitated.

Now! It had to be now.

Fionn, sensing something important was happening, the way dogs do, was waiting by the door. Marcus folded his arms across his chest in his sleep and sighed. The dog scratched at the door as if to say, 'Get a move on.'

Lucy Spoon took one last look around the room. At her husband. At what had been her life for the past twenty years, then walked away.

Chapter Four

They were all set. Corky was due any minute with the sawn-off. Bosco's guts were in a knot. It was a combination of fear and excitement. But it was his show. His idea. He had done all the planning. He felt proud of himself. This was the big one. After this job he'd be set up for life. He pulled open the drawer of the dresser and rummaged in the back, before taking out the hand-gun. OK, so it was only a replica, but yer man wouldn't know that. He stood in front of the mirror and pointed the gun at his reflection.

'Make my day, punk,' he said. 'Make my friggin' day.' He sniggered, then heard a noise outside in the passage and only just managed to shove the gun under his jumper before his mother put her head round the door of his room.

'Oh, there y'are, Son. Are yeh goin' out?'

'No, Ma. Not yet. Corky's comin' later on.'

'Right y'are. Well I'm off to the Bingo. I'll see yez later.'

'Bye, Ma.' And she was gone.

Bosco Biddle was nineteen years old and lived alone with his mother, Mary Ann. She loved him as only a mother could, and he thought the world of her. He was doing this job just for her. He wanted to buy her things. He wanted to be able to tell her that she didn't have to get up at the crack of dawn to sell fruit and veg all day on her stall in Moore Street, come hail, rain or shine. He wanted her to take things easy for a change.

She'd had a hard life. Abandoned by Bosco's father, she'd had to struggle to raise her son. But it was no pity. His father had given her a dog's life. She was better off without him. Bosco saw him once in the pub. Sally, his mother's friend, had pointed him out. He was drunk, but Sally said he was always that way. She said it was the drink caused all the problems between him and his ma. Sally had a lot of drink taken herself at the time and was maudlin. Up until then, Bosco had sworn that if he ever saw his father he'd beat the shite out of him. He even went over to him. But when it came to the point, he couldn't. He looked into his father's watery, pale, bloodshot eyes, and he couldn't. The man was a wreck. A shell. Destroyed by the demon drink. He didn't recognise Bosco. How could he? He hadn't laid an eye on him since he was a baby.

Because of his father, Bosco never took a drink himself. It wasn't that he disapproved of drink as such, but he was terrified that he'd end up like his old man. He'd heard talk of alcoholism being in the blood and, even though he'd only seen his father the once, even though the old man was bloated and grey-looking, Bosco could see himself thirty years down the line. He was his father's son all right. Same slight build. Same receding hair. Same pale eyes.

He pulled open the drawer again and took out the ski mask and gloves. No point in taking any chances. He'd told his ma that he needed a ski mask to keep out the cold, and she had insisted on knitting it for him. He hadn't the heart to say anything when it was finished. She had knitted it in black with white rims for the eye holes and the gap for the mouth, and, in a burst of creativity, had added two little red blobs for the nose, and yellow chain-stitch eyebrows.

The first time Corky saw it, he nearly fell on the floor, helpless. 'Yeh look like a bleedin' minstrel,' he gasped between fits of hysteria.

Bosco was not amused. 'Shurrup,' he barked. 'Me ma made it. It's a fuckin' disguise. It's not a friggin' fashion statement.'

Corky was still helpless. 'Righ'! Yez'll blend right inta the bleedin' background wearin' that!'

The door chime bing-bonged. Corky Ryan had arrived. Bosco hurried out to the hall, opened the door and Corky hustled in. He had a holdall with him, and looked extremely shifty and very nervous.

'Yeh got it, then?' Bosco asked.

'Yeah. Got it all right,' Corky confirmed. They went straight to Bosco's room. 'Where's yer old lady?'

'Bingo,' Bosco said.

Corky dumped the holdall on the bed and unzipped it.

Bosco put on his gloves – you can't be too careful – and picked out the customised shotgun. 'Loaded?' he asked.

Corky shook his head and rooted a box of cartridges out of his pocket.

Bosco examined the gun. He didn't know much about them, except that when you waved one in someone's face you were inclined to catch their undivided attention. The power excited Bosco. He had only tasted it the one time when he'd used the replica to rob the Paki off-licence. He'd got just fifty quid, but yer man didn't put up an argument. He was in and out. He was secretly a bit peeved that he didn't make the security-video slot on *Crimeline*, but hey, maybe next time, yeah?

Corky Ryan was thinly built like his friend Bosco, and about ten inches taller. They had been friends all through school, sitting next to each other since first class. Corky came from a large family. Even he was unsure of how many brothers and sisters he had, due to the fact that his mother had been dropping one or two babies a year since she married Corky's father, forty-odd years before. He had never seen three of his brothers and two sisters, who had emigrated to America before he was born. Deficient in the visa department, they were afraid to come home in case they weren't allowed back in. He, like Bosco, lived at home with his mother, along with five of his sisters and nine brothers, in two adjoining flats on the estate. His father was at sea. He saw him twice a year, but at this stage his mother was too old to have any more babies. Two of his sisters had a snapper each.

'So what's the story?' Corky asked, flopping down on the bed.

Bosco looked at his watch, then cleared his throat. He affected a haughty expression. 'Righ'. At twenty-three hundred hours we proceed in the vee-hicular transport to the rendezvous, where the subject will be alone in the house. At twenty-three thirty we gain entry to the house an' we abduct the subject by force.'

'Wha'?'

Bosco sighed. 'At eleven o'clock, go to yer man's gaff in the knocked-off van an' lift the bugger. Righ'?'

Chapter Five

—

The concierge tried to catch her attention as she hurried through the foyer but Jodie McDeal stared straight ahead, and then smiled and waved at an imaginary chum in the general direction of the Horseshoe bar. She did one circuit, then sneaked out and up to her suite. Better make the most of it. When they checked out her credit card they would start hassling her for payment.

She had tried to get hold of Rogan at every number she could think of but she couldn't track him down. Gnasher must have been telling the truth for once. He was obviously out of the country. The coward! Didn't even have the guts to face her himself. The situation had taken a very serious turn. Now that her anger had run out of steam, it was rapidly dawning on her that she was penniless and homeless, with only the clothes she stood up in to her name. She was irked that she hadn't dressed more cost effectively that morning. It just shows you that it pays to be prepared for every eventuality. It reminded her of her grandmother fussing to make sure she put on clean underwear every day, in case she got knocked down by a bus.

Around seven, Jodie ordered dinner and a good bottle of wine, but when it arrived she wasn't hungry. It's amazing how staring penury in the face can suddenly stunt your appetite. What the hell was she to do now? She was very high maintenance. Rogan had made her that way. Who would pay the bills now that he had abdicated his responsibility?

Then, ever the pragmatist, it occurred to Jodie that she had a house full of clothes and jewellery. She could sell the jewellery. That would give her a start. She had all the props to snare some other poor sucker. Feeling more positive, she poured herself another glass of wine and started to formulate a plan.

So Rogan had dumped her, but she was still young, still beautiful. That was a given. She also had certain unique talents. She hadn't even set out to snare Rogan. How much better could she do for herself if she really worked at it? She would find herself someone else. Someone richer than Rogan bloody Hogan. Someone seriously, obscenely, opulently, sumptuously rich. She would move to Cork. No one knew her in Cork and there were bound to be rich people there. She had heard that lots of the Glitterati had second homes in the area. Or was that West Cork? Never mind, she would head in that general direction and figure out the details on the way. She would appear out of the blue. A beautiful, ostensibly rich, well-groomed, designer-clad woman of mystery.

A woman of mystery. The notion appealed.

At ten forty-five, Jodie McDeal collected the car from the hotel garage and drove to Ballsbridge. She parked at the end of Wellington Road and checked out the house. It was in darkness. There was no car parked in the driveway. No sign of Gnasher Gill.

She drove in through the gates and parked the car in the garage, carefully closing and locking the door behind her. It wasn't too hard breaking in to the house. When Gnasher had changed the locks he had forgotten that she still had the key to the alarm. She hurried through to the hall and disabled it. Things were looking up, or so she thought. She hadn't anticipated the depth of Gnasher's loathing.

It was evident the moment she walked into her bedroom that things had very quickly taken a further, more sinister turn for the worse. Her wardrobes were empty. In a state of panic, she checked the tallboy. Not so much as a pair of knickers. In desperation she moved to the back bedroom. And, hallelujah, her dry-cleaning was still hanging on the back of the door. At least she had the black Emporio Armani dress and long jacket to fall back on. She was ecstatic until reality set in. Great! One frigging designer suit. Nothing to wear under it. No shoes to go with it, not even a clean pair of knickers. Granny McDeal would be spinning in her grave. Except, as far as Jodie knew, she wasn't dead.

She sat despondently on the end of the bed. 'OK,' she said to her reflection in the dressing-table mirror. 'OK. Don't panic. What are my options? Think!'

Her options were ever more limited by the minute. She took a wander round the house to see if she could find anything she could convert into cash. But there was nothing of obvious value that was easily saleable. It made her realise how little she actually owned. How little of herself she had invested in the house. It was just somewhere to live, albeit in comfort; somewhere to pass the time in between shopping, lunching and attending to her body while waiting for Rogan to show up. In some small way, the thought comforted her. Leaving the house would be no hardship in itself. It was just the terrifying notion of being cast aside.

She was ruminating on this thought when she had a minor brainwave. Her jewellery. Of course! The shock of finding that all her clothes had been swiped had pushed thoughts of the jewellery from her mind. She had oodles of gold. Brash, chunky pieces she hated. Stuff Rogan bought for her, then whinged because she never wore it. Like she wanted to be mistaken for a female football manager? Pity he never bought diamonds. Never mind. Too late to moan about that now.

She raced upstairs and into the box-room, where Rogan had hidden the safe in the floor at the back of a built-in cupboard. Her hands were shaking as she inserted the key in the lock. She took a deep breath, turned the key and heaved the door open. Her heart sank. The safe was empty except for an attaché case about twelve inches square. She had never seen it before. She had no idea how long it had been *in situ*.

The last time she had opened the safe was – at least five weeks ago. She leaned over the opening and grabbed the handle, which was on top of the lid. It was unexpectedly heavy and she had to brace her bum against the wall before she managed to hoist it out. It was a tapestry, box-like affair, with black leather trim. More like the sort of vanity case super-models lug their make-up around in. Twelve by twelve, by about twelve inches deep. She kneeled down and felt around the bottom of the safe to see if she had missed any small morsel of gold, but no luck.

The case was locked. One of those combination efforts. No problem. Rogan, who had an abysmal memory for numbers, always used 666. Jodie placed the case on the dressing-table and flipped the little wheels of the lock into place. It sprang open as she slid the levers. Click, click.

'Please be full of cash,' she said aloud. 'Please, please be overflowing with used notes.' She lifted the lid, eyes closed. After about five seconds she opened her eyes and looked inside. Nothing. It was empty. But why was it so heavy? It didn't make sense.

She examined the case. That was when she noticed that, about five inches from the bottom, there was a zip running round all four sides. She took out her nail-file and forced the clasp before unzipping it slowly. Then she flipped the upper part of the case back. Nestling in the base of the innocent-looking tapestry bag were two tightly wrapped packages.

Jodie didn't need to open one. She knew exactly what they were. She had carried enough of them through customs. She became conscious that she was holding her breath, and exhaled.

Chapter Six

He opened his eyes and, for a minute, hadn't a clue where he was. He felt groggy and more than a little nauseous. He also badly needed to empty his bladder.

Then Monty came to his senses. It all came back to him. The ring on the doorbell. The gun thrust into his face by the small one wearing the minstrel mask. Had it been the week before he would have thought they were just kids trick-or-treating in silly get-ups. The taller one had a stocking pulled over his face. There was a ladder running up his left cheek which had been mended crudely. It was over in less than half a minute. They were both shouting at him, but he was so startled and disorientated that he couldn't make out the words. The taller one grabbed him from behind and bundled him into the back of the van. He had opened his mouth and went through the motions of screaming, but no sound came out. It had been surreal.

Monty's mental replay was now in slow motion. The small one had pushed him back and handcuffed his hands together in front of his body. Monty was thankful they hadn't forced his hands behind his back because he had a large stomach and short arms. Instinct made him keep his head down and his eyes shut. The side door of the van slid shut. A blanket was thrown over him and the vehicle screeched away. His head had smashed against the wheel arch knocking him senseless.

Monty's hands were numb and he couldn't see anything, though he was aware that the van was still moving. He also had a splitting headache. For a moment the thought of blindness crossed his mind, then he realised that there was some sort of blindfold over his eyes. He was glad. He had read about kidnappings. He knew he had a better chance of survival if he was unable to identify his abductors.

He struggled on to his side. 'I have to pass water,' he shouted.

Monty George was a rich man. He had made his money the hard way, working all the hours God sent. He started with one van, hocked his soul, bought a lorry and, after that, a second-hand almost clapped-out articulated rig. In twenty years, the business grew from one to sixty new articulated rigs, twenty-one refrigerated trucks and twelve eighteen-hundred-weight courier vans. He had the third largest distribution network in Europe. But that was only part of his empire. He had diversified. When the company went public, he was worth forty-two point two million pounds overnight. The money didn't matter a jot to him. Oh, he enjoyed the life-style, but the cash was only the measure of his success. To succeed was everything. However small the objective, success was the aim. He was still hands-on. Even after a heart attack the previous year, he couldn't take his hands off the reins. It was his life. It was what made him tick. The excitement of it. The cut and thrust.

He had a deal on the boil to take over a TV satellite channel. He was doing that for Cindy, his second wife. Cindy wanted to be a TV presenter, but she was so blatantly untalented, Monty knew the only way he could make her dream come true was to buy his own TV station. Where women were concerned Monty was naïve, but not that naïve. Why would a gorgeous twenty-five-year-old even look at the likes of him, short, fat, fifty and unattractive, if it weren't for the money? Cindy claimed to love him. That would do. She kept him young and he had no illusions. In that area, money did have its uses. After Monica died, he had expected to spend the rest of his days alone. He had never expected to fall in love again at his age.

'I have to pass water,' he repeated.

Corky touched Bosco on the shoulder. 'He wants t'pee.'

Bosco looked over to where Monty lay in the back. He thought of letting him wet himself, just to show him they were hard-men, tough bastards who didn't give a toss, but then good sense kicked in. The old wanker was going to be with them for the best part of a week, and if he pissed himself he'd be pretty whiffy at the end of it.

'OK. I'll pull over when we get round the next bend,' he said.

It had been raining steadily since they left Monty's mansion in Sandycove. The forecast wasn't good, predicting high winds and heavy rain over the next three days. The tail end of hurricane Brenda or Biddy or something. All the better, Bosco thought. The cops won't be too keen on going out in the bad weather. He drove round the bend in the road and was about to pull in to the verge when, by the light of the headlamps, he saw a rusty Hiace van parked, with the lights off. The windows were steamed up. He smirked. It was probably a couple of knackers shagging on the quiet.

He drove by at speed and stopped thirty yards further on, round the next corner.

A van sped past and Lucy Spoon stirred in her sleep as the Hiace rattled. She was warm and cosy wrapped in her sleeping bag. Fionn was lying next to her in the back. Not long after eleven she had pulled in to the side of the road and climbed into the back of the van. She was tired. Emotionally drained. Her eyes ached. She was exhausted by the events of the day, and by driving at night in the pouring rain. The storm had caused widespread flooding and there had been many diversions, the result of which was that for two hours she had been driving in circles. She knew that she hadn't got very far, but what matter? She was free. She hadn't the first idea where she was heading. She was not even certain what road she was on, but life was going to be good from here on in.

The van creaked as Lucy turned over. She sighed and dreamed happy dreams as the rain drummed a tattoo on the roof.

Chapter Seven

As the lights changed from red to green at the junction of Stephen's Green and Kildare Street, Jodie McDeal saw Gnasher Gill lumbering up the steps of the Shelbourne through the teeming rain. Shit! she thought. How the fuck did he find me?

Her foot hit the accelerator, and she swerved to avoid a shunt with a black stretch-limo bearing diplomatic plates. She caught sight of the startled face of the driver out of the corner of her eye as she sped past, fighting with the steering wheel, struggling to keep the Merc under control on the slippery surface of the rain-lashed street. She screeched into Nassau Street on two wheels, breaking a red light, and her heart only slowed to a moderate gallop as she hit Merrion Square against the flow of the one-way system.

Under normal circumstances the sight of Gnasher Gill wouldn't have knocked a feather out of Jodie, but things had changed. At first when she'd found the two kilos of Smack she'd thought all her troubles were over. Then it dawned that it was no good to her. She had no way of selling it. In fact, she balked at the thought of dealing drugs. Even though she had personally been responsible for hauling over thirty kilos of the stuff into the country, her selective morality couldn't deal with supplying the drugs to snivelling junkies, in the same way that she could only eat meat as long as the finished dish bore no resemblance to anything living.

She hadn't eaten turkey since the day she witnessed her father ringing Gobbler's neck. He'd brought Gobbler home as a chick and they'd hand-reared him. She couldn't bring herself to eat someone she knew by name. Plucked and ready for the oven, he had looked like a dead baby. Her mother couldn't see what Jodie's problem was. A turkey's a turkey. But she took Jodie's side anyway just to annoy her husband – it was only a couple of weeks before she bolted. Young as she was, Jodie saw through her mother's sudden indignation and they spent a dismal Christmas with no one in the house speaking to anyone else. Happy days.

After her initial disappointment about the Smack, Jodie had had a rethink. OK, so she couldn't turn the Smack into cash by conventional means. Apart from her squeamishness, she didn't have the time or facilities to cut it and bag it, it would all take far too long and she needed to get away fast. Rogan would go ballistic when he found it was gone. Her plan was to hold the Smack hostage for a while, and then do a deal with Rogan. Most sane people would think this plan downright suicidal, considering Rogan Hogan's reputation but, basically, Jodie was fresh out of options. Rogan had thrown her penniless on to the street. And after all she'd done for him too! She was bloody angry. Angry and humiliated. Drastic circumstances call for even more drastic action, and to hell with the consequences. Even though she felt smug and a little excited about her new plan, Jodie was terrified. The way you are at the top of the ski-run you think is a tad too steep, just before you launch yourself into infinity and beyond.

She had zippered the bottom section of the attaché case closed, and dumped her cosmetics and toothbrush into the top part. Another quick search of the house gleaned a pair of black 501s that were stiff as a board, six pairs of knickers in the tumble-dryer, her scruffy trainers, a fleece in the utility room, and two really awful, cutesy Barbie-pink T-shirts that she got for free from the gym and wouldn't be seen dead in. Unfortunate choice of words, considering.

Jodie had packed the Emporio Armani, jeans, the trainers, knickers and awful T-shirts into a soft Louis Vuitton holdall and put it, and the attaché case, in the car. She was irritated to find that although she still had her bank card, she only had three cheques left in her cheque-book. Sod it! She emptied her wallet and all the loose change from her bag and counted it. Sixteen pounds and thirty-four pence between her and total insolvency. Further hunting revealed a petrol charge card. If the gods could bring themselves to give her even a tiny smirk, Rogan would have forgotten about the fuel charge card. Her plan was to shoot back to the Shelbourne, sleep the night, skip first thing after breakfast and head south. But Gnasher's visit to the hotel had put paid to that. She wondered if he knew about the Smack. Surely not. It was too soon. Her stomach did a somersault. What if he'd come back to the house and found her there all ready to hop it with Rogan's merchandise. Jodie shuddered at the thought. He was gagging to give her a wallop. She could sense it.

There was nothing for it. As she was far too hyper to sleep, she hit the road.

'Where the fuck are we?' Bosco's erratic driving had just lurched Corky awake. He rubbed his eyes.

'Not far now,' Bosco reassured his friend. 'Abou' another couple of miles an' we're there. How's yer man?'

Corky looked over to where Monty was lying, either asleep, or feigning sleep. He was curled up like a baby with his two hands clamped between his thighs. 'He's sleepin'. Wha' time is it?'

Bosco squinted at his watch. 'Quarter to two.' They drove on in silence. Bosco hadn't taken the diabolical weather into account and had underestimated how long their journey would take. The roads were very bad and they had encountered several detours because of flooding and fallen trees. He was heading for his Auntie Maureen's caravan, which was permanently parked in what the owners of the field called a 'Holiday Village', but was really a field. A muddy field with cement pads for the vans. His Auntie Maureen referred to it as a mobile home, but you couldn't call a ten-foot trailer anything other than a caravan. The site also boasted an unspeakable toilet block, and what was laughingly called a shower room.

After another fifteen minutes, when he hadn't come across the Happy Dayz Holiday Village sign, Bosco pulled in to the side of the road. 'Must've missed the turn-off,' he said to Corky, who hadn't asked. He did a three-point turn and headed back up the road. He crawled along at about five miles an hour, peering through the blackness for the sign. After several minutes he saw it. It had been blown over and was resting in the hedge.

'Here we are. Give yer man a shove.'

Corky leaned over and shook Monty's shoulder. Monty stirred, then jolted awake. 'Wha – ?'

Bosco parked the van round the side of the caravan. It looked smaller than he remembered, and a lot shabbier. Still, it would serve their purpose. They'd be warm and dry, and out of sight. No one came near the place at this time of year.

Corky gave Monty a poke with his foot. 'Time t'go, Granpa,' he said. He slid the door open and between them he and Bosco helped their handcuffed and temporarily blind hostage out of the van.

The rain was still coming down in buckets and the ground was squelchy under their feet. Corky held the torch while Bosco fumbled with the keys. The inside of Auntie Maureen's caravan gave them no surprises. It was as shabby and down at heel as the exterior.

'Jeasus! This place bleedin' stinks.' Corky pushed Monty ahead of him, and Monty stumbled and ended up on an upholstered bench by the wall. In the late fifties, when the caravan had been built, it had probably been described as an all-purpose sofa-bed, but really it was just a chip-board bench covered in foam that folded out into a very narrow bed with wonky fold-down legs.

'It's just a bit damp,' Bosco said defensively. 'It'll be grand when we get the heat goin'.'

Corky misheard him. 'It's a bit of a dump, all righ'.'

Irritated that Corky was slagging off his Auntie Maureen's holiday home, Bosco assumed his Boss role. 'Go get the stuff from the bleedin' van. I'll get the heatin' sorted out.'

Corky did as he was told. Bosco kneeled down and, after three abortive attempts, managed to coax the ancient miniature gas fire to life. It spluttered and popped, but pretty soon glowed red.

Everything about Auntie Maureen's caravan was in miniature. From the minuscule steel sink and stove to the tiny, handy fold-away table in red-speckled Formica. The overhead, or in this case, mid-chest-level, lockers were just big enough to hold the little pillows, with built-in essence of mildew.

A rush of cold air made the fire pop violently as Corky struggled back inside with a box of provisions. He dumped it on the floor and went back for the second load. Bosco held the door closed until he returned with a black bin liner full of sleeping bags, then shot the bolt to prevent the storm from blowing it open.

Half an hour later the kettle had almost boiled and the fire had warmed the cramped space up to a sub-tropical temperature. The windows and walls were running with condensation and their wet clothes were steaming. From time to time a gust of wind battered the caravan. The camping gas lantern cast a weird bluish light over everything.

Bosco made the tea and handed a mug to Monty. 'Here y'are. Mind yeh don't spill it.'

Monty was grateful. His throat was dry as a bone. He sat silently on the bench listening to the two villains slagging each other off as they tried to make the place more comfortable. One of them switched on a radio and fiddled with the stations until he found Atlantic 252. Monty was a good judge of character, but he couldn't figure them out. They sounded more like a couple of kids on a camping trip than dangerous criminals, yet they'd pushed a sawn-off shotgun in his face and dragged him away in the middle of the night. He decided he had better not underestimate them if he wanted to survive the episode. 'Are you paramilitaries?' he asked. 'Are you Republicans?'

Bosco turned his head and looked at Monty. It was the first time the man had uttered a full sentence. He was surprised at the question. It hadn't occurred to him that Monty would make that assumption. He thought about lying, just to put the fear of God into him, but changed his mind. It stuck in his craw to be associated with that crowd. 'No, we're not the bleedin' IRA,' he said. 'Bu' tha' doesn't mean we're not mad bastards. If I were youz, I'd be afraid' – meaningful pause – 'I'd be *very* afraid.' He had wanted to say that to someone ever since he had heard Clint Eastwood say it in a *Dirty Harry* movie. 'Be very afraid,' he repeated for good measure, loading his voice with menace. He couldn't gauge Monty's reaction because of the blindfold.

'What are you going to do with me?' Monty asked after a pause.

'Wha' are we goin' t'do wit ya?' Bosco repeated. 'Wha' d'ya think we're goin' t'bleedin' do?'

Monty thought for a few seconds before answering. 'Well. I suppose you want money. Am I right?'

Bosco laughed. 'Well spotted, Granpa. That's jus' wha' we want. Yer auld woman should cough up a few quid t'get yeh back in one piece.'

'Yes,' Monty said. 'Erm . . . How much d'you want?'

'We were thinkin' in the region of abou' a hundred grand.' Corky looked over at Bosco, waiting to see what Monty would make of that.

Monty was surprised. It just showed that they could have absolutely no idea of how much he was worth.

'So – em – So I suppose you've sent a ransom note to my wife.'

'Left it on yer hall table,' Bosco said. 'She'll've read it when she got home from her actin' class.' He winked at his friend.

'How did you know –' Monty started, then stopped as he copped on. 'How long were you watching us?'

33

Bosco stood up and stretched, and in doing so whacked his hands off the roof. It stung. He winced. The space they were currently sharing was nothing if not intimate. 'Long enough,' he said non-committally.

He picked up a sleeping bag and tossed it at Monty. It hit him in the chest. 'Lie back there,' Bosco ordered. Monty complied meekly. Then he taped the older man's ankles together. 'Don't ge' any daft ideas abou' makin' a run for it,' Bosco said, trying to sound dangerous.

Monty hadn't a notion.

Chapter Eight

Tuesday, 5 November, eight thirty a.m.

The sound of a reluctant starter motor whirring and whining dragged Jodie from sleep. She looked at the clock on the dashboard. It was eight thirty. Just after two she had found she was wall-falling and had pulled in at the next transport stop she came to, to avoid falling asleep at the wheel.

It was only as she settled herself down for the night that she realised how ill equipped she was. A small travel rug and a leather jacket between her and hypothermia. She was stiff as a board and freezing. She struggled into a sitting position and pressed the lever to pull the seat upright. The windows were all steamed up. She rubbed a hole in the mist and squinted out. The car-park was half full of trucks, vans and container lorries. She was thirsty and her saliva tasted strong enough to strip paint.

She pulled down the sun visor and peered at her reflection in the vanity mirror. The trip through the downpour to the ladies' toilet the night before hadn't done her any favours. Her hair hung like rats' tails where it had dried and there was a frizzy clump at the back of the crown. She dug out her hairbrush and did running repairs, then licked her finger and attempted to wipe away the smudged mascara from under her eyes. It was waterproof. At thirty quid a shot, what did she expect? It wouldn't budge.

Dumping the hairbrush back in the vanity case, she threw the rug on to the back seat and struggled into her leather jacket. Then, grabbing her bag and the vanity case, she climbed stiffly out of the car. The rain had eased to a light misty drizzle, almost qualifying for 'soft day' status. A rusty Hiace van was parked in the space next to her. A ginger dog was sitting in the passenger seat looking out. It barked as she walked past.

She stopped by the window. 'Calm down, doggy,' she said to the animal. 'I'm not Jimmy fucking Saville. I only look like him.'

She headed towards the ladies' toilet where she had a rudimentary wash, cleaned her teeth and replaced her make-up. A splash of water through her hair, followed by a blow dry under the hand thingy and she felt almost human. Breakfast was calling. A big fry seemed both necessary and appropriate.

Lucy mopped up the last of the egg-yolk with bread and popped it into her mouth. It tasted good. As little as twenty-four hours before, if she had done that with her egg, Marcus would have gone into a sulk claiming that she was disgusting and she'd put him off his food. For a slob, Marcus could be very fastidious about some things. And this from the man who ate his own ear-wax.

She rolled herself a cigarette and lit up. Best smoke of the day. The transport café was busy, with most of the tables occupied. She had eaten a hearty breakfast. Beside her on the table she had a cheeseburger in a carton for Fionn's breakfast. Not the best diet for a dog, but she wouldn't eat dog food if there was even a suspicion of anything tastier, and who could blame her?

Once, after a particularly awful incident, Marcus had kept her up three nights in succession, ranting and raving because she had laughed when he said that he thought he was descended from a higher alien life form – he'd just read Erich von Daniken's *Chariot of the Gods*, subtitle, *Was God an Astronaut?*. The previous day he had dragged her to the top field behind the house to assist him in rigging up torches to act as landing lights to guide in any stray spacecraft that might happen by. With hindsight, the silliest part of the incident was that she had found herself apologising and agreeing with him, even suggesting that perhaps they should lay out the lights in a circular pattern as that appeared to be the accepted shape of spacecraft. Grudgingly, he had agreed to her idea, furious that he hadn't thought of it first. Marcus had a talent for argument, for the sake of it. He always managed to browbeat her into submission. He would confuse her, switching his arguments around until she was totally befuddled.

After three nights without sleep, Marcus's manic episode finally ran its course and he went to bed. He woke up ten hours later full of the joys of spring. Chatting away as if nothing had happened. Lucy was exhausted as she had only managed to doze on the sofa for a couple of hours. In a fit of malevolence, she made him a Spag Bol using dog food. She added a tin of tomatoes and liberally laced it with oregano, chopped onion and garlic. She declined to eat, claiming a stomach upset. He complimented her on the sauce, and didn't seem to notice that Fionn turned up her nose at the leftovers. Obviously nine out of ten extraterrestrials prefer Pedigree Chum.

'Do you mind if I sit here?' A pretty young woman wearing an expensive leather jacket stood by the table. She was struggling with her bag slung over one shoulder, and was carrying a small vanity case while balancing a loaded tray on her forearm.

'Sure,' Lucy said. 'Help yourself.' She pushed her empty plate out of the way. 'Do you mind?' She held up her cigarette.

The girl shook her head and smiled. She slid the tray on to the table, put her bags on the inside seat next to the wall and sat down.

Lucy realised on second glance that she wasn't just pretty, she was really beautiful. She had smooth, fair skin, blonde hair and dazzling violet eyes. Lucy wouldn't normally have noticed, but the girl's eyes were really startling. She found she was staring, so she looked down at the table top.

The girl ate ravenously. When she had finished, she pushed away her plate and sat back in her seat. 'Sorry,' she said, by way of conversational opening. 'But could I bum a cigarette off you?'

'Sure.' Lucy pushed her pack of tobacco and Rizla across the table. 'Can you manage?'

Jodie nodded, expertly rolled a cigarette, lit it and sighed contentedly as she exhaled the smoke. 'Best smoke of the day.'

Lucy agreed.

'Em . . . Where exactly is this?' Jodie asked.

'I'm not altogether sure. I was driving round in circles last night because of the storm. Why is it that in this country, the word diversion just means "Don't go this way"? Why don't they sign an alternative route?'

'Got me there.' Jodie took another drag on the cigarette.

'Where've you come from?' Lucy asked.

'Dublin.'

'And where are you headed?'

'South.' Jodie hoped this middle-aged hippie didn't want a lift.

'Then I suppose we're somewhere between Dublin and the South,' Lucy said. 'Or, in other words, about twenty miles from where I used to live in the Wicklow mountains.'

Smartarse. Jodie inhaled on the last of the cigarette. 'How about you? Where are you headed?'

Lucy shrugged again. 'I don't know.' As soon as she said it, she realised that it sounded feeble. 'Haven't made up my mind yet,' she added.

'Oh . . . Right.' Jodie indicated the cheeseburger box. 'Aren't you hungry?'

'It's the dog's breakfast.'

'Bummer.'

Lucy laughed. 'No. I mean it's *really* the dog's breakfast.'

They laughed together at the misunderstanding. Jodie needed to laugh. She was brittle from stress. Once she started, she found it hard to stop. Every time she thought she had it under control another fit of giggling escaped. She was unable to speak. Lucy stared at her across the table. Jesus! It wasn't that fucking funny, she thought. Out of the frying pan into the fire. Have I a sign stuck to my forehead saying, nutters over here?

Jodie regained control of her faculties. 'Sorry,' she explained. 'I had the day from hell yesterday. I guess it just caught up with me.' Embarrassed, she stood up and picked up her bag and the attaché case. 'Well, must be off. Nice meeting you.'

'Take care.' Lucy watched Jodie walk from the café. She wasn't the only one. Every pair of eyes in the place followed her progress as she glided towards the door.

Jodie stood motionless, staring at the dry, empty space where she had parked the Merc. Common sense told her that she must have parked it somewhere else. It couldn't just vanish. The rusty Hiace with the ginger dog was there. With the Pat the Baker van on the other side.

She was still staring at the gap when Lucy walked up.

'Are you OK?'

'It's gone. My fucking car's gone. Some bastard's nicked my fucking car!' Jodie wailed.

'Are you sure?'

'Of course I'm fucking sure. It was here. Right bloody here.' She leaned against the Hiace and let out a low moan. 'Oh shit! My bag. The Emporio Armani. They took the frigging Emporio Armani. What am I going to do now?'

Lucy was more than a little bemused. This girl really was crazy. 'I dare say you'll live without the *Emporio Armani*,' she said, heavy on the irony. 'You should call the cops, though. It can't have been gone that long.'

What the hell did she know, this smartarsed elderly new-age traveller? Of course she couldn't call the bloody cops. The car was in Rogan Hogan's name. If she reported it stolen and the cops contacted him, he'd know where she was heading.

'Come on,' Lucy said. 'There's a phone in the café.' But Jodie didn't budge. Lucy stood awkwardly, waiting for her to say something. It seemed a tad harsh just to get into the Hiace and drive away. The girl was very obviously not the full shilling.

'You don't understand,' Jodie said. 'The car belongs to my ex-boyfriend. If I call the cops he'll find out where I am.'

'You stole it?'

'Yes – No – Sort of. We split up and he took all my stuff, so I took the car.' It bore a passing resemblance to the truth.

'Oh, I see.' Lucy gave a sympathetic sort of nod. She could relate to that. They were both fleeing someone. 'So what are you going to do?'

Jodie shrugged. 'Plan A was that I'd go down to Cork.' She was more gutted about the Emporio Armani than she was about the car. The clothes maketh the man, or in this case the woman. How the hell was she going to snare a new man now?

'Have you friends down there?' Lucy opened the passenger door of the Hiace. Fionn jumped out, wagging her tail with a smiley expression on her face. It wasn't just the smell of the cheeseburger. Fionn was always like that.

'Never been there,' Jodie said. 'How about you?'

'I've a couple of mates down there, but I haven't seen them in years.'

Jodie rubbed Fionn's head, and tickled her behind the ear. 'Nice dog,' she said.

Lucy opened the burger box and put it on the ground. Fionn nudged the top of the bun off with her nose, anxious to get to the best bit first.

'More reliable than a man any day,' Lucy said. Jodie felt inclined to agree. They watched the dog gobbling up the burger.

When she had finished, Lucy picked up the empty container. 'I'm going to take the dog for a walk,' she said. 'Why don't you come? It'll clear your head and help to get things in perspective.'

'I suppose so.' Jodie felt low. She was too used to easy living these days to manage without unlimited cash and a gold Visa card. At least she still had the Smack. If all else failed – What was she thinking? All else *had* failed, and failed spectacularly. The Smack was her only option now. Unconsciously she hugged the attaché case to her chest.

'Would you like to leave the case in the Hiace?' Lucy asked. 'It looks heavy.'

Jodie gripped it even more firmly. She had no intention of letting the only thing between her and destitution out of her sight.

Lucy gave her a weird look. 'Please yourself,' she said and set off at a hearty clip towards the forest.

Chapter Nine

Tuesday, 5 November, nine thirty a.m.

Mornings weren't the best time for Cindy George. She didn't really come to until after eleven, so it was not surprising that the first she knew of her husband's kidnapping was when Bosco phoned at nine fifteen. To begin with, she didn't have the slightest idea what he was talking about. She hadn't found the ransom note the night before when she got in. She did wonder why all the lights were on, though. Monty wasn't one to waste electricity, but she was dog-tired after her class and went straight to bed. She assumed that Monty had gone out for some reason, and would lock up when he came home.

After a frustrating couple of minutes, Bosco finally got it through to her. He kept repeating, 'No cops,' and 'Yer aul' fella gets it if I even smell a cop.' It was all very dramatic.

'But what do you want?' Cindy was sitting up in bed now, looking at Monty's empty, undisturbed, space in the bed next to her. She bit her lip.

'A hundred grand. I want it in used notes. I'll call yeh later to arrange the drop,' Bosco said, adding ominously, 'An' remember, no cops, or he dies, an' then I'll come an' find you and you'll die too – Goddit?'

'Got it,' Cindy squeaked.

Bosco hung up. He was pleased with himself, but Jeasus, was yer woman thick or what? She hadn't even noticed he was gone. Maybe they sleep in separate beds, he thought. He wouldn't have been surprised. He'd seen Cindy. She was a cracker. Blonde with big bazookas. He loved blondes with big bazookas. He had never had a woman like Cindy. In the biblical sense he had only ever had Natasha. He loved Natasha, but she wasn't in Cindy's league. Natasha's bazookas were a bit on the small side, no more than a handful. But he loved Natasha, and Natasha wasn't thick. When I get the money, he thought, I'll get Natasha the best pair of bazookas money can buy. Now that was a present!

He stepped out of the phone box and walked towards the van. The plan was that he would give Cindy a few hours to arrange the cash, then he'd phone her again and tell her where to bring it. Simple as that. She wouldn't dare call the cops. He felt confident that he had put the fear of God into her on that score. Things were going well. He felt powerful.

He started the van and drove off. Suddenly a red Mercedes 280SL convertible zoomed out of a side road, directly across his path. The soft-top was down and three gurriers were roaring and shouting and giving him the finger. He jammed on the brakes and swerved, nearly landing in the ditch.

'Stupid fuckin' eejits!' he yelled after them. His heart was pounding. Joy-riding was one thing, but right now it didn't suit Bosco to get killed. Not when he was so close to more money than he had ever even dreamed of.

After his heart slowed down, Bosco set off again, back towards the camp site. He hoped that Corky would have the breakfast cooked. His guts were rumbling. He had been too wound up to eat properly the day before. The wiper blades scraped on the windscreen so he switched them off. He was glad the rain had stopped. Life in the caravan was more bearable if they could leave the door open. Three men in that tiny space generated some body odour. Yer man, Aiden Nulty on the 2FM weather forecast, said the storm would pick up again later in the day. He looked up at the sky. It was murky all right. Bosco signalled right, and turned into the gate.

'How'd it go?' Corky asked.

'Fine. I'll give her another ring later on, when she's had a chance to ge' the cash.' Bosco folded a slice of bread round the sausage and bacon Corky had cooked. He poured himself a mug of tea and piled in two sugars. It hit the spot. Monty, despite the circumstances in which he found himself, was hungry too. Corky handed him a rasher sandwich, and when he had eaten it, a mug of tea. Then he sat down at the red-speckled Formica table and had his own breakfast. They all ate in silence.

Monty wondered how Cindy was and if she'd had the gumption to call the police. He felt sure that the small one would have warned her against such action, but he hoped that she had anyway. It wasn't so much that he was afraid of dying. The doctor had told him he'd been clinically dead when he had his heart attack the previous year. The ambulance man had brought him back to life, they said. He'd been completely out of it. He couldn't recall any visions of the dark tunnel and the blinding light, or the sense of overwhelming peace that people sometimes talked about. All he remembered was a pain in his chest and then waking up in hospital.

It was just at the moment he was enjoying himself. He had spent the major part of his life working, and although he got huge satisfaction out of his success, since marrying Cindy he had discovered that there was more to it. She had given him back the youth he had missed while he was making a quid, or in Monty's case, forty-two point two million quid. He had to admit that he felt proud when he walked into a room with Cindy. He could feel the envy of men. It had all come as a surprise to him.

He and Monica had never really socialised much. She was a home body, and had been a good wife. In the early days, when he drove the rigs himself, she would invariably have food on the table however late he came home. He always had clean clothes. His only sorrow was that she couldn't give him children. He would have liked children. He knew Cindy wasn't keen, but at fifty years of age he was well aware that life was a trade-off. Anyway, he was too old. If he had a child now, it was odds on, with his heart condition, he'd never live to see it grow up.

Bosco chomped on his sandwich and day-dreamed about Natasha and her new bazookas. Corky, on the other hand, was thinking about dogs. He planned to buy a greyhound when he got his cut.

The sound of a car engine brought Bosco back to reality. He looked out of the window and his heart did a backward summersault as he recognised the Day-Glo slash along the side of the cop car.

'Fuck!' He leaped to his feet and pulled the door closed. 'It's the friggin' cops.'

Corky, who was jammed behind the table, struggled to free himself, then grabbed the sawn-off and joined Bosco as he peeked out through Auntie Maureen's net curtain. 'What's he doin'? What's he fuckin' want?'

The patrol car was over beside the toilet block. They watched as the driver did a three-point turn and headed back towards the gate. 'He's only lookin',' Corky said, trying to sound confident. The car slowed down and stopped near Auntie Maureen's caravan.

'Shit!' Bosco made a dash for the door. 'Keep yer man quiet.' Corky turned and pushed the shotgun tight up against Monty's temple.

Bosco took a deep breath and, after opening the door a crack, eased himself outside and closed it, leaning his back against it to be assured that it would stay shut. The cop wound down the window.

'How're doin'?' said Bosco.

'Bit cold to be camping,' the cop observed. 'And who would you be?' He had a strong West of Ireland accent.

Thinking on his feet, Bosco said, 'Liam Gallagher,' then winced. It was the first name that came to mind. 'I'm stayin' in me cousin's caravan fer a couple a' days.'

He saw the cop giving the van the once-over. 'Where're yeh from?' he asked.

Bosco thought about lying, but he knew his accent was a dead give-away. 'Dublin.'

'That your van?'

'Yeah.' He hoped the culchie cop wouldn't ask him for documents.

The cop nodded. 'On yer own?'

'No. There's a couple of us. Stag do las' nigh'.' How that came into his head he had no idea.

'Is that right?' the cop said, loosening up a bit. 'Few sore heads, I suppose.'

Bosco gave him a strained smile. His top lip stuck to his teeth and his throat had dried out. 'Yeah! Somethin' like tha' all righ',' he croaked.

The cop put the car into gear. 'Right y'are. Well watch yerselves,' he said and drove off.

Bosco heaved a sigh of relief, and waited until the cop car was well out of sight before he went back inside. Suddenly, things weren't going according to plan. 'We gotta get outta here,' he said.

Corky was in full agreement. Seeing the cop had frightened the life out of him too. He was all too aware that firearm offences were serious shit. And you didn't even have to shoot anyone. 'Did yeh see 'im givin' the van the bleedin' once-over?'

But Bosco was way ahead of him, and was jamming the food and stuff back in the box. Corky realised what he was doing and grabbed the sleeping bags.

'What's going on?' Monty asked.

Corky yanked him to his feet. 'We're movin' house, Granpa.' He tried to sound fearless. Bosco was already out of the caravan and had dumped the box in the back of the van. Corky helped Monty down the step and frog-marched him towards the sliding side door.

'Could I lie on a sleeping bag this time?' Monty asked. 'The floor of the van's very hard.' Corky looked at Bosco for an opinion.

'Suppose it can't do any harm,' Bosco said.

Corky spread the padded sleeping bag out in the back, then helped Monty climb inside. 'Keep yer bleedin' head down,' he barked. He didn't want Monty to think he was a push-over just because he had done him a favour.

Chapter Ten

Tuesday, 5 November, eleven a.m.

Common sense told Gnasher Gill that it couldn't have gone.
He'd put the Smack in the safe himself only four days
previously.

   He closed the door and opened it again, hoping that
somehow the attaché case would reappear, but it didn't. The
safe was still as empty as his guts felt now. Gnasher was not
the panicky type, so the sensation was unfamiliar to him.
This was all down to that screaming stuck-up slapper. It had
to be. He wanted to kick himself. He'd had no idea that she
had a key to the safe. Was Hogan mad, or what? Giving that
one a key to the safe? Thinking with his prick, that was the
only explanation. Hogan wasn't a stupid man. Far from it,
but that one got away with murder. If she was his woman
he'd keep her in line all right. He wouldn't put up with the
shit Hogan put up with. A hefty clatter was what the bitch
needed. He'd never liked her. So he may have fancied the
knickers off her. May have passed comment to some of his
mates that he'd like to give 'er one, the way blokes do, but
he'd never liked her. He felt vindicated now that she had
done a runner with Hogan's Smack. Vindicated, but a little
on the iffy side. What if Hogan held him responsible? He
thought again. How could he? Hogan was the one who gave
the silly bitch the bloody key, not him.

   He closed the safe and locked it again. She'd been there. He
knew it. The alarm was off and the kitchen window broken.
Mentally he kicked himself again, for being so stupid as to
forget that she had an alarm key. Hogan would blow a gasket.

Gnasher comforted himself with the memory of telling Jodie that she was past her sell-by date. The look on her face, wha'? This small thought was some consolation. He smiled.

At exactly the same time that Gnasher was ruminating on the downfall of Jodie McDeal, Rogan Hogan was walking through the front door of his Templebar penthouse apartment with Angelica Quinn. He looked relaxed and tanned after five days in Morocco setting up a deal with a new supplier.

So did Angelica. She had spent half her time by the pool improving her tan, the rest, either shopping in the Souk, snorting coke, or gratifying Rogan in their sumptuous suite. Angelica was not as beautiful as Jodie. For one thing she was very tall and skinny, but that was down to her being a model. She was Rogan Hogan's new trophy girlfriend. She was a rising star in the international modelling firmament. She also had a serious cocaine habit, which was very useful to Hogan. The fashion for heroin waifs on the catwalk suited her look perfectly, and she didn't even need make-up to look the part. He'd been mad about Jodie once, but she was getting too old and too demanding for too little return. All she was good for these days was a good fuck, and even her appeal in that department was wearing thin. Angelica was different. She was financially independent. And it was like shagging a boy, without actually having to shag a boy. Angelica's slim, androgynous body and cropped hair turned him on, and made him confront feelings he hadn't openly acknowledged in himself before. It was tough, particularly as Rogan Hogan was unashamedly homophobic.

Angelica was as ditzy as first impressions suggested. She was also totally lacking in judgement. At eighteen she'd been around the block a few times. Four years ago she had been discovered walking down Grafton Street by an agency scout and this had led to a contract with a top London agency. Four *Vogue* covers, a high-profile ad campaign and two engagements were behind her, the first to an Irish rock superstar, the second to an international photographer. She dumped the rock star for the photographer, thinking that he would be better for her career, only to have him drown in the Jacuzzi while under the influence of various substances. She'd been with Rogan Hogan for six weeks now. They met in the VIP room of his newest club, the Python Nest. She had been feeling alone and vulnerable. Same old story.

He picked up the mail and scanned it as he made his way through to the kitchen where Angelica was busy fumbling with the coffee maker. The doorbell rang. When he looked at the video screen he was surprised to see a uniformed cop standing in the outer lobby of the building. He buzzed him in. He never had any dealings with the cops these days. His only arrest was as a juvenile, when he had been caught shoplifting. He had got away with a caution.

Rogan Hogan wasn't your stereotypical underclass criminal. He was from a stoutly middle-class family, his father a solicitor, his mother a nurse. And he had been mortified when he was caught. Not with remorse, but because he hated the fact that he had failed. To prove to himself that he wasn't a complete spa, he went out the next day and stole a cassette recorder, which he sold to one of his school friends for ten pounds. Easy-peasy.

From humble beginnings his empire grew. He was a clever boy and, despite his extramural activities, did well at school. He went on to university and did business studies, for no other reason than he felt that learning the nuts and bolts about business would be invaluable in his chosen career. And Rogan Hogan planned to make crime his career. He was clever, because he wasn't greedy. He planned every move and paid his associates well. But he was also a vicious and sadistic bastard, so his reputation went before him. Disloyalty in any shape or form was not tolerated. Better not mess with Hogan, you could end up with your legs ripped off – or worse.

'Mister Hogan?' the cop enquired. Hogan nodded, arching his eyebrow in a question mark. 'We found yer car, Sir.'

Hogan stared at him. Noticing the blank expression, the cop continued, 'Red Mercedes 280SL convertible?' He read the licence number from his notebook. 'We arrested two juveniles, a third got away.'

'You mean they stole it?' The cop was looking at him now as if he were a simpleton. Hogan explained. 'I'm sorry, Officer, you see I've been away. I only just got back and I had no idea that the car was even missing. Is there any damage?'

The cop nodded. ''Fraid so, Sir. The front off-side wing took a shunt and the side window's broken.' The cop carried on explaining to Rogan about the car, and where it was now, but he wasn't listening. He was seething inside. How dare they! How bloody dare the little fuckers steal his car.

After the cop had gone he called Gnasher on his mobile.

'Did you get the keys from Jodie?' he snapped, without so much as a hello. Gnasher's heart jumped into his throat.

'I changed the locks, Boss,' he said.

'What about the keys to the Merc?'

'Erm . . . No, Boss. Bu' I figured she wasn't goin' nowhere I couldn't find her.'

'Well, I just had the fucking cops on my doorstep. Three gurriers ripped the Merc off and smashed it up.'

Shit! Gnasher swallowed hard.

'The only up side is that at least the bitch isn't still driving it.' Gnasher felt a whiff of hope. 'I want you personally to find out who the three little fuckers are who ripped the car off, and bring them to me at the Python Nest later. Got that?'

Gnasher cleared his throat. 'Got tha', Misther Hogan. Erm . . . One other thing – '

'What?' Hogan sounded really pissed off.

Gnasher bit the bullet. 'The . . . eh . . . the case you left in the safe – '

'What about it?'

'Yer woman took it.' He braced himself for the explosion.

*

After she'd phoned the bank and the various building socie-
ties, Cindy had a leisurely breakfast, then went to her aero-
bics class. After that, she drove into town to the hairdresser's
and had her roots touched up.

'Bu' where're we goin' t'fuckin' go?' Corky asked Bosco
under his breath.

They were driving south. Monty was lying in the back
trussed like a turkey, and Corky was up front with his friend
and fellow conspirator.

'Chill out,' Bosco said. 'We'll find somewhere. There's lots
a' empty holiday homes round here. We'll just keep a look-
out.'

It wasn't an act. Bosco was feeling as up-beat as he
sounded. He'd had time to think about the situation and
moving on was only a precaution as far as he was concerned.
The plan was going well. It would all pan out. At the end of
it he would be able to buy Natasha her new bazookas as
well as helping his ma out and he would still have plenty left
for himself. The wind had picked up again and rain was
battering against the windscreen. Corky leaned over and
turned up the heater.

'Keep an eye out fer empty holiday homes,' Bosco
instructed. Corky wasn't sure what an empty holiday home
looked like, but didn't want to sound like a spa by asking.
He rubbed away the mist from the passenger side window
and peered through the lashing rain.

The rain started again so unexpectedly that they were caught
in the middle of the forest. They made a run for it. Fionn
lolloped along beside them as if it were a game.

After about fifty yards, Lucy grabbed Jodie's arm. 'It's
pointless running,' she gasped. 'We can't get any wetter even
if we walk.'

Jodie slowed down to a trot. She was breathless and
wheezing. She made a mental note to pack up smoking. The
track was muddy and her Gucci loafers were destroyed. They

must have walked for about three miles. Jodie found her companion laid back and easy to talk to so she unburdened herself and told Lucy her story, or at least the edited highlights.

'So what's in the case that's so valuable?' Lucy asked, never one to beat about the bush, except where Marcus was concerned.

Jodie hesitated. She had only just met this woman. Common sense told her that it was not the smartest idea to blab about having a case full of hard drugs in your possession to just anyone. But Lucy probably took drugs anyway. She looked the type. Hell, she could smell it on her.

Lucy noticed Jodie's reticence. 'Hey. It's cool. It's your business,' she said good-humouredly.

Sod it. 'Well, actually,' Jodie said. 'It's two kilos of one-hundred-per-cent-pure Smack.'

Lucy stopped dead in her tracks. 'Jesus! No shit?'

'No shit,' Jodie said. 'Erm . . . Did I mention that my boyfriend was a drug dealer?'

'No,' Lucy said. 'You only mentioned *rich* and *businessman*.'

'Add psycho to that.'

'Hm. A psycho drug dealer. He sounds like a piece of work.'

'Only if he's pissed off. When things between us were good, they were very good,' Jodie said wistfully.

They were in sight of the truck stop now. Lucy was right, they weren't any wetter than if they had run all the way. Jodie's feet were squelching in her shoes. The Timberlands had kept Lucy's feet as dry as a bone. 'So what are you going to do?' she asked.

'I'll call him and try to cut a deal.'

It sounded a very simplistic plan to Lucy. 'But if he's such a dangerous character, don't you think that would be . . . well – dangerous?'

'What else can I do?' Jodie was being practical now. 'I've no money, only the clothes I'm wearing. The bastard shafted me. The least he could have done was to give me some sort of warning. What the hell did I ever do to him? He didn't have to be like this.' Jodie found that she felt hurt and rejected more than she felt angry, though that's not to say she wasn't very angry. It was just a matter of degree.

They stopped by the Hiace. Lucy opened the door and Fionn shook herself and jumped inside.

Jodie caught sight of her reflection in the window. 'Shit! Look at me.' Her hair was wet and stuck to her head again, and her clothes were sodden. Thank God for the waterproof mascara at thirty quid a shot. At least she was spared from looking like a panda. She rung out the ends of her hair.

Lucy climbed into the back of the Hiace. 'You can wear some of my stuff 'til yours dries out,' she said, rummaging in a bag. 'Haven't any other shoes, I'm afraid, only these wellies.' She jumped down. She had a pair of bright custard-yellow wellies and a holdall in her hand. 'Come on. Let's get ourselves fixed up in the bog.'

Jodie didn't object. She was worn out. It was good to have someone else to make decisions for her right now. She squelched her way across the lorry park in the wake of the hippie and the dog.

Chapter Eleven

The cottage looked deserted, but it was hard to tell. Bosco cupped his hands against the mucky window and peered into the dimness. There were no obvious signs of occupation. It was quite sparsely furnished, but neat and tidy. No bits and pieces were lying around. No old newspapers, or dishes on the drainer. He decided to take the chance. He went back to the van to get a screwdriver.

'This place looks OK,' he said to Corky. 'Get yer man sorted out, while I force the door open.' He didn't wait for any objections. The visit from the cop had left Corky on the edgy side of jumpy. He felt it better to assume command. The last thing he needed was Corky throwing a wobbler.

The back door afforded him no problems and the lock gave way easily. The place smelled damp and cold. He clicked the light switch but nothing happened. He tried again. Same result. Power must be off, he thought. Further proof that the place was uninhabited.

Corky followed him in, leading the still blindfolded Monty, who stumbled over the step. He settled their hostage on a chair. 'This place is bleedin' freezin',' Corky remarked. He was pissing Bosco off ever so slightly.

'Stop whingin',' Bosco barked. 'It'll be grand when we get a fire goin'.' He looked around for the makings, but all he found were a few damp wood blocks. Neither he nor Corky was a smoker so they didn't have a match between them. To forestall further moans from his partner, Bosco made for the door. 'I'll nip back to that truck stop we passed. There was a shop. They'll have coal an' stuff.'

Monty cleared his throat. 'Er – could you get me some chocolate.' Bosco looked back. 'I need chocolate or I get hypoglycaemic,' Monty said with a tinge of urgency.

'Wha'?'

'I get hypoglycaemic. My blood sugar drops and I pass out.'

'Oh . . . Righ',' Bosco said. 'Any particular kind?' He didn't fancy carting an unconscious Monty around. He dropped his voice two octaves, giving it a sarcastic note. 'Any *particular* kind,' he repeated, remembering that he was supposed to be a ruthless hard-man. Corky gave him a weird look.

'Dairy Milk's fine,' Monty said. Bosco thought he was very calm for a man in a life-threatening situation. Just as well, Corky was wound up enough for all of them.

As it was over two hours since he had first contacted Cindy, he decided it wouldn't do any harm to give her another call, to see how her arrangements for the cash were coming on. He drove to the truck stop and parked as near as he could to the public phones to avoid getting any wetter than necessary.

When he didn't get a reply, he felt a bit anxious until he rationalised that she was probably out at the bank. He hung up, and made a run through the downpour to the shop. He picked up a couple of mega bars of Dairy Milk and a few Mars Bars to help him work rest and play, put them in the wire basket, then looked around until he found Firelighters and matches and, as an afterthought, a bundle of candles. On the way past the fridge he picked up a litre of milk and a fresh loaf from the bread shelf. He had seen coal and peat briquettes stacked outside the shop door. He paid for the contents of the basket and told the sales girl to take for a bag of coal and a bale of briquettes.

It was as he was stuffing his shopping into a plastic carrier bag that he first noticed the patrol car. He walked over to the window and looked out at the lorry park. The car had stopped right in front of the van and he could see the cop through the windscreen talking into his radio. Bosco fought the urge to panic and stood where he was, weighing up the situation. What if the cop at the caravan site had checked up on the van's plate and found out it was nicked? These guys could be on the look-out. He took a couple of deep breaths and watched and waited. The cop finished talking into the radio just as his oppo came out of the café carrying two take-away cups of coffee. They sat there and drank their coffee, chatting together.

Bosco took the bull by the horns. Picking up his shopping, he pulled up his coat collar and headed outside. He heaved the bag of coal on to his shoulder and took the bale of briquettes in his free hand. Instead of walking by the cop car, he made his way round the back of the van and checked the lorry park for a likely vehicle to steal. Most of them were big trucks. The only possible was a beat-up looking Hiace. Nonchalantly, he walked up to it and peered through the side window. He tried the door. It slid open easily.

With her hair dry and her make-up fixed, Jodie felt a lot better. She had warmed up now she was out of her wet clothes. The ladies' toilet was cosy and very clean. There was an electric storage heater against one wall and she had put her soaking wet jeans, sweater and shoes on top, next to Lucy's skirt. They were steaming nicely now and wouldn't take too long to dry. Her leather jacket was in a sorry state, but Lucy cheered her up by drawing her attention to the fact that cows generally lived out in the open air, so it was very probable that it would dry out fine. In front of her on the vanity unit, Lucy had laid out an Indian print skirt, a pair of thick woollen socks and a heavy hand-knit jumper that looked as if it had seen the boil wash more than once. Clothes that, in normal circumstances, she wouldn't have been seen dead in. But she was grateful. She dressed and pulled on the wellies over the thick socks. She felt toasty warm. It was a comfort.

'Are you going to call your friend now?' Lucy asked.

Jodie had been putting it off. 'I suppose I should get it over with,' she said.

Lucy fished inside the holdall and dragged out a plastic rain-mac. It was one of those transparent efforts that folds up into the size of a postcard. It was wrinkled and sorry-looking. Jodie caught sight of her reflection in the mirror. A fucking hippie in yellow wellies. She smirked at the thought that anything could make her look worse. She smoothed out some of the wrinkles and slipped into the waterproof coat. It reached down to her ankles.

Lucy looked her up and down. She still looked beautiful. How did she do that? Although she had been reasonably good-looking when she was younger, she'd never looked that good. This girl had the ability to appear amazing in anything. She even managed to make yellow wellies into a fashion statement.

Lucy felt sad. Watching Jodie brought it home to her that she was middle-aged. She stared at her reflection in the glass. The black eye pencil that rimmed her eyelids was bleeding into the creases. She licked her finger and wiped away the smudges, then lifted the drooping skin at the corners of her eyes. All that did was to make her look both oriental and old. I should make the effort, she thought. But she knew it was a sow's-ear job. What the hell am I playing at? she asked herself. In three month's time, I'll be the big four-o and what have I got to show for it? Twenty years of living like a hermit with a manic depressive.

Lucy began to have serious doubts about her future. What was there out there for her? All she really knew was that she didn't like her life the way it was, but she had no clear plan of how she would want it to be. Her entire being had been so wrapped up in the dream of getting away that she had never thought past the leaving. It was like having a chronic toothache and only being able to focus on the pain, not on how to fix it. Her subconscious nudged her with scraps of feelings about there being a certain comfort in the familiar, however awful it was. She jabbed the thoughts aside. This is stupid, she told herself. To hell with the familiar. For the past twenty years, I've just been making do. Living in a situation that's totally unsatisfactory in every sense, just because I'm afraid of being on my own.

'Are you OK?' Jodie's voice intruded on her thoughts.

'I'm fine. I was just having an argument with myself. I'm fine.' Lucy had a lump in her throat and her voice had a strangled quality to it.

'Are you sure?'

Fionn was asleep under the storage heater. Lucy bent down and stroked her back. Her fur was hard where the hot air from the heater had force-dried it. She stirred and licked Lucy's hand. The concern in Jodie's voice had touched Lucy. She sank down to the floor beside the dog and started to cry.

Jodie stood by, not sure what to do. She was embarrassed and, to some extent, shocked. The woman had seemed so together, so in control until now. She crouched down and put a comforting arm around Lucy's shoulder, still unsure of what to say. She was uncomfortable with the situation, but at the same time felt unable to walk away from it, particularly as Lucy had helped her, apparently without a second thought.

'Look ... Is there anything I can do?' she asked awkwardly.

Lucy pulled herself together and wiped her eyes on her sleeve. 'I'm sorry. I was just being miserable.' She stumbled to her feet. 'I'm in pretty much the same boat as you. I've just walked out on my husband after twenty years, you see. And I'm not sure where to go from here.'

'Twenty years! Wow,' Jodie said. 'That's a long time.'

'Better late than never.' Lucy spoke with a false breeziness. 'I'll survive. I've managed so far, despite Marcus. Come on, let's get this show on the road.' She picked up her skirt from the heater and rolled it up. 'We can hang these in the Hiace. The heater should finish drying them off by the time we get to Cork.'

Jodie was relieved that the difficult situation had passed.

She wasn't very good when it came to empathising with women. For some reason unknown to her, most women were hostile. She found she usually got on better with men, with the exception of Gnasher Gill. It suddenly dawned on her what Lucy had said. 'You'll drive me to Cork?' She was astounded.

'It's as good a place as any. And I don't have any other pressing plans.'

Jodie collected her damp clothes and rolled them up with Lucy's skirt, before stuffing them in a bin liner that Lucy miraculously produced from her apparently bottomless holdall.

It was one of those situations when you're not sure if you are actually going mad. The two women stood in the rain staring at the empty spot where the Hiace had been parked not an hour before.

'This isn't happening,' Jodie said. 'This can't be fucking happening.'

Lucy was equally stunned. Who in their right mind would be desperate enough to steal the Hiace? It was a rust bucket.

'Did you lock it?' Jodie asked.

'What for? Only a complete card-carrying crazy looper would want that wreck.'

Jodie laughed at the idiocy of it all. 'From the sublime to the ridiculous. First the Merc, now the Hiace! It looks like we found ourselves the luckiest crazy looper in – wherever this is!'

'Shit! All my camping stuff was in that bloody van.' Lucy caught sight of the patrol car. 'Look. There's a cop car. I'll go and report it.' Without waiting for a reply, she hurried off. Seeing no point in standing in torrents of rain so soon after getting herself dry, Jodie trailed after her.

The cops had difficulty keeping a straight face when Lucy gave them the description of the Hiace, but they did their best and even radioed in the report.

Meanwhile Jodie walked over to the public phones and dialled Rogan Hogan's mobile number.

Chapter Twelve

Cindy George ate a leisurely lunch at La Stampa and, as she handed over her platinum Visa card to pay her bill, noticed that it was still raining. She thought it would be nice to go and shop for a new pair of winter boots.

Rogan Hogan was beside himself with rage. Unless you were well acquainted with him, however, you wouldn't be aware of this, because Rogan Hogan never showed his true feelings to those around him. To any of the others sitting in his office that Tuesday afternoon, he was just mildly irritated. Gnasher Gill knew different, but only because he had been with Hogan for a very long time. The meeting broke up and those present, with the exception of Gnasher and Hogan, went about their various missions, all of which related to the apprehension of the three gurriers who had been foolhardy enough to knock off the Merc. Hogan sat behind his desk deep in thought.

Gnasher was puzzled. He couldn't understand why his boss was so concerned about a poxy car, which was leased in any case, when yer woman had legged it with two Ks of top-quality Smack. He intimated as much to Hogan.

'Find where they lifted the car and we have some idea where the bitch is,' Hogan said simply.

Gnasher nodded. 'Righ'.'

Jodie had kept the call simple. All she had said was, 'If you were wondering where the stuff from the safe is, I've got it.' She knew very well that he would have had no doubt about who had it, but it was as good a way as any to open negotiations. 'I need cash, Rogan. I haven't a penny. I want to do a deal.'

Do a deal? Give her money for what was rightfully his? As if! He really wanted to tell her to go to hell. He truly wanted to call her a slag, a slapper and every other name he could think of. Threaten her with serious bodily harm and worse. But Rogan Hogan, as always, kept his head. The ability to keep his anger under control was one of the things that made him so dangerous. The wrath of Rogan Hogan was always studied and planned, never knee-jerk.

'OK.' His voice was reasonable. 'I suppose I was a bit rough on you. We can deal. No hard feelings?'

Jodie knew Hogan too well to feel reassured by his manner, but she played along. 'I don't want a lot, Rogan. I only want enough to give me a new start.'

'How much, Honey? How much d'you need?' Over-the-top reasonable.

'A hundred grand should do it.' Jodie had thought of asking for a lot more but, weighing up the pros and cons, she estimated that the figure was just about low enough for him to agree without a fight. More, and he might get iffy. The Smack must be worth twenty times that to him. 'Look on it as my pension,' she added. 'And you'll never hear from me again.'

'OK, Sweetie. I guess I owe you that. Where are you?'

Alarm bells. 'I'll call you later,' she said, at once paranoid, and slammed down the phone.

Rogan could be at his most dangerous when he sounded that calm. She'd seen him in action enough times to know that much. She found her hands were shaking. Jodie leaned her back against the wall and closed her eyes. What the hell am I doing? she thought. If he catches up with me he'll fucking kill me. She knew she had to dream up a decent plan fast or she could well find herself the subject of a lurid tabloid headline. The rain was beating against the back of the phone box. She could see Lucy sitting in the Garda car talking to the cops. She was suddenly very depressed. Thus far anger, denial and bloody-mindedness had kept her going. Now she was running on empty. Her reflection mocked her. Even if she got to Cork, she was hardly likely to nab a megamillionaire looking like some fugitive from Woodstock. She watched as Lucy got out of the patrol car and made a dash for the café, closely followed by the dog. At least *she* had the dog. Jodie felt alone and abandoned. She picked up the attaché case and her bag from the floor, pulled up the hood of the plastic mac, and headed across the lorry park to the café.

Bosco had a good fire going. He felt that seeing the cop at the caravan site had been a blessing in disguise. He said as much to Corky.

'How d'ya make that out?' Corky asked.

'Is this place better or wha'?' Bosco asked. 'It's warm, isn't it?' Corky shrugged, then gave a grudging nod. 'There's more room, isn't there?'

Corky nodded again.

'From my point of view, it's much more comfortable,' Monty piped up. They had seated him in an armchair by the fire. His hands were still cuffed and his eyes covered, but Bosco had taken off the tape that bound his ankles before they left the caravan. He was far too heavy to lug around. Better and easier if he was able to walk. 'The chocolate was good too. Thanks.'

'Yer grand,' Bosco said, forgetting that he was supposed to be a psychopath. He found it weird when Monty spoke. It was something about the way he pointed his blindfolded eyes in exactly the wrong direction that was unnerving. Bosco sat in the chair at the other side of the fireplace and stretched out his legs towards the warmth. Corky had relaxed a bit and was lying full length on a rickety sofa, which he had pulled up to within three feet of the fire. It was a cosy candle-lit scene.

After ten minutes or so Bosco said, 'Aren't yeh 'fraid?'

Monty looked over in approximately the direction of Corky's feet and said, 'Afraid of what?'

'Aren't yeh 'fraid we'll kill yeh? Aren't yeh afraid a' dyin'?'

Monty shrugged and addressed his answer to Corky's size tens. 'What's to be afraid of? Dying isn't hard. I died last year when I had a heart attack. The paramedic brought me back to life. There was nothing to it.' He paused, then qualified his statement in case his abductors got the idea that it was an invitation to help him on his way to the hereafter. 'Of course, I don't *want* to die. Who does? But I'm not afraid of it. Anyway, I don't think you want to kill me. You want money, right? Why would you kill me? I can't identify you, and my wife'll pay you whatever you want.'

Black soft leather, to just below the knee, with a three-inch heel. Cindy dithered. Not about the three-hundred-and-fifty-pound price tag, but would they go with red Versace? She decided that they would. 'I'll take them,' she said.

Marcus Pyle stirred and opened his eyes. He was cold and his head was splitting. It took him a minute to realise that he was lying on the sofa, not in his own bed. A fit of coughing overtook him and he struggled into a sitting position. His mouth was dry. He licked his lips and, with effort, stood up. The room swam and he staggered.

'Lucy!' he called. 'Lucy, where the fuck are you?' He waited for a reply. Silence. He was puzzled when he noticed the pile of fivers on the table, then smiled to himself as he remembered his win-double at the bookie's the day before. He pulled back the curtain and looked out into the yard. The Hiace was gone. What day was it? Tuesday. Dole day. What the fuck was Lucy doing? She knew he needed the van. It was dole day! He had to sign on. Irritated now, he filled a pint glass with water and took a long drink. Why hadn't she woken him? He looked at the clock on the mantelpiece. 'Shit!' It was after one. His sign-on time was eleven. What the hell was she thinking about, the stupid, selfish bitch?

'Lucy!' Yelling now. Angrier. 'Lucy! Get back here now, you moron!'

After he had eaten his lunch, Jake Devine put on his oilskins and headed out through the rain to the barn. He had a mug of tea in his hand. Only Ozzie's legs were visible, protruding from under the front of the bus. He stood and waited. Ozzie was humming an unrecognisable tune as he worked. After a minute or so, he stopped humming and slid out on the trolley.

'I fixed the gearbox but yer track rod ends need replacing.'

'Can you do it?'

'Yeah, no probs. I'll have it ready in a couple of hours, OK?'

Jake looked at his watch and nodded. 'Fine. About threeish, then?'

'Yeah.' Ozzie looked at the steaming mug of tea. 'That for me?'

Jake handed him the mug and the mechanic cupped his hands around it. 'Should go like a dream then.'

'Great,' Jake said. 'Thanks.' He turned and walked back to the house. A man of few words.

Chapter Thirteen

Tuesday, 5 November, three p.m.

They were killing time.

Lucy and Jodie were on their third pot of tea and had run out of things to talk about. During the previous couple of hours Lucy had related her story to Jodie. The telling made her cringe. She sounded so wet! Who else in their right mind would have put up with Marcus's appalling behaviour for so long? It was only as she told her story that she realised the insanity of it all. Assisted by Jodie's reaction to some of the more eccentric incidents, it struck her that until that exact moment, the bizarre nature of her everyday life had sailed way over her head. To her it was normal. That your spouse thought that he was descended from a higher alien life form was not at all unusual. To find oneself routinely responding to the name of Fuck-face or Pea-brain or Youstupidfuckingbitch didn't seem odd. Not nice, maybe, but certainly not odd.

When she dwelled on it she recognised the reason for this state of affairs was its insidious nature. In the beginning, she had been so besotted with Marcus she hadn't noticed how weird and hung-up he was. She had had utter faith in his outlandish plans and ideas, in his ability to accomplish whatever he set out to do. When his schemes didn't pan out and he had blamed her, instead of talking it through and looking for the real reasons, she was so desperate for his approval, so caught up in the myth that she had created in her own mind, that she would apologise and promise to do better the next time. She truly believed that it was all her fault, that she had let him down in some way. Bad idea. She realised now that Marcus had leaped on her insecurity and exploited it. If he wasn't in the humour for an argument, he had learned that the silent treatment was just as good a tool as any for getting his own way or for having Lucy feed his self-esteem by acknowledging her own ineptitude.

Sitting in a steamy café at the truck stop, Lucy grasped the nettle and finally accepted the basic fact that she had spent the past twenty years humouring a madman. She said as much to Jodie.

'Well spotted,' was Jodie's jaded reply. She was fed up. You can only take so much of other people's problems on board, and she had troubles of her own to sort out. Lucy chatted on, but Jodie wasn't listening. It didn't matter, Lucy didn't require any answers. She was talking to herself, really. Sort of do-it-yourself psychotherapy. Talking through and analysing the past.

'What time is this bus due?' Jodie asked suddenly.

Lucy stopped in mid sentence and looked at her watch. 'Another hour.'

'Are you sure your friends won't mind?'

'Of course not. No way. The last time I heard they were living in a squat. It's open house. It'll be cool. Don't worry.'

Jodie cringed. A squat. Only one step up from a cardboard box in a shop doorway. How much further down the social ladder could she slither? 'I've known them since I was at college. We all lived in a sort of commune.' Lucy went on. She stared wistfully at a point somewhere above Jodie's head, remembering better times.

Middle-aged brown-rice types, Jodie thought. Worse and worse. They probably vote for the Monster Raving Green Party and wear sandals with socks.

They had learned about the bus from the petrol pump attendant. It was a private bus that did the trip to Cork every Tuesday, returning on Thursday, or so the man said. The normal departure time was two o'clock, but they were in luck because the driver had called in to say that he would be delayed until four due to a technical problem.

It cheered the two women up a little that at least something was going right for them. He further advised them that the fare was six pounds and that they must purchase the tickets from him in advance to avoid disappointment should the bus be booked out. They parted with their money, Lucy less reluctantly than Jodie, who was now down to her last tenner.

Jodie rubbed a hole in the steamy window and looked out. The rain had stopped at last and the wind seemed to have died down. 'It's brightening up,' she commented, the way you do. 'I think I'll call Rogan again. I've thought of a cunning plan.'

Bosco parked the Hiace well down the road from the truck stop. He hid it in a lane-way, and finished the trip on foot. He was glad that the rain had stopped.

Cindy answered on the tenth ring. He counted. By the fifth ring he became anxious that she wasn't in, but he relaxed again when he heard her singsong, slightly breathless, childish voice on the line. 'Cindy George speaking.'

'Yeh. Got the cash?'

'Well . . . I wanted to talk about that.'

'Whatcha mean?' – sharply.

'Oh, there's no problem,' she added quickly. 'I can get the money, it's just – '

'Just wha', Missus? No tricks or yer aul' fella gets it.' Tough talk.

'You asked for a hundred thousand pounds *not* to kill my husband, right?'

'Yeah?'

'Well, the thing is, what if I gave you one hundred and fifty thousand, on condition that you *do* kill him?'

It took a couple of seconds for it to sink in. 'Wha'? Yeh want me *t'kill* yer aul' fella?'

'That's right. I'll give you one hundred and fifty thousand pounds in used notes.'

Bosco was dumbstruck.

'After I give you the money, I'll wait a day before I call the police, to give you the chance to cover your tracks – ' Cindy had obviously thought it all out. Bosco's heart was pounding in his chest. '. . . Then, I'll call them and report the kidnapping, and that I paid the ransom, and that the kidnappers haven't returned my poor husband home.'

'Yeh want me *t'fuckin' kill* yer aul' fella?' When Cindy didn't reply immediately, he added, 'I don't understand.'

'What's not to understand?' Cindy's voice lost all its softness. 'I'll give you a hundred and fifty grand if you make me a widow. What's hard about that?'

'A hundred an' fifty grand?' Bosco repeated.

Cindy was well aggravated now. 'Oh, all right. Two hundred grand and that's my final offer.'

'Two hundred grand t'pop yer aul' fella? Yeh want me t'pop yer aul' fella fer two hundred grand?'

Cindy felt a tinge of anxiety. She hadn't expected that she'd have to haggle. She wanted to close the deal as soon as possible. Working on the assumption that a bird in the hand is worth two in the bush, she continued, 'I can have the cash by tomorrow. By this time tomorrow, you could be rich.'

Bosco's internal organs were doing a jig. Apart from his heart, his digestive tract was making weird rumbling noises.

Cindy mistook his confusion for cool bargaining technique. 'OK. Two hundred and fifty grand, and that's it. No more. What d'you say?'

Good question. What do you say to someone who has just offered you a small fortune to make them a widow? Bosco gulped. 'Yeh can get the cash by t'morra?' He needed time to think.

'By tomorrow,' Cindy repeated.

'OK. Get the cash sorted. I'll call yeh t'morra.' He slammed down the phone. His hands were shaking and although the temperature was only about two degrees above freezing, he was sweating profusely. 'Jeasus fuckin' Christ!'

He pushed open the door of the kiosk. A blonde hippie type was outside, waiting to use the phone. He held the door for her, then walked off in a daze.

He had no recollection of the drive back to the hide-out. He was on auto-pilot. It only occurred to him as he pulled up at the back of the house that Cindy had just offered him a quarter of a million quid to off her old man. To kill Monty. A quarter of a million! It was like sharing the Lotto.

But there was a catch. He wasn't sure he *could* kill another human being. And how would he do it anyway? Put the sawn-off against the poor bastard's temple and blast his brains out? Stick it in his mouth and pull the trigger? Bosco was in shock. His hands were still shaking and there was a weakness around his knees. That, and the rumblings in his gut, he put down to Corky's greasy fry. He sat in the Hiace for a few minutes more, wondering what to do. Should he tell Corky? Should he tell Monty? Suddenly he felt sorry for Monty. The poor sod. How could he tell him Cindy had just offered a fortune to be rid of him? Make me a widow. Her words echoed round his brain. Hard bitch. Big bazookas or not, she was still a hard bitch.

Corky was in what passed for the kitchen when Bosco walked in. He pulled the door to the sitting-room closed. He didn't want Monty to overhear what he was about to tell his partner.

Corky was standing at a rusty old stove that ran from a gas cylinder. He was heating up soup and was he pleased with himself. 'Got this yoke goin',' he said proudly. 'What did yer woman say? Did she ge' the cash?'

Bosco nodded. 'In a way.'

'Wha'?' Corky stopped stirring the soup.

'She offered us a – ' He hesitated. 'She offered us a hundred an' *fifty* grand.'

He'd never held out on Corky before, but the prospect of an extra hundred grand all to himself got the better of him.

Corky's jaw dropped. 'Bu' we on'y asked fer the ton. Why'd she – ?' He was staggered. Why would someone bargain upwards. 'Jeasus, she mus' think an awful lot 've her aul' fella.'

'Not exactly,' Bosco said. 'She on'y wants us t'fuckin' do away with the poor twat.'

'Wha'? Like kill him?'

Bosco nodded.

'Bloody Nora! What'll we do?'

Bosco shrugged. 'Dunno . . . What d'yeh think?'

Corky shook his head. 'Dunno. But it's worth thinkin' about. A hundred an' fifty grand! Jesus, that's a lotta cash – I know of fellas who'd cut yer arm off t'do it fer five grand.'

'We could always *say* we did it. Dig a hole in the woods an' fill it in again, yeh know? Make it look like a grave.'

Corky switched off the soup. 'Yeah, bu' wha' if she wants t'see the friggin' body? What'll we do then?'

'Shit! I dunno.'

Corky was feeling sorry for Monty too. 'Poor bastard. Poor fuckin' bastard.' A thought struck him. 'Hey. Wha' if we tell yer man his missus wants rid of him. He migh' give us two-hundred grand *not* t'do it.'

That plan didn't suit Bosco at all. That was fifty grand less than he had in the bag already. Shit, he thought, why did I tell the lie? Corky's was a good plan. If he hadn't lied to him in the first place they could have done a deal with Monty for three hundred grand. Shit! Shit! Shit! And bollocks! He made a quick decision. 'We won't say a word yet. I'll tell yer woman we'll do it, an' get the cash. We can worry abou' the rest again.'

Corky looked uncertain. Why settle for a hundred and fifty if they could get more?

Bosco guessed how his mind was working. 'We can't take a chance that she'll get pissed off. She could go t'the cops if we don't play it her way.' The logic was a bit iffy, but Corky seemed to buy it.

At the back of his mind, Bosco knew he couldn't pass up the chance of a lifetime. If push came to shove and Cindy got awkward, he'd just have to grit his teeth and do it.

He looked down at his feet. The white swooch on his Nike trainers said it all. *Just do it.* Suddenly he felt invincible. It's amazing how empowering the promise of a quarter of a million can be. Just do it! Anyway, Monty had said he wasn't afraid of dying. He said it, there, in the room. OK, so he also said he didn't want to die, but hey, who does?

Corky was thinking along the same lines though, being of a squeamish nature, he was rather hoping that if any killing had to be done, Bosco would take care of it. He poured the soup into three mugs. 'Give us a hand,' he said.

Bosco picked up the sliced loaf and followed him out to the sitting-room.

Chapter Fourteen

Tuesday, 5 November, three fifty p.m.

The three lads were terrified.

Decco, the leader, was trying to hide it, not wanting to lose face in front of the other two. He was the one who'd spotted the shiny red Merc in the first place. It was he who had expertly hot-wired it in a new world record time. And why not? It was miles ahead of the crummy Japanese job they'd lifted in Templebar. He cursed Robbo. The stupid little prat. It had been his idea to drive down the country for a spin so they could open it up on the motorway and feel the speed. It was a pseudo sports jobby and as cramped as a sardine can. The bastard thing wouldn't do over seventy-five without the wheels wobbling and the engine knocking like fuck. Then the gearbox had packed up, mainly because it was an automatic, and Robbo, never having driven a car with automatic transmission before, insisted on trying to keep changing gear. At the time it had seemed it was all for luck. They'd abandoned the knackered car and were in search of a substitute. The Merc was sitting there in the lorry park, begging to be lifted. *Deadly*!

Anto, the youngest, and Decco's brother, whimpered. He was standing next to Decco. Decco gave him a sidelong glance. Yes, he was crying all right. Shit! His ma would kill him when she saw the state Anto was in. As if it was his fault.

They were alone in the cellar except for Gnasher Gill. He was sitting on a big crate, cleaning his fingernails with a flick-knife. The blade gleamed as it caught the light. Decco cringed. He hated knives. He'd heard the stories too. Looking around the dimly lit room he wondered if this was the place they did all that stuff. His legs were aching. He felt as if he'd been standing there for ever. He shifted his weight on to his other leg. His back hurt where one of Gnasher Gill's heavies had whacked him in the kidneys just for the laugh. There had been no need. The sight of the two of them standing at the door with baseball bats had been enough. He hadn't put up a struggle.

Anto snivelled and wiped his sleeve across his face. Decco looked at him again and noticed a dark patch on his jeans where he'd wet himself. He heard Robbo cough behind him. At first when they'd been picked up, Decco thought it was about the money he owed Pius Gibney for the couple of rocks of Crack he'd let him have on a promise. He knew Gibney worked for Hogan. But they never even mentioned the Crack, so neither did he. He kept asking what he'd done, why they were kicking the shite out of him, but they didn't say a word, just dumped him in the boot of the car and brought him to this cellar. Robbo and Anto were already there, both bearing the marks of a beating. He could see that Robbo's nose was broken. It was twisted to one side and the front of his T-shirt was caked with blood.

It was Gill who had first mentioned the Merc. Decco nearly shit himself when Gill told him who the Merc belonged to. Of all the Mercs in all the world, why did he have to knock off Rogan Hogan's? And worse, smash it up. Half of him wished they'd just get on with what-ever they were going to do, the other half quaked at the possibilities.

A door behind Gnasher Gill opened and Rogan Hogan walked into the room. Decco held on tight and clamped his buttocks together as his bowels turned to water. Anto lost it and started to wail, crumpling to the floor. Gnasher Gill merely looked up to see what the noise was. Hogan was smiling, but it wasn't an evil smile. It was friendly. Decco was confused.

'Now, lads, I think it's time we had a little chat,' Hogan began.

'So did you talk to your boyfriend?' The conversation had died some minutes before and, as she had been talking about herself for most of the afternoon, Lucy felt it only polite to show some interest in her companion's problems.

'Ex-boyfriend,' Jodie clarified. 'Yes, I talked to him.' She reached for her bag then remembered that she had no cigarettes. Lucy pushed the tin of tobacco across the table. Jodie rolled and lit up, inhaling the comforting smoke deeply into her lungs, then she exhaled through her nose. 'I told him the plan.' She picked a shred of stray tobacco off the tip of her tongue.

'So what is the plan?' Lucy asked.

Surprised by her directness, Jodie told her. 'The deal is, he pays a large sum of money into my bank account, and I return the – his property.'

It sounded rather simplistic to Lucy, particularly after the picture Jodie had painted of a shrewd, psychopathic drug dealer/businessman. 'And he trusts you to return the dr – stuff after he's deposited the cash?'

'He's no choice,' Jodie said. 'He'll just have to look on it as a leap of faith.' She didn't believe for a second that Rogan would trust her to return the Smack, but it was up to him to devise the actual plan to suit both their requirements. If he wanted the Smack, he'd just have to bloody well work it out. She knew for sure that he didn't doubt her threat that she'd dump it down the toilet. Another thing she was sure of was that he hadn't even the tiniest hope of finding her. Holding on to that thought quelled the fear.

'Big leap of faith,' Lucy commented. 'Fucking huge, mega, Olympic standard, leap of faith, if you don't mind me saying.'

Jodie did, but, not wanting to get into a discussion on the matter, made no further comment.

At five to four the bus pulled up in front of the truck stop café. The two women gathered their things together and headed outside. Jodie was dubious. The aged vehicle was a blast from the past. Brown and cream coachwork. Fat, bulbous mudguards. Split windscreen with one tiny wiper. The engine was rumbling and black exhaust gases were belching from the rear. *Veruuumm. Verumm.*

'D'you think it'll make it?' Jodie asked.

'Why not? What's wrong with it?' Lucy said, but then she was used to driving around in the Hiace.

Jodie, grasping the fact, just shook her head. 'Never mind.'

The door was open so they clambered up the four steep steps. Jodie, unaccustomed to long skirts flapping round her ankles, experienced some difficulty. The driver's seat was empty, as was the rest of the bus.

'Good job we booked in advance to avoid disappointment.' Lucy swung her bottomless holdall up on to the luggage rack.

Jodie, unwilling to tempt fate a second time, hugged the attaché case to her chest, and took a window seat about five rows from the front. Lucy sat in the aisle seat next to her, while Fionn settled down on their feet. After about five minutes, an elderly couple got on and sat down at the back.

Jodie looked at her watch. It was nearly ten past four. 'I thought this thing was supposed to leave at four.' She was grumpy, worn out from lack of sleep and adrenalin overload. She was also in desperate need of a long hot bath as the plastic mac made her feel tacky and damp.

At twenty past, a tall man wearing a long waxed trench-coat got on and walked down to the back of the bus. He had dark features, a five-o'clock shadow and hooded eyes, which gave him a brooding look. Jodie guessed he was around the forty mark. On his head, he wore a cowboy hat with a thin silver band. He reminded her of a bounty hunter. She stared at his feet as he walked down the bus. Yes, he was wearing cowboy boots under his black jeans, but no spurs. She turned and looked at him over the back of her seat after he had passed. A skinny pony-tail hung down past his shoulder-blades. He had a rolling, easy gait.

She nudged Lucy. 'The man with no name.' She cast her eyes to the ceiling.

The elderly couple handed the man with no name their tickets. He seemed to know them. The old man said something Jodie couldn't make out and he replied, then she heard them all laugh. Jodie turned back in her seat. Lucy was sitting bolt upright, staring straight ahead.

'What's up?' Jodie asked.

'I think I know that guy,' she whispered.

'So?' Jodie turned in her seat to look at him again.

Lucy grabbed her arm. 'No. Don't look!' she hissed. 'I mean I know him from years back. From when I was at college.'

'So what?' Jodie repeated.

'So, the last time I saw him I stole fifty quid from him. That's what!'

'No shit! Then you'd better keep your head down so he won't recognise you,' Jodie hissed back.

The man with no name strode back down the bus and stopped by their seat.

'What time will we get into Cork?' Jodie asked as she handed over their tickets. Lucy, who had sunk down in her seat, was paying particular attention to the toe of her left boot.

'About six thirty,' the man with no name said. 'Barring floods, that is.' Jodie, who, carried away by first impressions, was expecting a Texan drawl, was surprised when he spoke with a sort of velvety West Brit accent. She stifled a snigger as he touched the brim of his hat with his forefinger in salute. He walked on down the bus towards the front, then stopped suddenly and turned. He stared straight at Lucy, who turned a whiter shade of pale, then shook his head and continued back down to the front where he slid behind the driver's seat. He closed the doors and moved off.

'Was it him?' Jodie asked.

Lucy nodded. She fought the urge to make a dash for it and leap from the moving bus, reasoning that she would only draw attention to herself. Suddenly she felt very ashamed. Jake Devine had been a friend of sorts, she had shared the squat with him and a bunch of other students, but she had stolen from him without a second thought. All because of Marcus. All because she'd been so desperate to follow him back to Ireland and didn't have the boat fare.

'D'you think he recognised you?' Jodie asked, digging her in the ribs with her elbow.

'Don't think so,' Lucy said. 'God, I hope not.'

Bosco and Corky drank their soup in silence. Monty, who had become accustomed to eating blindfold, was dunking his bread in the soup and munching away happily. Bosco couldn't get over how calm he was. He must trust his old lady to pay up, no problem, he thought. Poor bastard. Then he checked himself. It didn't do to feel sorry for your victim. If he started to feel even the slightest sympathy for Monty, he knew he would never be able to finish the job. And a quarter of a million is a quarter of a million at the end of the day.

Monty was as relaxed as he appeared. He had total faith in Cindy. In some ways he found it all rather exciting. Being in the company of his two kidnappers, hearing their banter, convinced him that they weren't as hard as they wanted him to believe. The small one had showed no reluctance to buy him the chocolate, had he? They'd let him lie on the sleeping bag in the van, hadn't they? He was fed and they allowed him to use the toilet. They were concerned for his comfort. He felt perfectly sure that he was safe as houses and that it was all a matter of time. At the back of his mind he wondered if Cindy would find him more exciting after this adventure. Would she value him more now that she had tasted the risk of losing him? Would she actually love him for real?

He remembered the first time he laid eyes on Cindy. He'd

thought she was gorgeous. He was a guest at his niece's wedding reception in the Shelbourne Hotel and was taking a breather in the lobby. He had found it difficult to mingle in large crowds for too long at a time as it was only about eighteen months since Monica's death.

Unaware that she knew exactly who he was and how much he was worth, he was highly flattered when she made a bee-line for him and, though it seemed corny, asked for a light for her cigarette. Flustered and embarrassed, he had dropped his lighter, and they both stooped together to retrieve it. Their hands had brushed and he felt a tingle of electricity. Thinking back, he couldn't recall their conversation, but he remembered how his ego was inflated to bursting by her undivided attention. Whatever his friends might say behind his back, and he had no illusions about that, he knew they all, without exception, secretly envied him.

'Did you speak to my wife?' he asked Corky's left foot.

'Yeah. She's gettin' the money. Yeh should be home by tomorra or the next day.' Bosco felt a bit guilty about lying to Monty. Was it fair to build up his hopes? But what did it matter? He was a gonner. He'd be dead. He wouldn't know the difference. Think of the money, he kept telling himself. Think of all that cash.

'What are you going to do with the money?' Monty enquired, as if reading his mind.

'I'm goin' t'buy a dog. A racin' dog,' Corky said. Bosco glared at him. What was he playing at? Carried away by his dream, Corky ignored him. 'I'd like t'breed 'em too. Get a good bitch an' breed pups.'

'Really?' Monty sounded surprised. 'I used to breed greyhounds. I had a Greyhound Derby winner back in the eighties. Bred him myself.'

Corky said, 'Yer kiddin'!'

Bosco lifted his boot and kicked Corky to catch his attention, then glared at him again.

Corky rubbed his wounded side and looked round at his partner. 'Wha'?'

Bosco put his finger to his lips and shook his head. Corky shrugged and went back to his soup. 'I was on'y sayin'.'

Monty sniffed the air. 'Is it only me, or can you smell gas?'

The explosion took them all by surprise. There was an almighty boom and the kitchen door flew open, followed by a tongue of flame. It all happened in slow motion after that.

Fortunately the kitchen was at the opposite end of the house from the front door so their means of escape wasn't blocked by falling debris. Bosco leaped up, grabbed Monty by the upper arms and, in a burst of adrenalin-fuelled strength, yanked him to his feet and made a run for the door. Corky grabbed the sawn-off and followed.

The sturdy stone walls saved them, but the corrugated tin roof was in bits and the rafters were ablaze. They heard the crash of the ceiling coming down as they were half-way through the door. No one looked back. A further massive explosion, as the gas cylinder ignited and took off like a rocket through the roof. The force of the explosion blew them off their feet and they ended up at the far side of the yard in a tangled and dazed heap. Bosco, lying on his back looking at the ruined, burning cottage thought, I'd better move the Hiace, just as the gas cylinder re-entered the earth's atmosphere and, making a loud whistling sound, plunged through the roof of the van.

'What's happening? What's happening?' Monty was very agitated.

'The fuckin' cooker blew up,' Corky said. 'An' it burned the friggin' house down.' He laughed uncontrollably. 'The bleedin' house is burned.'

Bosco struggled to his feet and ran over to the remains of the Hiace. There was a perfectly neat hole in the roof where the cylinder had penetrated the rusty metal. It was wedged between the front seats, half-way through the floor. It was obvious that the gearbox was banjaxed. He stared in disbelief. The house was well ablaze now, and he realised that their jackets, cash and all their stuff – with the exception of his knitted ski mask, which was mocking him from the front seat of the Hiace – were inside. Corky was still laughing like an eejit. Monty had lifted the blindfold and was staring at the burning building, mouth agape. And, as if that wasn't enough, it started to rain again.

Bosco sat down in the dirt yard with his back against the Hiace. Why? Why the fuck did this have to happen when everything was going so well? He looked up at the dark, angry sky and, as the rain lashed down into his face, yelled at the top of his voice, 'Well, fuck you, God! Fuck you too!'

Confident that Jake had not recognised her, Lucy began to relax. To be on the safe side, she said in a low voice to Jodie, 'Whatever you do, don't call me Lucy. Call me something else.'

Jodie shrugged. 'OK. Whatever.' She felt more comfortable with her travelling companion since her admission of larceny. Up until then she had had the feeling that the hippie had the upper hand, knowing that she was carrying two K of Smack in her hand luggage. She wasn't altogether sure that an attack of moral indignation might not have led Lucy to turn her in to the cops. Now at least they were on equal terms in the moral high ground stakes.

The bus slowed down and stopped. Ahead of them, they could see the flashing blue lights of a cop car, a big breakdown truck and an ambulance. A large wagon had overturned and was partially blocking the road. Jake slid his side window open and stuck his head out. They heard him talking to someone but couldn't make out the conversation. After a few minutes he slid the window shut and eased himself out from behind the wheel. Instinctively Lucy shrank down in her seat again and looked at the floor.

'Sorry, folks. Small delay 'til they move the wagon off the highway.'

'What happened?' Jodie asked. Lucy could have strangled

her. Why did she have to talk to him? He was standing right beside her seat now.

'Circus wagon skidded on mud and lost control on the bend back there,' he said, pointing out of the back window of the bus. 'The trailer went right over the bank.'

'Anyone hurt, Jake?' the elderly man asked.

Lucy exhaled as he moved away and joined the two at the rear of the bus. 'Not seriously,' he said.

'Chill out, Lucy,' Jodie said in a low voice. 'If I didn't know better, I'd think your body language was very suspect.'

'What?'

'Relax! He hasn't recognised you. But the way you're going on, you're drawing attention to yourself.'

'Really?'

'Trust me.'

Lucy tried to relax, but her spine was as tense as a steel rod and her shoulders hunched up round her ears. Jake was still sitting at the back of the bus in conversation with the elderly couple, whom he called Jon-Joe and Biddy. They seemed like a happy pair.

Jake liked them a lot. They were regulars and he'd known them since he had started to do the Cork run two years before. Going Tuesdays returning Thursdays suited them well. They visited their daughter and stayed over, baby-sitting the three grandchildren so she and her husband could have a night out.

Jake enjoyed life in rural Ireland. It was a far cry from the rat-race of London. He knew how lucky he was that he'd been able to leave it behind before burn-out set in. Often he reflected on the strange twists and turns of fate. After leaving art college he had started his career in graphic design. He had hated it. Hated the regimentation of having to work to a deadline and a brief. It didn't suit his temperament. He loved a challenge, but he needed a project to pick to pieces and reassemble in his own time. He was frequently fired. He didn't care. He developed an interest in computers and started designing computer games along with Craig Wilson, a friend who was not only computer-mad, but also a marketing executive. He had found his niche. He devised formats, designed the graphics, and between them they worked on the software nuts and bolts that made the programs work. Their games were imaginative and exciting, and the graphics far superior compared with anything that was on offer at the time. In the first three years of operation they snatched the largest slice of an ever growing market.

After five years Jake became disillusioned. It wasn't fun any more. He was under pressure again. Deadlines and balance sheets reared their ugly heads. He was just thinking about jacking it all in and walking away when, in the early nineties, a Japanese multinational bought out the company for an obscene amount of money and set him free. He retreated to Ireland, bought a derelict water-mill and some land, and set about restoring and rebuilding it. He took up singing again and had a regular gig with a country music band in Cork on Tuesday and Wednesday nights. He'd inherited the bus when he bought the mill. He liked the idea of being the local bus driver. He also loved to drive the bus. It was like being a kid again, but with a life-sized Dinky toy. He felt it made him part of the community.

Jon-Joe was telling him a story about a ewe he'd bought the week before, but Jake couldn't concentrate and, with Jon-Joe's accent and the fact that he didn't wear his top set of dentures, it was essential to concentrate in order to understand what he was saying. Jake's lack of concentration wasn't due to any deficit in the interest department, but to the woman sitting in the aisle seat mid-way down the bus. She reminded him of someone but he couldn't place her and it was bugging him. Jon-Joe finished his story and Biddy laughed enthusiastically. Jake took her cue and joined in.

A cop pushed open the door. 'You should be able to get past now if you're careful,' he told them.

Jake made his way back to the driver's seat, studying the woman's profile as he passed her, but he was none the wiser because she turned her head away just as he drew level. With the cop guiding him, he carefully manoeuvred round the partially moved wreckage of the wagon. Before he drove away the cop warned him to watch out for fallen trees.

From time to time he looked at the woman through the rear-view mirror. He estimated that she was about his own age. He hadn't heard her speak so he had no idea where she was from. Was it London or Ireland? The information was sitting somewhere at the back of his brain and he couldn't retrieve it.

Unaware of Jake's interest, Lucy had relaxed again and she and Jodie were chatting.

'What are you going to do when we get to Cork?' Jodie asked.

'I suppose I'll hang out with my friends for a while and see what's going on. What about you?'

'When Rogan pays up, I'll kit myself out in designer gear and snare me a rich man.' She paused. 'In fact, that's what you should do. It's time someone looked after you for a change.'

Lucy snorted. 'Yeah, right.'

'Why not? You've done your stint with that gobshite. Now it's time for you to sit back and be spoiled.'

'Look at me, Jodie. At my age, statistically I'm more likely to be involved in a terrorist incident than I am to meet a suitable man.'

At that moment they were both thrown forward in their seats as Jake slammed on the brakes and the bus skidded to a halt.

The next moment Bosco erupted through the doors waving the sawn-off and wearing his mother's knitted ski mask. 'This is a hijack!' he yelled. 'Everyone stay still and no one gets hort.'

Chapter Fifteen

Tuesday, 5 November, five p.m.

It just wasn't Cathy Grady's day. Pulled off an interview with Mel Gibson, who was in the country scouting for locations for his new movie, she'd been sent off at a moment's notice to cover the storms.

'Nothing the viewers like better than a good dose of death and destruction, Cathy,' her boss and anchor-man, Liam Goggin had said. That he didn't attempt to hide the smirk that accompanied the remark didn't help her humour.

'I mean, Mel Gibson. Hunky, gorgeous Mel Gibson, and where am I going?' she raged at herself that morning in the mirror. 'To the back end of bloody beyond, and in shite weather to boot.'

And as if missing out on the delectable Mel wasn't bad enough, Liam Goggin had allocated Micky Folan as her cameraman. Micky bloody Folan of all people.

'That spawn of Satan,' she hissed at the mirror as she aggressively attacked the tangles in her hair with her hairbrush.

Micky Folan. Everyone's best friend. 'Sure isn't Micky only gas,' 'Isn't Micky great crack,' was the general consensus around Madigan's Pub. Sure enough, he was a great cameraman. Got the footage when push came to shove. God knows he should be good. He'd been at it long enough. Sometimes she wondered what she had ever done to Micky to provoke his merciless practical jokes, of most of which she was the victim.

Despite Cathy Grady's unswerving contention that Micky

Folan was out to get her, this wasn't strictly true. At least, not in the sense Cathy imagined. The reason that she was so regularly the butt of Micky's juvenile sense of humour was because he looked on her as a challenge. In all his forty-five years on the planet, he had never come across anyone so completely devoid of a sense of humour as Cathy Grady. He took every opportunity to prove to himself that somewhere in her tight-arsed body there had to be at least one tiny grain of fun.

In some ways Cathy Grady's paranoia was understandable. It had not been a good six months for her. She blushed as she recalled the incident when she mistook Abe Horovitz, an eccentric American billionaire about to invest heavily in a software operation in Carlow, for Woody Allen and asked him, on air, about his relationship with Soon Yee.

'I didn't know they were staying in the same hotel.' She cringed at the memory. That little disaster was down to Micky bloody Folan. The man was sick.

'Quick, Cathy! It's Woody Allen. Quick, I'm rolling.'

She would never forgive him either for letting her interview Dick Spring, a three-minute in-depth piece in which she questioned him about his views on the forthcoming visit of President Clinton and the effects of the visit on the peace process, with a small chunk of broccoli stuck to her left front incisor.

It wasn't meant to be like this. By now, two years into her contract with RTE, Cathy had expected more. Unlike her sister Megan, who sailed through school and college, seemingly without opening a book, Cathy had to work at it. And she had. Late into the night. At weekends, when all her friends were out on the town, Cathy had worked single-mindedly towards her goal. She achieved a respectable degree in Political Science and Journalism at UCD. She worked first for the *Indo*, then got a staff job at the *Irish Times*. Things were going according to plan.

Cathy wanted to be the best. She wanted to get into television. She even took a pay cut to that end when the job with RTE came up. She wanted to front programmes like *Prime Time*. Like *Questions and Answers*. Maybe even move to the Beeb and do *Panorama*. Perhaps cross the pond and join CNN as an anchor-woman. She fantasised sometimes, staring at her reflection in the bathroom mirror. 'This is Cathy Grady, for World News' – pause – 'CNN, Atlanta.'

Now, standing in front of the wreckage of a circus wagon in the teeming rain, her hair blowing in her face, she felt like signing off, 'Cathy Grady, RTE News, cold, wet and hungry, and thoroughly pissed off.' But she was too professional for that.

'OK, Micky. Let's go for a take. Three . . . two . . . one . . .' She took a deep breath, arranged a serious but suitably concerned expression on her face and looked straight into the camera.

'The crash took place shortly after three thirty this afternoon on the Boran road, when the lorry skidded on a mud slide causing the circus trailer to jack-knife. The driver lost control and sustained two broken legs and head injuries. He was taken by air ambulance to the Mater hospital where his condition is described as comfortable.' She ended the report: 'When asked about the rumour that several of the circus animals had escaped, a spokesman stated that this was the case, but that the animals in question were docile and not dangerous. He also said that they had every confidence the animals would be recaptured very soon. He would not specify what species were at large. The public are warned, however, not to approach an animal should they come across one, but to inform the Gardai immediately.' She paused, then signed off, 'Cathy Grady, RTE News, Boran.'

Micky smirked. 'Sorry, Cath, have to go again. Yer hair was all over the place.' He handed her his woolly hat. 'Try this.'

Cathy jammed the hat on her head. 'This never happens to Kate fucking Adie,' she muttered viciously. Then, rearranging her face, counted back from three again.

*

Decco couldn't remember the name of the place where they'd knocked off the Merc, neither could the other two.

Rogan Hogan was close to losing patience. It was evident to Gnasher Gill because, even though Hogan was still smiling pleasantly at the three gurriers, his eyes were steely cold.

Decco saved their hides by suggesting that he'd know the place when he saw it again, if he did the same journey. It was the best plan on offer.

Gnasher grabbed Decco by the left ear and twisted it violently. 'Don't do any messin' or ye'll be carryin' yer bleedin' ears home in yer pocket, righ'?'

'Riiiigh'!' Decco's reply came out in a sort of strangled yelp.

Gnasher let go of his ear and gave him a shove in the back. It caught Decco in the tender part of his kidneys. The pain was so intense he wanted to crumple to the floor and cry like his younger brother, but he was bright enough to know that it was not a good idea to give Gnasher Gill any excuse to lay the boot in. He gingerly patted his ear to make sure it was still attached to the side of his head.

Robbo and Anto were cowering in the shadows, trying to be invisible.

Hogan said, 'Take him, Gnasher. Drive there and ask around. She's no transport now, so see what you can find out and call me later.' He picked up his briefcase and headed for the door.

'What'll I do with *them*?' Gnasher asked, indicating the other two-thirds of the trio. They shrank even further in size.

Hogan, without breaking his stride, waved a dismissive hand in their general direction. 'Get the lads to give them a smack and then let them go.'

Anto wet himself again.

In some twisted, misguided way Decco saw the situation as an opportunity. The best break he had ever had in all of his fifteen years on earth. If he could impress Rogan Hogan, if he could only make Hogan see that he was smart, there was a chance that he would give him an opportunity to make something of himself. He knew he was way smarter than that psycho gobshite Gill, and he'd sell a lot more gear than that loser, Pius Gibney.

The pain in his back had subsided to a dull ache by the time Gnasher Gill hit the motorway. Decco enjoyed the comfort and speed of the top-of-the-range BMW as it purred effortlessly along.

One day, he thought, one day I'll have one a' these.

Wesley looked back up the hill and blinked his beady eyes as the bright lights of the TV crew and mobile crane momentarily dazzled him. He was disorientated and groggy. His ribs hurt where he'd been slammed into the side of the truck. He'd remembered nothing further about the crash when he came to, lying in a heap in the undergrowth at the bottom of the hill. The ground beneath him was soft and muddy.

Wesley watched the people milling around at the top of the hill. Snatches of shouts and the rumble of the crane's machinery were carried down by the wind. He knew if he was to survive he would have to make it up to the top of the hill. Stiff and sore, Wesley concentrated his mind. The longest journey starts with the first step he told himself.

When he heard the vehicle driving into the yard, Marcus thought it was Lucy and the anger rose again in his chest. He had been muttering to himself all day, rehearsing what he would say to her when she finally put in an appearance.

He sat in his chair, staring into the fire. Depending on her attitude, he'd either give her the silent treatment for a couple of hours or, if she showed any sign of aggression, he would launch straight into a row.

He felt closer than he had ever felt to slapping her. No – punching her. In fact, he was looking forward to it. She had pushed him far too close to the wire lately. Her attitude had changed for the worse over the last few months and she was arguing back. And what did she know? Wasn't it he who had taught her everything? Before she met him, she knew nothing. Hadn't he worked his fingers to the bone to give them a good life? And all she could do was spoil everything. Mess up every opportunity. If it weren't for her negativity about the individual trifle deal, they'd be rich now. But no. She couldn't bear to see him succeed. She was jealous of his mind; of his superior intellect.

A sharp rap on the door made him jump. He sat tight. Another rap. Irritated, he thought, so she thinks she's smart? Then, inasmuch as Marcus Pyle's bulk could facilitate leaping of any kind, he leaped from the chair.

'Mister Mark Pyke?' the cop enquired.

Taken aback that it wasn't Lucy standing there on the step, it took a moment for the cop's words to register. 'Marcus,' he stuttered. 'Marcus Pyle. P-Y-L-E.' He spelled the word out slowly. 'Who are you? What do you want?'

'I'm Sergeant Mulligan,' the cop replied, as if Marcus should know. 'Are you the registered owner of a maroon Hiace van?' He read the registration from his notebook.

Marcus nodded. 'Yes. Well, no. My wife's the registered owner. Why?'

Mulligan handed him a crumpled piece of paper. 'I found your ESB bill in the Hiace. It's overdue.'

'What?'

'You'd better pay it or they'll cut you off.'

Marcus stared at him open-mouthed. Since when did the cops start chasing up debts for the ESB?

Sergeant Mulligan looked down at his notebook and produced the stubby remains of a pencil from his pocket. Marcus continued to stare at him. Who was this pig-thick eejit? He was half expecting him to lick the point of the pencil.

'Where were you at approximately four o'clock this afternoon, Mister Pyke?' the policeman asked.

Marcus had already taken a strong dislike to Sergeant Mulligan. 'The name's Pyle, not Pyke, and I was here. Why?'

'Is your wife at home, Mister Pyke?'

What was this fat bastard going on about? 'No, she isn't here at the moment. She's off somewhere in the van.'

'*She* has the van? And what's her name?'

'Lucy. My wife's name is Lucy Spoon. What's this about?'

'Quare sort of a name,' Mulligan muttered as he looked over Marcus's shoulder. 'Could we go inside?' Reluctantly Marcus stood back and the cop walked past him into the living-room.

He was a big man and he didn't look very fit to Marcus who always thought cops were supposed to be athletic. He was suddenly anxious. The notion that Lucy had been in an accident crossed his mind.

Mulligan did a quick appraisal of the room and then stood with his back to the range, warming his backside. 'If she's your wife, why has she a different name to you?'

'She just has,' Marcus replied impatiently. 'Has something happened to her? Has there been an accident?'

Mulligan ignored the question. 'Do you know if your wife belongs to any of the proscribed organisations?'

'What?'

Mulligan gave him a let's-not-play-games look. 'Is your wife a Republican, Mister Pyke?'

A cross between a snort and a cough exploded from somewhere inside Marcus. 'Phwaah! A Republican? Are you crazy?'

Mulligan just stared steadily at him, saying nothing. He couldn't stand these hippie types. All drop-outs living off the state. New-age travellers they called themselves these days. New-age knackers more like.

When Marcus had recovered his wits enough to see that the cop was serious, he said, 'What's this about? Where's my wife?'

The sergeant walked over to the window and looked out into the yard. He spoke with his back to Marcus. 'At four o'clock this afternoon there was an explosion at a property on the Boran road. The house was destroyed along with the Hiace van your wife was allegedly driving. At this point in time, we suspect the house was being used as a bomb factory.'

Marcus was lost for words.

Mulligan allowed a while for the information to sink in, then continued: 'Preliminary examination of the premises has revealed a quantity of fertiliser, the type used in home-made explosives. At the moment we're waiting for the specialist anti-terrorist technical team to come from Dublin to examine the scene.' In reality, Mulligan hadn't phoned Dublin yet. He wanted to have a good start on them, so he was delaying the call for as long as possible.

Still speechless, Marcus gaped at the cop. That Lucy could be a terrorist was the most bizarre notion he had ever heard. She hadn't the imagination for one thing. 'But my wife's English,' he spluttered.

Mulligan raised his eyebrows. 'English?' he said, half to himself. 'Hm. Is she a left footer then?'

'What?'

'You know. A left footer? A Prod.' Eugene Mulligan wasn't into this new fangled politically correct rubbish. He believed in calling a spade a spade.

Marcus said, 'I suppose so. I don't know. We've never talked about it.'

'Never talked about it? And why would that be, Mr Pyke? Would it be because she's a member of the UFF? Or the UVF maybe?' Mulligan felt a surge of excitement. This was just the sort of incident he needed. If he could steal a march on that snotty crew, soon to be on their way from Dublin, he'd be made. He'd show the bastards he could do the job as well, if not better, than they could with all their courses. Common sense, that's what good police work was. Common sense, not seminars. He was sick of their sneering and the way they took over as soon as a good case came along. Thirty years he'd been in the job. Thirty years. Some of the little snother-boxes weren't even that age. They were still wet behind the ears. He cocked an eyebrow at Marcus, waiting for a reaction.

Marcus was horrified.

'What time did your wife go out, Mister Pyke?'

Marcus shook his head. 'I don't know. She was gone when I woke up.'

'And what time was that?'

'Around one. I remember looking at the clock, and I was annoyed that she hadn't woken me. I was supposed to sign on at eleven.' Marcus wasn't normally given to talking to the police so freely, but he was still in a state of shock at the thought of Lucy being an IRA or UFF or whatever kind of bomber. Once he started, he couldn't shut up. 'She knew I needed the van. You see, I always go into town to sign on Tuesdays.'

Mulligan was pleased to see that he had rattled Marcus who was just babbling now. He raised his voice to cut across him. 'Mister Pyke?'

Marcus fell silent. He had a weakness at the knees so he sat down at the table.

'We haven't found any bodies yet so we don't think she was hurt.'

Marcus stared at the table top, his head a jumble of conflicting emotions. He heard Mulligan moving around the room picking things up and putting them down again.

'Is this your wife?'

Marcus looked up. Mulligan was holding a snapshot of Lucy and the dog. He remembered taking it five summers before when he was toying with the idea of becoming a photographer. He nodded.

Mulligan put the photo in his pocket. 'I'll borrow this, if you don't mind.' He didn't wait for any objection.

'Was she alone?' The assumption of another man had seeped into Marcus's head. She must have another man. How else would she have become involved with a terrorist group? That was it! She had an IRA or UFF or whatever lover. That would explain her change of attitude. That Lucy didn't have the opportunity to become involved with another man simply because he watched her like a hawk – knew exactly where she was at any given time – didn't occur to Marcus. It had taken approximately twenty seconds for

Mulligan to convince him that his wife of twenty years was a subversive. Not surprising, considering that Marcus Pyle routinely thought the worst of Lucy Spoon.

'Why d'you ask if there was another man? Do you know something?'

Marcus shook his head violently from side to side. 'No. No. I just wondered, that's all.'

Sure, thought Mulligan. We'll get back to that one. 'We don't know for certain if she was alone,' he said aloud. 'Some charred men's clothing was found at the scene, so it's probable that she wasn't. These terrorist cells are usually a group of three or four individuals.'

As he was speaking, Marcus heard another vehicle drive into the yard. His first thought was that it was Lucy until he remembered that the cop had said the Hiace was destroyed.

Sergeant Mulligan looked out of the window, then made straight for the door. 'My colleague,' he said. 'You don't mind if we take a little look around?'

'What?'

He opened the door. 'Your wife is a fugitive, Mister Pyke. I'm sure you'll have no objections to us searching the place. You'll find my colleague has a warrant in any case.'

Unaware that she was currently at the top of the Boran Garda Siochana's most wanted list, Lucy Spoon had other things on her mind. She was sitting on the floor in the corner of Jake Devine's living-room, along with Jodie McDeal and the dog.

Huddled together at one end of a sofa, next to the short, heavy-set man who appeared to be a hostage, were Jon-Joe and Biddy. The hostage was unshaven and he looked as if he had been sleeping in his clothes. Jake was sitting on the bottom step of the stairs and the two terrorists were muttering together in the corner, while the small one kept them covered with the shotgun. They were all nursing mugs of tea that Biddy had made.

After the small one with the ski mask had appeared,

waving a shotgun, a taller thinner gurrier, with what looked like half a pair of tights pulled down over his face, yanked the little fat man aboard. The one with the ski mask seemed to be the ringleader. It was he who was shouting instructions that they were not to move, and they were to sit still and stuff. In the same breath, he yelled at the two women to go down to the back of the bus and to sit with Biddy and Jon-Joe, though obviously he didn't refer to them by name.

'We can't sit still *and* go down to the back,' Jodie said in a very peeved voice.

Fionn, with bared teeth, growled at Bosco. He wasn't fond of dogs at the best of times. Lucy held on tight to her collar as the animal strained against it. She was terrified the dog would be shot.

'Just do it!' Bosco barked. 'And keep that friggin' hound quiet or I'll shoot the fucker!'

Jodie still hadn't made a move. That blonde one had a serious attitude problem. He'd show the stupid cow to have a bit of respect.

Lucy shushed Fionn and stroked her head. The dog was still not happy and continued to growl.

Jodie gave an exaggerated sigh and cast her eyes to the ceiling. Bosco wasn't sure she was going to do as he had told her. He stood his ground and glared at her, though she wasn't aware of it because she couldn't see his face under the ski mask. It was hard to take someone seriously when they looked like a Jolly Minstrel, even if they were waving a sawn-off shotgun around.

Lucy had also made no attempt to move, though in her case it was because she was still stunned by the suddenness of it. No sooner were the words *terrorist incident* out of her mouth, than two bloody terrorists popped up from nowhere screaming and shouting.

Bosco gave them some gentle encouragement. 'Move!' he yelled in his hard-man voice.

They stood up. With a jaded air Jodie, clutching the attaché case, followed Lucy, still clinging on to Fionn's collar for dear life, down the bus to sit in the seat across the aisle from Jon-Joe and Biddy.

Jodie muttered something Bosco couldn't make out. He let it go. She wasn't being particularly brave. She was just behaving instinctively. Six years as Rogan Hogan's woman, four years of carrying countless Ks of hard drugs through customs, had left her with a certain disdain for bottom-of-the-heap gougers like the two who had taken over the bus. It had also given her a talent for bluffing when under severe pressure. In reality she didn't like the situation. The leader looked jumpy, as if he didn't know what he was about. She wondered who they were and who their hostage was. He didn't look terribly worried or afraid. That gave her some comfort. She sat on the edge of her seat and hugged her future against her chest. She fervently hoped that the two gurriers wouldn't do a Dick Turpin and steal their luggage.

Corky shoved Monty down the bus to sit in the seat in front of Biddy and Jon-Joe. Fionn sat by Lucy's seat, throwing the occasional growl in Bosco's direction, just so as he would be in no doubt of her opinion of him.

Bosco stood by the driver's seat, covering everyone with the sawn-off. He hadn't the slightest idea what to do next. Grabbing the bus had been an impulse, prompted by the fact that he was cold and wet, and was panicking ever so slightly that they had nowhere to go and had found no alternative means of transport.

'Where to?' Jake asked.

Bosco didn't know, but he didn't want to show it to Jake. The explosion had frightened the life out of him. And things had been going so well up until then. He tried to buck himself up. There was quarter of a million up for grabs if he used his head. If only he could hold it all together. He didn't want to think about the details. Particularly the one involving the killing of Monty in order to get the cash.

Corky thought it was all a huge joke, but Bosco made allowances for that. Corky wasn't the brightest.

Right now they needed somewhere to stay. Somewhere

with a phone. Somewhere safe. If he could manage that, they were half-way to being home free. There was a chance they could still pull it off.

'Where d'you live?' he asked Jake.

'What?'

Bosco shoved the barrel of the sawn-off in Jake's face. 'I'm askin' the questions,' he growled. 'Where d'you feckin' live, Punk?' He saw Jake flinch back in his seat. He was pleased with the reaction. It restored his confidence a bit.

'About a mile down the road.'

'Then that's where we're goin'.'

Jake pushed the barrel of the firearm away from his face with his index finger. 'There's no need to stick that thing in my face. I get your drift.'

At once Bosco's confidence faltered again, but he rallied and reminded himself that he was the one holding the sawn-off. He thought of whacking the smartarsed bastard across the side of the head with the heavy wooden stock of the gun, just to make an example of him to the others, but changed his mind. He needed him to do the driving.

'Get movin',' he barked. 'And the rest of yez, sit there an' keep bleedin' quiet.'

Jake set off again.

'D'yeh've a phone?' Bosco was sitting with the sawn-off cradled across his lap and with his back braced against the windscreen so he had a view of the whole bus.

'Yep,' Jake replied. 'Are you IRA?'

'Mind yer own friggin' business!' Bosco snapped, half pleased at Jake's assumption. If he figured him for a terrorist, he'd hardly doubt that he was dangerous.

It was dark by the time Jake parked the bus in the barn. Bosco herded everyone off and they all trooped into Jake's house, with Corky bringing up the rear.

'Is *this* where you live, Jake?' Biddy asked, when they were all inside.

'I told you he'd bought the old mill, an' done it up,' Jon-Joe said.

'Well, you made a grand job of it, Jake,' Biddy said. 'Will I make tea?'

'I'd love a cup, thanks,' said Monty. He rummaged in his pocket and took out a large bar of chocolate he had left from the supply Bosco had bought him earlier. 'Anyone like some chocolate?'

'Shaddup!' Bosco yelled. This was getting out of hand. Were these people crazy? Didn't they realise he was a dangerous criminal? Hadn't they noticed that he had a sawn-off shotgun?

How could he know that Biddy was a quarter of the way through her own private journey towards senile dementia? Bosco's yell registered through the fog, though. Biddy looked shaken.

Suddenly Bosco felt guilty. She reminded him of his ma. He'd hate it if anyone spoke to her like that. Jon-Joe put a protective arm around Biddy's shoulder and puffed out his chest like a turkey cock protecting his harem. Although Bosco was only about five seven and thinly built, Jon-Joe was less than five foot two and Biddy was even smaller.

Bosco felt ashamed. 'Sorry, Missus. Make tea fer us, if yez like.' Biddy gave him an uncertain smile. 'Go with her,' he said to Corky. Better to be safe than sorry.

Lucy cupped her hands round the comforting mug of tea. She'd been giving Jake the odd covert glance to see if he showed any signs of recognition, and was relieved when he didn't catch her eye. Anyway, judging by his house, he had done well for himself. He didn't seem to have missed the fifty quid.

Why didn't that thought comfort her? Probably because she was generally an honest person. The thought of stealing was repugnant to her. She had even stood up to Marcus on that point and refused to sign on because she was working in the market. It only brought home to her what a mistake Marcus had been. How badly he had influenced her. She would never have dreamed of stealing had he not threatened to go off without her.

'The devine Jake' the other girls in her college year used to call him. They had all fancied him like mad and were jealous as hell of Lucy when she got a room in the same squat. He wasn't her type – probably because he didn't have 'lazy control-freak psycho' tattooed on his forehead. She didn't have a lot to do with him after the foundation year because they took different courses. He did the graphic-design course and she settled on fine art. Apart from that, he was into country music big-time which, although he was considered cute to look at, made him a nerd as far as she was concerned, albeit a pleasant enough one.

Jodie nudged her in the ribs. 'Who d'you think they are?' she whispered.

'I don't know. IRA perhaps?'

'I don't think so,' Jodie said. 'For one thing, they only seem to have the one gun. I'd say they're just gurriers. Who d'you reckon yer man is?'

'Maybe they tried to rob a bank and it went wrong, so they grabbed him as a hostage,' Lucy surmised. 'He might be a bank manager or something. Pity we missed the news.'

From his vantage point on the stairs, Jake was watching Bosco and Corky too, and making similar assumptions. He wasn't sure what to make of them. The smaller one was obviously the boss, the tougher of the two. It was transparently clear that they didn't have a plan of any sort. Something had gone wrong for them, and he and the group around him were unlucky enough to be in the wrong place at the wrong time.

His gaze switched to Monty, who was chomping away on his chocolate bar, apparently unconcerned. He watched as Monty offered a chunk to Biddy and Jon-Joe. Jon-Joe gave a gummy smile and took the chunk of confectionery, broke it into two pieces and handed one to Biddy, who immediately dunked it into the hot tea and fed it to her toothless husband.

They were something else, those three. Here they all were in a very ugly situation, and they were munching chocolate, drinking tea and generally acting as if nothing were amiss.

Knowing Biddy and Jon-Joe Horan, he could make allowances for them, but what was it with the other guy?

His gaze continued round the room and landed on the two hippies. The older one *was* very familiar. Suddenly he had it. She was the dead spit of a girl he had known when he was at college. One of the fine-art students. Lucy something. He couldn't recall. It was an odd name. The name of an object. He trawled his memory. Lucy Door. Lucy Tree, Lucy . . . Lucy Spoon. That was it, Lucy Spoon.

She was talking to the younger woman. He studied Lucy's face. She was quite handsome in an unstructured sort of way. Her hair could do with a bit of attention but, apart from a slight bagginess around the eyes, she didn't look a lot different. He wondered if the girl was her daughter. He decided not. She wasn't young enough. She was perhaps twenty-five or six. She had a classy air and the clothes she had on looked strangely out of place on her. A moment more appraising her and he had it. It was her hands. They were smooth and white, and her nails were perfectly manicured and varnished. Her hair, too. Although it looked as if it could do with a wash, it was definitely the result of a fifty-quid haircut.

Lucy looked up and caught his eye. She blushed immediately and cast down her eyes. What was her problem? Maybe she didn't recognise him.

Bosco, meanwhile, was reviewing the situation with Corky. His panic had subsided now. As he always did, he concentrated on the positive. It was a talent he had. He had convinced himself that they were even better off than they had been at the cottage.

'How d'yeh bleedin' make that out?' asked the more negatively minded Corky. 'In case yeh hadn't noticed, we was nearly blown t'bits. The fuckin' van's knackered, an' we've this crowd of eejits t'sort out. How're we bleedin' better off?'

'For one thing,' Bosco said in soothing tones, 'we got a phone. I can call yer woman without havin' to leave the house. There's less chance of the fuzz picking us up now we're not drivin' round in a fuckin' knocked-off van.'

Corky didn't look convinced.

Bosco tried another tack. The last thing he needed right now was for Corky to bottle out on him. 'Anyway. They migh' be a crowd of eejits, but they're not givin' us any trouble, are they?'

'S'pose not,' Corky said half-heartedly. 'So what's the plan?'

'I'll ring yer woman again,' said Bosco. 'If she's the money sorted, by this time t'morra we could be home free.'

He hoped Corky wouldn't bring up the small matter of the five other hostages again. He hadn't figured that one out yet.

'Um . . . Excuse me?' The younger hippie, the pretty one, was looking in his direction. 'Excuse me?' she repeated, holding up her hand as if she were in school and wanted a pee.

'Wha'?'

The hippie stood up and made her way across the room towards him. Bosco noticed for the first time how beautiful she was and what amazing eyes she had. He had never seen eyes that colour before. They were an unbelievable shade of violet.

'Excuse me, but my friend Edith and I were wondering what you are going to do with us?'

She was standing a couple of feet away from him now. She was drop-dead gorgeous. He couldn't really judge what kind of body she had under the baggy clothes, but he decided with a face like that she was bound to have big bazookas. Big, white, squashy bazookas. His heart was fluttering. He pulled himself together and cleared his throat. 'Nothin',' he said. 'At least nothin' if yez all behave yerselves.'

'That's all well and good. But some of us had other plans. Can you tell me how long you think you'll be keeping us here?'

He found her coolness and beauty completely intimidating.

Corky saved him. 'Fer as long as it takes, Missus,' he said. 'Now go an' sit down again an' don't ask questions.'

Jodie gave him a withering glance. An I-was-speaking-to-the-organ-grinder-not-the-monkey sort of glance.

It wasn't lost on Corky. He raised his hand as if he was going to hit her.

Bosco shot his arm in front of Corky's hand. 'Do as he says, Missus,' he blurted, with an unsaid *please* in the tone.

Jodie returned to her place in the corner.

'Whatcha stop me for?' Corky said under his breath to his partner in crime.

'I told yeh before. Yeh shouldn't hit women,' Bosco replied.

He had not had the benefit of Corky's role model, his father, who routinely battered his mother the couple of times a year he was home, with or without the benefit of drink. He was a truculent man, drunk or sober. Although Corky loved and respected his mother, he knew no better. All his brothers hit their girlfriends, and all his sisters, with the exception of Edel, who was in a battered wives shelter, put up with it from their partners.

On his Communion day, as he watched his mother disguising a black eye with the pink make-up she kept for the purpose, he asked her why his da hit her. 'Because he loves me, pet,' she replied. 'Because yer da loves me. He wouldn't do it if he didn't love me.' That was the set of values that Corky's parents handed down to their kids.

'Where's yer phone,' Bosco, who had now regained his composure, barked at Jake.

Jake pointed to a door to Bosco's right. 'In the office.'

Bosco had decided it was time to get things moving and make the call. He handed the sawn-off to Corky. 'Don't take any crap off them,' he said in his Dirty Harry voice.

After the way the woman had looked at him, Corky didn't need to be told. He settled himself in an armchair with the sawn-off at the ready.

Bosco returned a couple of minutes later. 'She's not there,' he said to Corky under his breath. 'I said I'd be callin'. Where is she?'

'Must be still fixin' up the money end a'things,' Corky said, for once the more up-beat of the two.

Bosco wasn't so sure. But what other reason could there be? It wasn't as if she'd be calling the cops. Not when she wanted her old man dead. Probably out celebratin', he told himself. 'Yeah,' he said to his friend. 'That'll be it.'

'*Edith*?' Lucy hissed. 'Where the hell did *Edith* come from?'

Jodie grinned at her. 'Well you said not to call you Lucy and Edith was the first name that came into my head.'

Chapter Sixteen

Angelica Quinn stretched languidly and stood up. 'Well, sweetie, I'm off,' she said. Then, in a baby voice, asked, 'Can Jellie have a little lifter to take with her?'

She was off to an all-night photo-shoot down at the docks. An assignment for *Marie Claire*. All out of focus, arty shots of her in evening wear, and the temperature plummeting by the minute. She anticipated that she'd be half frozen to death before the photographer got the moody shots he wanted. She'd need a little pick-me-up to get through it. It wasn't as if she had any body fat to keep her warm. Still, that's what it was all about. Who said modelling was glamorous? It was bloody hard work.

Hogan had other things on his mind. When he didn't reply, Angelica draped herself across his knee, wrapping her slender arms around his neck. 'How about it, Honey Bunny? Jellie will be weely weely gwateful.' She nibbled his ear. She was hard to ignore.

'How grateful?' he asked, running his hand up her silky thigh and under her skirt.

'Weeeely gwateful.' She stuck her tongue in his ear.

He opened the buttons of her shirt and slid his hand inside. The feel of her flat boyish chest and small hard nipples made him catch his breath.

Angelica purred in his ear, 'Just a couple of gwamms, Baby, to keep me going 'til later. Jellie will be weely *weeeely* gwateful.'

'How grateful?' Hogan lowered his head and bit her nipple

hard. He felt her flinch. He bit harder. She yelped and pulled away. 'I thought you said you'd be grateful,' he said.

She closed her eyes and leaned back towards him. He liked that about her. She was compliant and obliging. Not like Jodie. It was a constant battle with Jodie. Angelica didn't have any fight left in her. He had found her at the right time. At her lowest ebb. In a perfect state of vulnerability. He bit her again and tasted blood. This time she didn't pull away.

The phone rang. He looked up at her. She had tears in her eyes. He liked that. It excited him. She slid off his knee and, as she fixed her clothes, he picked up the receiver.

'It's me, Boss. I'm at a lorry park outside some hole in the wall called Boran.'

'Just a minute.' Hogan reached into his inside pocket and pulled out a small plastic envelope of white powder that he had placed there earlier for the purpose. He held it out to Angelica, whose face immediately lit up. 'Here you are, Babes.' She grabbed the bag and hurried towards the door. Rogan Hogan watched her leave. As she reached the door, he said, 'We'll pick up where we left off when you get back, Babe.'

Angelica cringed, but hid it well. She turned and ran her tongue suggestively over her lips.

'OK. Go ahead. What did you find out?'

'This is the place alrigh'. I asked around an' yer wan in the café remembered her,' Gnasher said.

'So where is she now?'

'She hooked up with some knacker. The fella at the pumps said they caught a bus to Cork.'

Jodie on a bus! That was a novel notion. Hogan found he was smiling. 'How long since she left?'

'The bus went at four.'

Shit! She'd be well there. 'OK. Go on down to Cork and see what you can find out.'

'OK, Boss,' Gnasher said. 'What'll I do with the young fella?'

Ah yes, the boy. Hogan remembered how desperate he was to please. 'Keep him with you. He could be useful – one way or another.'

Gnasher put down the phone. Decco was lounging against the car, waiting for him. He had two cartons of coffee in his hands and a couple of burger boxes balanced in the crook of his arm. Gnasher took a burger and sat in the driver's seat with his legs still outside the car. Decco handed him a polystyrene cup of coffee.

They ate in silence. Decco was ravenous. He watched Gnasher as he chewed and decided that he wasn't as bad as people said. In fact, he'd been quite nice to him on the drive down.

Decco was relieved that he had recognised the correct motorway turn-off and had managed to find the right truck stop. At first he was chancing his arm, not at all sure if this was the one. He hadn't paid much attention the last visit. Robbo's driving was outrageous at the best of times. The whole place looked different in the dark, but he told Gnasher Gill this was it. He said it with perfect certainty, secure in the knowledge that no one could prove otherwise. That it *was* the right place was a bonus. When the woman in the café had told Gill that she remembered the female he was looking for, he had to stop himself from blurting out '*Really, Missus?*'

When they were back outside, Gill slapped him on the shoulder. It was the closest, he knew, he'd ever get to praise from someone with Gill's reputation as a hard-man. He felt, after that, that Gnasher Gill liked him, and he decided to go for broke and ask him outright if there was any chance of a job.

In actuality, Gnasher was just relieved that they had the right place and a lead he could pass on to Hogan. He wasn't altogether sure he was off the hook in Hogan's eyes regarding the loss of the Smack.

When Gnasher Gill had finished his snack he tossed the empty containers at Decco. Decco looked around and then dropped them on the ground.

'Pick that up!' Gill barked. 'Haven't yeh heard of protectin' the bleedin' environment. It's gobshites like you who're killin' the feckin' countryside.'

Decco cringed, picked up the litter and postponed his job application.

Jeannie Horan-Evens was worried. Very worried. It was all Jeremy's fault. If he'd come home on time to mind the kids, as he'd promised, she wouldn't have been five minutes late meeting the bus.

At first she had been relieved when she hadn't seen her parents waiting in the doorway of Marks & Spencer's, imagining that the bus was late. She had sat in the car and waited. Her father had phoned earlier in the day to say that the bus wouldn't be leaving Boran until four o'clock, because of some problem. The estimated time of arrival should have been six thirty. It was now well after seven. What if there'd been an accident? The weather was awful for travelling.

She opened the driver's door a crack so the interior light lit up and squinted at her watch. Seven twenty. It was nearly an hour late. She was really anxious now.

It was Jeremy's fault, she thought again. She had wanted to call off their night out on account of the weather, but he wouldn't hear of it. She checked herself. That wasn't fair. At least he wanted to go out with her. Spend some time together. Lots of her friends' husbands never took them outside the door.

Jeannie Horan-Evens locked her car and walked to the nearest phone box, where she dialled her parents' phone number. No one answered. She hung up and redialled in case she had misdialled the first time. The phone rang and rang and rang.

*

Marcus Pyle had backache. The chair on which he had been sitting for the last two hours seemed to be designed for maximum discomfort. Or at least that's how it felt. Whichever way he shifted his weight, he couldn't find even an iota of ease.

The room in the Boran Garda station was a dismal affair. Small and painted cream. Only a table, which was screwed to the floor, and two chairs. No window as such, just a square of glass bricks set high in the wall behind him.

The ashtray on the table in front of him was full of his cigarette ends and the air was correspondingly foggy. He had smoked nearly a full packet of Golden Virginia. There was enough left for one more, but he was out of papers and matches.

He stood up and stretched his back, then closed his eyes as he rubbed his pounding temples. What was taking so long? It wasn't anything to do with him. He didn't even know Lucy was a terrorist bomber until the cop, Mulligan, had told him the story.

At first he couldn't take it in, but the cop was sure of it. And she *was* at the explosion house. What did Mulligan call it? The bomb factory. What was she doing there if she wasn't in it up to her neck? Marcus winced. They couldn't possibly think he had anything to do with it.

Marcus Pyle rotated his head in a circle. His neck and shoulder muscles were in knots. He heard the bones in his neck crunching as he completed the circle. A second rotation in the opposite direction and he felt better. He opened his eyes. The harsh light from the fluorescent tube overhead sent a dart of pain through his head. He closed his eyes again and rubbed the heel of his hand in the sockets. That made it easier.

He wondered if the door was locked. He hadn't heard a key turning or a bolt sliding. He walked over and tried it tentatively. The handle slid down easily and he pulled the door inwards.

He could hear voices in the public office down the hall. He poked his head out and listened. The conversation was indistinct. He coughed.

The conversation ceased.

'Hello?' he called timidly. This was unlike Marcus, but he didn't want to antagonise Sergeant Mulligan any further. Sergeant Mulligan's assessment of him could mean the difference between walking away or being dragged into the whole awful business. It was a nightmare. My wife the terrorist.

The conversation resumed down the hall. Marcus raised his voice a couple of decibels, being careful not to let any note of impatience creep in. 'Eh . . . Excuse me?'

Mulligan had heard Marcus the first time but he was letting him stew. A search of the house had turned up nothing incriminating or subversive, except an ancient copy of *Playboy* which Mulligan had secreted about his person for perusal at his leisure later on.

Marcus hadn't asked to see the warrant, which was a good job considering that the thing didn't exist. What did come to light, though, was the fact that Lucy Spoon had moved on. Most of her clothes were missing with, according to the now effusively co-operative Marcus, sundry camping equipment, two sleeping bags, a sum of money and a dog.

The interview had lasted an hour. Marcus had told Mulligan all he knew about Lucy. How they had met. How long they had been together, that kind of thing, protesting his innocence at every opportunity. Mulligan let him talk himself out, using the technique of allowing silences to hang in the air, the theory being that the interviewee would feel obliged to fill the void with more information than he had intended in the initial instance.

At the first significant hiatus, Mulligan had said, 'Who's the other man you thought she was with?'

'What other man?' Marcus asked.

'You asked me if she was with anyone at the house where the explosion took place. You know something about that, don't you? You know about the other man.' Mulligan was leaning across the table towards Marcus, staring into his eyes. Marcus could feel little globules of spit landing on his cheek as the cop got into his stride. 'You knew full well that your wife was mixed up with a paramilitary organisation.'

'I didn't,' Marcus protested, horrified. 'I knew nothing about it.' He was close to tears.

Mulligan leaned back in his chair and snorted. 'You're trying to tell me that you lived with this woman in the same house for twenty years, and you had no idea she was mixed up with that crowd?'

'No idea at all,' Marcus pleaded. 'Really. I hadn't a clue.'

'And where d'you think she'd go in a situation like this? Where d'you think she is now?' More head shaking from Marcus. 'You look like an intelligent man.' This was stretching the truth as far as Mulligan was concerned, but needs must. Flattery can sometimes pay off. 'I can't believe you didn't notice *something* strange about her behaviour?'

Marcus jumped on the remark. 'Well, now that you come to mention it, she has changed over the past few months.'

'In what way?'

Marcus paused to get it straight in his mind. 'Well, it's her attitude. She's more argumentative, for one thing. And she seems to have *opinions*.'

'Opinions?'

'Well, yes. She never expressed *opinions* before. Now, suddenly she's full of *opinions* about everything.'

'And does she have *opinions* about the North?'

Marcus was into his stride now. 'Well, funnily enough, she never talks about the North, but then she wouldn't would she? If she's involved the way you say, that's the last thing she'd talk about.'

Mulligan played the silence card again, a half-sneer on his lips. As the pause became uncomfortable, Marcus continued, 'She must have been a mole or a sleeper – or something.'

'You seem to know a lot about it for someone who claims not to know a lot, if you don't mind me saying so,' Mulligan said.

It took a moment for Marcus to unscramble that statement. He wanted to be sick. His stomach was churning. This was a waking nightmare.

'No, I don't. I mean I don't know about paramilitaries. I read a lot of spy books. Haven't you read James Bond or John le Carré?'

'Can't say I have.' Mulligan had seen James Bond films on the telly of course, but he didn't mention that.

Marcus carried on. His voice had a desperate edge to it now. 'A sleeper's someone planted by the enemy who does nothing for years and years, then gets called out for a specific operation. Maybe that's it.'

Mulligan didn't look impressed. 'And what about a mole?'

'It's a person who . . . Well, em – A mole's like a sleeper, only the one side thinks that they're working for them, when the whole time they're working for the other lot.'

Mulligan stood up and slid his hands into his pockets. He was shaking his head and had a sort of half-smile on his face. 'Moles and sleepers is it, Mister Pyke?'

It was a Pyke too far. Marcus saw red. He jumped up from his chair and grabbed Mulligan by the lapels. 'Look here, shit for brains! The name's Pyle.' He spelled it out again, this time enunciating the letters with exaggerated clarity. 'P . . . Y . . . L . . . E. It's not Pyke, or Poke or even Peak, it's Pyle. I didn't know that my wife was mixed up in anything iffy. I don't know where she is right now, and as far as I'm concerned, I never want to lay eyes on her again. Got that straight, Mister Plod?'

Without saying a word, the policeman took his hands out of his pockets and, as Marcus stood there seething and fuming, caught hold of him by the upper arms and kneed him hard in the groin.

Needless to say, Marcus let go of his lapels immediately, doubled over and grabbed his balls, letting out a strangled bellow. Mulligan waited. After a suitable interval, when the pain and feeling of nausea had subsided, Marcus eased himself gently down on to the chair.

'That wasn't very smart was it, Mister Pyke?' said Mulligan. 'I wouldn't do that again if I was you, or I'll have to charge you with assaulting a member of the Gardai, and you wouldn't be wanting that, would you?'

'No,' Marcus whinged piteously.

Mulligan had left the room, shaking his head and with the silly grin still on his face.

That had been over an hour ago. Marcus closed the door quietly and, gingerly, sat back down at the table. What if they'd caught up with Lucy and she'd told them a pack of lies about him being involved, just to save her own hide? She'd do that. He knew she'd do that, just to get back at him. He was suddenly panic-stricken. For the first time it occurred to him that maybe he should have been kinder to Lucy. If he had, maybe she wouldn't feel the need to drop him in it.

His remorse didn't last long. In the next breath he was telling himself what a good husband he had been to her through the years. If it weren't for him, etc. How soon would he be saying, if it weren't for her? And would it be from a prison cell?

Footsteps outside, and Mulligan walked in. Marcus didn't bother to get up. Suddenly he was weary beyond belief. The cop sat down at the table, took out a packet of cigarettes and a box of matches and slid them across. Marcus hesitated. Mulligan gave the packet another shove in Marcus's direction. Grateful for the show of compassion, he lit up.

Mulligan said nothing until Marcus stubbed the butt out in the ashtray. Then he stood up. 'OK, Mister Pyle. You can go now.'

It took a second for the words to register. A wave of relief washed over Marcus and he had to fight hard to stop himself from breaking down. He didn't wait for a second invitation and limped to the door. He needed a drink, and badly. A strong one.

Mulligan escorted him to the front door of the Garda

station. 'Don't you want to know if we found your wife, Mister Pyle?' he said.

Marcus stopped. He didn't care if he never saw his wife again, not after all the trouble she'd caused him. 'And have you?' he asked, for appearance's sake.

Mulligan shook his head. 'No, Mister Pyle. Don't forget to call us if she gets in touch.'

'Absolutely,' Marcus said with conviction. 'Abso-bloody-lutely.'

Mulligan watched him as he hobbled down the street and disappeared into the pub. He could have hung on to him for a further four hours, but what was the point? It was obvious he hadn't a clue where she was.

Joe Flynn walked out of the door and stood beside him on the step. 'What a wanker!' Mulligan muttered.

'Why d'you let him go, Sarge?'

'Because I didn't want the bother of giving him a free dinner,' Mulligan said. 'Anyway, he'll be back here like a dog with its arse on fire if she puts in an appearance.'

'D'you think so, Sarge?'

'I'd put money on it, Son.'

Mulligan shivered as a freezing gust of wind blew straight into his face. With a heavy heart he turned and went back into the office. The evil hour had come. He couldn't put off the call to Dublin any longer.

Cathy Grady's feet were frozen. The wind and rain had left her carefully straightened hair looking not unlike Margaret Thatcher's, and she had a splitting headache. But at least they'd filed the piece for the nine o'clock news in time. It wasn't all bad.

She eased her feet out of her shoes and stretched them towards the fire. The shoes were ruined. Two hundred and fifty quid down the drain. She wondered if she'd be able to claim them on expenses, then dismissed the idea. She knew what her boss would say about that. Her fault for wearing totally unsuitable footwear. What did he know? When she'd dressed that morning it was with Mel Gibson in mind, not hurricane bloody Bridget.

She picked up her glass of hot whiskey and took a sip. The steaming liquid warmed her throat and the heat penetrated as far as her stomach. She began to relax a little.

A puff of smoke from the chimney as the pub door opened caused Cathy to lean away from the fire.

A tall, miserable-looking, bearded hippie limped in and leaned up against the bar. 'Pint of Guinness and a large Bushmills, please,' he said to the barman. His voice had a strangled quality as if he were in pain.

The barman drew the whiskey from the optic and passed it across the bar. The man knocked back the amber liquid and seemed to exhale the woes of the world. The barman handed him the pint of Guinness and money changed hands.

The door opened again and Micky blustered in. He had the look of a fire-fighter or a traffic cop in his waterproofs with yellow fluorescent strips on the back and the sleeves. He scanned the half-empty bar, then made a bee-line towards the fireplace.

Cathy felt a wave of coldness radiating off his jacket. He held out his hands to the flames and rubbed them together.

'Got us a B&B,' he said. 'Only the one room, though, so you'll have to share with me, Cath.'

'In your dreams,' was all Cathy could come up with. She wasn't in the mood for banter.

Micky picked up the pint Cathy had got in for him and took a long swallow, just as a young girl, probably the publican's daughter judging by her age, brought over a tray with two baskets of chicken and chips.

Ravenous, they ate in silence. Cathy hadn't had anything since her breakfast Weetabix, and she was aware that her empty stomach was partly responsible for her ill temper. She'd long since come to terms with missing out on the Mel Gibson interview. In fact, it had been she who persuaded Liam to let them stay put with the OB satellite truck to follow up the escaped animal story. Although the circus management was making light of it, she had heard from one of the animal trainers that a couple of geriatric tigers and a crocodile were still at large. How often did a story like that come along? Liam had got the *destruction*. Would he look more favourably on her if she was able to deliver the dose of *death*? Not that she wished anyone ill, but a couple of mauled and mangled sheep or cattle would make for a good story. *Fear grips this small rural community* – at least it would by the time she was through.

Cathy pushed the remains of her chicken in a basket to one side and took out her notebook. 'I talked to the post mistress,' she said in a low voice to Micky. 'And she's agreeable to giving us a sound bite or two after she's got her kids to bed. Apparently that stretch of road's an accident black spot.'

'And did you ask her what she thought about fuckin' Tigger the Tiger and his mate?' Micky enquired, grinning.

'I wasn't going to. I wanted to get her reaction on camera, but she'd already heard. She told me that the trainer guy was pretty specific. It's definitely two tigers and a crocodile.'

'I thought yer man said they weren't dangerous.'

'Well they would say that, wouldn't they?'

As Cathy leaned back in her chair, stretching to ease her aching back, her attention was drawn to the hippie as he downed his pint of Guinness in one long swallow.

He sighed loudly, wiped his mouth with the back of his hand and pushed the empty glass across the bar for a refill.

The barman topped up a settling pint. 'Drownin' yer sorras?'

Marcus shrugged. 'Something like that.'

'Ah, sure nothin's so bad that it doesn't look better through the bottom of a glass,' said the barman, dispensing the usual home-spun clichés along with the drink.

Cathy smirked at Micky, then cast her eyes skywards.

'That's all you fucking know,' Marcus snarled. He took a sip of the fresh pint. 'Does *your* wife run a frigging bomb factory behind your back?'

The barman laughed. 'Jeasus! Was it her blew up the place on the Boran road, then?'

Marcus drained his Guinness in another gulp and slammed the empty glass on the bar along with the exact payment. 'Apparently.'

By the time Cathy had kicked her faculties into gear, the hippie had stormed out into the night. Micky didn't react at all. He hadn't been listening.

Up at the bar, our intrepid reporter ordered another round. As Micky's pint was settling, she smiled engagingly at the barman. 'Now, about this explosion . . .'

Unaware that she had just missed Bosco's call, Cindy George closed the front door behind her, put on the chain and set the alarm. The last thing she needed right now was to risk a burglary. Not with two hundred and fifty grand in the house. The case was heavy. Not as big as she had expected, but still heavy.

It had taken her most of the afternoon to collect the cash from various deposit boxes and building society accounts around the city. Monty didn't believe in having all his eggs in the one basket.

She was annoyed with herself for having offered the extra fifty grand. But that couldn't be helped now, even though it left her short of ready cash. But there was the Isle of Man account if she was stuck before probate was sorted out and, if she felt like a holiday – quite necessary for a grieving widow – there was the account in the Cayman Islands. At the end of the day, it was a small price to pay. Two hundred and fifty thousand didn't put too much of a dent in forty-two point two million quid. The shares were probably worth even more now.

Holding that happy thought, Cindy George picked up the case of cash and lugged it down to the basement, where she hid it in the industrial-sized tumble-dryer. She then took a couple of clean linen sheets from the pile sitting ready for the linen cupboard, opened them out and shoved them in the dryer on top of the case. That should do the trick, she thought. No one would think of looking there.

Upstairs in the drawing-room she poured herself a large gin and tonic – lemon, no ice – and settled down in front of the TV waiting for the phone to ring.

She felt a certain sense of excitement. When she had married Monty, she had thought he was on his last legs. Fat and red-faced, he looked like a candidate for a heart attack any day.

Her hopes were raised when he collapsed the previous year, but he was in the office at the time and, as his secretary got immediate help, he survived. She found it particularly hard to hide her disappointment when the nurse at the Mater Private informed her proudly that the paramedics had brought Monty back from the dead in the ambulance.

It wasn't that she didn't like Monty. He had been good to her and she knew he loved her dearly, but it just wasn't the plan. He was supposed to have died and left her a wealthy widow long ago.

Cindy had always wanted to be rich. Even at primary school, when the class was asked by the teacher what they wanted to be when they grew up, Cindy had answered every time, 'I want to be rich, Miss.' She couldn't understand why her reply never satisfied the teacher. Why would she want to be a nurse? Why a teacher like the other girls, for heaven's sake? Even at seven, the thought of working for a living didn't appeal to Cindy. She wanted to be a princess.

Though far from stupid, Cindy just coasted through school. She scraped through her leaving certificate and, at a total loss as far as career choices were concerned, took a post-leaving-certificate course in beauty therapy. She hated it. Removing superfluous hair and tending to open pores was not her idea of a good time.

After the first year she dropped out and took a modelling course. Her proportions were all wrong for the catwalk, and she got little work, so she was forced to supplement her income by waiting on tables. One night a photographer spotted her in the night-club restaurant where she was working at the time, and offered her glamour work. She was suspicious to begin with, and surprisingly shy about baring her best assets, but after a bit of gentle persuasion and a couple of tequila slammers she lost her inhibitions. Her proudest moment was when she made the front page of the *Sun*, advertising their *Supa Million Pound Bingo* promotion.

That break led to other work and soon she was doing quite well. Her minor celebrity status gave her the opportunity to meet other celebs, footballers and the like. She would attend the opening of an envelope if she thought it would give her the chance to meet the right people. She took to calling herself an actress when interviewed. It wasn't too far from the truth. She *was* attending acting classes, and felt that it was the next logical step in her pursuit of her mission statement, which, put simply, was I want to be filthy rich by the time I'm twenty-five.

Meeting Monty was a case of serendipity. She'd had no intention of calling in to the Shelbourne that evening. Not that it wasn't a regular hunting venue for Cindy, but she had spent the previous three hours being photographed with a randy one-armed Lotto winner from Finglas, who couldn't keep his hand to himself, and she needed a drink.

She recognised Monty at once. At the time of the stock flotation he had made the front page of the *Irish Times* financial section – essential reading for Cindy. He was smaller than she had expected and not quite as fat. As a model she was aware that the camera lens puts on at least seven pounds, but it was still a surprise.

A further surprise was that she found she quite liked him. He was in no way brash, as she had expected. And he kept his hands to himself, which was a welcome change after her day so far.

By the end of the evening they were getting on like a house on fire, but it was left to her to ask him out. He blushed when she asked – another endearing surprise – but agreed enthusiastically. He courted her in the old-fashioned way and they married six months later. She thought she had realised her greatest ambition.

But life pretty soon became boring. Even though Monty was generous to a fault, it was the little things that started to niggle at her. The way he switched off lights. The way he clipped and saved supermarket coupons, which she binned rather than endure the humiliation of producing them at Superquinn. Monty still bought his clothes from a chain store and had his shoes mended. He couldn't see the point of eating out unless it was a special occasion. She succeeded in coaxing him out to charity functions reasonably often, even managing a film première once – but she was still fed up.

When the boredom got too hard to bear, Cindy decided that she wanted to be a TV presenter. She had continued with her acting lessons and felt she was ready. Bad call, but her private acting coach could hardly justify the lessons, three a week for the past four years, if he didn't stretch the truth to breaking point. As luck would have it, Monty was in the process of buying a TV station of his very own, and promised her a presenter's job. She was elated. Real fame was at last in sight.

She would have happily gone along with the prospect, had not this opportunity presented itself. How could she let it go? Monty kidnapped. Monty out of the way. At first she thought of refusing to pay the ransom so that they'd kill him. But further consideration made her realise that, if Monty escaped, he might be ever so slightly annoyed that she'd left him to the mercy of the kidnappers. The only solution was to offer them more cash in order to make certain that Monty never came back.

She felt genuine regret that Monty had to die, but as far as she could see there was no other solution. She couldn't wait for ever. Monty hadn't kept his side of the unspoken bargain as far as she was concerned. OK, so he wasn't aware that there had been that sort of bargain, but why did he think she married him? He wasn't stupid. You didn't get to make forty-two point two million quid if you were stupid.

And she was close to her twenty-sixth birthday. She'd soon be over the hill. Too old to enjoy herself.

Cindy George got up, poured herself another drink, then sat in front of the TV and waited for the phone to ring.

Chapter Seventeen

Tuesday, 5 November, nine thirty p.m.

Worried about Biddy's and Jon-Joe's welfare, Jake suggested that someone should go to the chipper for food. Monty was relieved. All his supply of chocolate was gone and he was beginning to feel a little light-headed. Corky's stomach was rumbling, as was Bosco's, so they didn't put up any argument.

Jake took the orders and stumped up the cash, then gave Corky the keys of his jeep and directions to the nearest chip shop. He had a half-baked notion of trying to get the two gurriers to relate to them all as human beings. He had read somewhere that that was the best thing to do in this situation. He had to get the two of them calling them all by their first names. If he could achieve that, there was less chance that they would be harmed.

The TV had been on since seven thirty. Jon-Joe had asked especially. He and Biddy were anxious to see *EastEnders*, Jon-Joe explained. 'That Grant fella from the pub finds out that the Pauline one from the launderette's his real mother.'

Bosco agreed to the request, mainly because he followed *EastEnders* too and was glad of a distraction. But the time crawled by. He'd zapped the remote to catch the RTE News at nine, and they'd seen pictures of the havoc the storm was causing in various parts of the country. They all paid attention when a shot of the crashed circus wagon flashed on the screen.

'The driver sustained two broken legs and head injuries. He was taken by air ambulance to the Mater hospital where his condition is described as comfortable,' Cathy Grady said earnestly to camera.

'How could he be bleedin' comfortable if he's two feckin' broken legs an' head injuries?' Corky asked no one in particular. He had broken his collarbone once and there was no way he would describe the experience as *comfortable*.

On to the screen flashed images of the crashed wagon and a shot of the trailer lying on its side half blocking the road, half over the embankment.

'When asked about the rumour that several of the circus animals had escaped, a spokesman stated that this was the case, but that the animals in question were docile and not dangerous . . .'

Everyone lost interest after that, so when an item about the Common Agricultural Policy came on, Jake had made the suggestion about the chipper.

'OK,' he began. 'My name's Jake. I'll make a list of what everyone wants. When I come to you, tell me your name and give me your order.' He looked straight at Jodie.

She shrugged. 'I don't know. Chips, anything.'

'What's your *name*,' Jake asked pointedly.

'Jodie,' she said, sounding bemused that he was making such a big deal out of it.

'OK, *Jodie*. Just chips.' He wrote it down, then he looked at Lucy. 'Ah yes, *Edith*. And what do you want, *Edith*?'

Lucy cringed. Shit! she thought, he does recognise me. 'Er . . . Just chips as well. Em . . . and a cheeseburger for the dog – if that's OK.'

Fionn, apparently lying asleep on the floor, wagged her tail at the mention of *cheeseburger*.

Monty was next. He announced his name and ordered a double cheeseburger, chips and curry sauce. Biddy and Jon-Joe joined in with the spirit of the game, each piping up their names, despite the fact that they'd known Jake for two years or more. Both ordered cod and chips. For himself, he ordered chicken breast and chips, then he looked at Bosco.

Without thinking, Bosco said, 'Bosco. I'll have . . .' Then

he realised what he had just done. He turned bright scarlet under his minstrel mask. 'That's just an alias,' he stuttered. 'Fer the purpose of the bleedin' list.'

'That's fine, Bosco. What would you like?' Jake asked.

He ordered a curryburger, chips and onion rings. Corky, smirking at Bosco's *faux pas*, said he'd decide what he wanted when he got to the chipper.

Jake handed him the list and a twenty-pound note. Biddy and Jon-Joe went to the kitchen to make tea. Bosco could see them clearly through the kitchen door from his armchair, so he didn't bother to kick up a fuss. He couldn't bring himself to upset Biddy anyway. This, too, was not lost on Jake.

Lucy, who was now seated with Jodie on a small two-seater sofa near the window, caught Jake's eye. He gave her a knowing wink and a sly smile. To hell with it, she thought, and smiled back.

Only Fools and Horses came on the television next. Monty, Biddy and Jon-Joe were engrossed.

Jodie was deep in thought, wondering how long before she'd be able to phone Rogan. She wasn't madly anxious about it. The fact was, she had the Smack however long it took. She didn't doubt for a minute that she would get out of the predicament in which she now found herself. These guys were just amateurs. If necessary, if push came to shove, she'd frighten the shite out of them and tell them who her boyfriend was. Well, her ex, but she wouldn't mention that small detail.

Lucy, meanwhile, was watching Jodie. She was impressed by how cool she was and how she had stood up to Bosco and the other one. She found it all the more incongruous that Jodie would have such old-fashioned values. *Find a rich man to look after you.* In her mind she could hear those words coming from her mother's mouth. All the more strange that an independent, strong woman like Jodie would think the same way.

Lucy had always felt that she was a constant source of disappointment to her mother because she didn't share her aspirations. She had no interest in clothes or make-up. Never had men chasing after her, the way her mother claimed to have had.

Violet Picket-Spoon would not have been seen dead without full make-up and every hair in place, rock hard and brittle with the aid of half a can of hairspray. She was small, and slim and pretty. Lucy, who took after her father, was tall and gangly, with limbs that appeared to be too long for her body, greasy hair and a terminal teenage slouch.

Lucy had memories of the shlep around the shops and her mother forcing her into neat little suits that had her looking middle-aged at thirteen. Neat little suits and American Tan tights that made her legs look orange. Lucy suspected that her mother was secretly pleased that she didn't measure up in the looks department.

After the divorce, her mother got custody. In those days it was more or less a foregone conclusion, though Lucy would have preferred to stay with her father. She didn't like Malcolm Bryant. Sorry, *Doctor* Malcolm Bryant. He had a PhD in something obscure, but her mother always referred to herself as Mrs *Doctor* Malcolm Bryant.

Violet was the archetypal snob, the prototype of Hyacinth Bucket. Lucy, who had no sense of rhythm, had to suffer the humiliation of ballet classes, tap classes, piano lessons and even singing lessons. Each fiasco lasted only one term, before her parent had to admit defeat. Horse riding lasted two terms, but only because Lucy had fallen off and sprained her ankle half-way through the first term, and the second term was well under way by the time she had recovered.

That Lucy's talents lay in another direction was something Violet would not acknowledge. What good was *drawing*, for God's sake? She also had the knack of causing Lucy huge embarrassment by cross-examining her friends about their backgrounds and prospects. Pretty soon, Lucy ceased to invite people round, and would never have dreamed of taking a boyfriend home – on the odd occasions that she had a boyfriend – as the cringe factor would have been way too high. Even thinking about it twenty-odd years later Lucy gave an involuntary shudder.

It was with great relief that she fled to art college at the age of seventeen and three-quarters. Her mother almost suffered a nervous breakdown as Lucy had omitted to mention her plan until it was a *fait accompli*, well aware of the commotion it would cause.

Lucy had attempted to keep in touch and, for the first couple of terms, had gone home for the occasional weekend, but Violet couldn't come to terms with the fact that her daughter was a grown-up. She criticised her clothes, her hair, her make-up, or the lack thereof, casting up what she perceived as the successes of the neighbours' children. Soon Lucy became heartily sick of hearing how Angela Williams was marrying an orthopaedic surgeon and Patricia Heart was engaged to a stockbroker, who was also a viscount.

When her father died at the end of her first college term, Lucy was left feeling empty. Her mother tried to be compassionate towards her, to be generous about her father. But long-remembered wounds and a couple too many at the funeral brought out some home truths, which Lucy didn't want to hear. There was a row and Lucy stormed out.

She attempted a reconciliation when she and Marcus married. She wrote and invited Violet and Malcolm to stay, but received no reply. She sent Christmas cards to her mother and sometimes a birthday card, if she remembered. They were never acknowledged.

Ten years after the rift, her stepfather wrote to say that her mother had died. Lucy travelled over to the funeral. She was angry with Violet for dying without making things right between them. She arrived at her stepfather's house full of resentment and guilt. Malcolm Bryant was kind to her. It touched her that he was so obviously devastated. The funeral was well attended and the vicar and friends of her mother all said nice things about her. Lucy didn't recognise the woman they were all talking about but, for Malcolm's sake, didn't make an issue of it.

She continued to send Christmas cards to Malcolm for a couple of years, then he remarried and communication sort of petered out. Six years after her mother's death she received a note from a neighbour to say that Malcolm had died as the result of a car crash. It was with an overwhelming sense of guilt that she realised that she felt more sadness about his passing than that of her own parent. From time to time, if she was feeling low and was in the humour to beat herself up, she wondered if she had made her life choices just to spite Violet. It wasn't something she was ready to confront, but sometimes it felt uncomfortably close to the truth. For what other reason could she have made such shit choices? Marcus was certainly any mother's nightmare.

After Corky arrived back with the food and had handed it round, he and Bosco took turns to sit out of sight in the kitchen to eat in comfort. It was a relief for them to spend some time minus their masks. When he and Bosco had finished, Bosco handed him the sawn-off and disappeared into the office to call Cindy.

Cindy was relieved to get the call. It was getting late and she was beginning to worry that something had gone wrong. Had you been Bosco, however, you wouldn't have suspected anything from her tone of voice. Maybe the acting lessons were paying off at last.

'You got the cash?'

'Yes. I have it. Where do you want me to bring it?'

He gave her directions to the truck stop. 'Bring it there tomorra at four o'clock.'

'OK. I'll do that.'

'What'll yeh be drivin'?'

'A silver BMW.'

'Righ'. Park near the gate that leads inta the woods. I'll meet yeh there.'

'But how will I know if you've kept your end of the deal? I'll need to have proof before I hand over the money.'

Jeasus, she's thick, Bosco thought. As if she could stop me takin' it off of her.

But Cindy was way ahead of him. 'I won't have the money with me. I'll need to see proof that you've done the business before I tell you where it is.'

'You'll get yer proof,' he said. 'Jus' bring the cash.'

'No problem. Tomorrow at four then.' She hung up.

Bosco, who still had the receiver to his ear, could feel his heart quicken. Up until then, the need to kill Monty in order to get the cash had been an abstract concept. Now he realised that if he wanted the money he would have to deliver. It was a weird sensation, knowing that he had the power of life and death over another human being.

When he had robbed the Paki off-licence, and the day before when he grabbed Monty, the thought of killing had never crossed his mind. He couldn't have killed the Paki in any case because the gun was only a replica. But even with Monty, the need to kill was removed by the threat of the gun. All he ever expected to use the sawn-off for was as an incentive to persuade Monty to go quietly. He knew of people who wouldn't think twice about shooting someone, but Bosco was aware that he wasn't in that league. He wasn't sure he wanted to be, but he wanted that money. He needed that money. He replaced the receiver. It was time to get a grip. Cash like that didn't come easy.

He sat in the green leather swivel chair and put his feet up on the desk. It was time to figure something out. Some sort of a proper plan.

Chapter Eighteen

Wednesday, 6 November, nine thirty a.m.

Gnasher was exhausted. He'd only had two hours' sleep in the back of the car. He was stiff, sore and bad-tempered.

Decco had been little help. Not that he lacked enthusiasm, but there was still no sign of Jodie McDeal or her knacker friend. He and Gnasher had scoured all the likely places that sort hung out at, but with no result. To avoid suspicion Gnasher had spun a story about needing to find her because her father had died suddenly. It was flimsy in the extreme, but a surprising number seemed to buy it. Only a few, who probably thought they were the drug squad, were less than forthcoming.

One bit of progress was that they discovered that the private bus, on which Jodie was travelling, never arrived in Cork. They only found that out by default when Gnasher got stroppy with a barman and stated in no uncertain terms that she had to be in Cork, because 'wasn't she on the friggin' bus from Boran'.

That was when the barman said that the bus had never arrived. He knew this, he said, because the driver, Jake, played a gig there every Tuesday and Wednesday night and he hadn't turned up. He pointed to a Day-Glo poster advertising live music with 'Jake and the Rustlers'.

'How'd you know the bus didn't feckin' arrive?' Gnasher barked. 'How'd you know he didn't just miss the feckin' thing?'

The barman was a big man himself and he didn't take kindly to Gnasher's attitude. Who the fuck did this thick

Dublin Jackeen think he was? 'Because he's the feckin' *driver*, ya gobshite!' the Cork man snarled back. Well accustomed to dealing with awkward bastards, he turned his back and carried on serving customers.

Decco saw Gnasher's face redden with anger. 'Thanks a million for the help. D'you know where this fella lives? This bus driver fella?' he said quickly to the barman's back.

The barman, who didn't pause from his task or turn round, sighed impatiently. 'Somewhere round Boran. His name's Jake Devine. If yeh see him, tell him t'give us a ring.'

It didn't make sense. He knew she had boarded the bus. The pump guy was certain about that because he sold them the tickets. 'And you wouldn't forget that young one in a hurry,' he'd said, salivating at the memory.

The woman in the café, too. She had no doubts because she remembered that they had a dog, and dogs weren't permitted. She tut-tutted that they'd smuggled the creature in and hidden it under a table. She'd only seen it when they were leaving and getting on the bus.

So where the hell was she? The bus couldn't have disappeared into thin air. This wasn't the *X Files*.

'Maybe it was the storm,' Decco speculated, trying to ingratiate himself with what he saw as a helpful suggestion.

He and Gnasher had gone in search of a decent breakfast and were sitting up at the bar of an early house. Gnasher had a half-full pint of Guinness in front of him. Decco had asked for the same but Gnasher ordered him a Coke. Decco was disgusted. He always drank Guinness, unless he could get alcopop, that was.

The woman of the house came out and plonked two plates of fry in front of them on the bar. Decco was starving. He gobbled up the rashers, egg, sausage and black pudding without drawing breath. Gnasher ate more slowly, turning over the possibilities in his mind. The boy had a point. The weather *was* shite. He'd had to take a couple of detours himself to avoid fallen trees and some flooding on the way down. Maybe the bus had turned back. Maybe the bitch was back in Boran.

'D'you've a phone book?' he asked the woman.

'Over there,' she replied, pointing at a once cream-now nicotine-coloured pay phone on the wall. Decco jumped down off the high stool and fetched the directory over to Gnasher.

Leafing through the pages the hard-man said, 'How d'yeh spell Devine?'

Spelling wasn't really Decco's strong point. He hadn't seen the inside of a classroom since he was twelve. He made a gallant, if lucky, stab at it. 'D-E-V-I-N-E, I think it is. Like the saints.'

Gnasher leafed through the pages until he came to the DEVs and his meaty finger traced down the list. There were only two J. Devines and, of those, only one had an address in Boran. He took out his mobile and dialled the number.

When the phone started to ring everyone who was awake froze and looked over in Bosco's direction. He was sitting in his chair with the sawn-off still across his knees. He and Corky had taken turns to sleep up in one of the bedrooms while the other guarded the hostages.

Jake had produced a blanket for everyone and they used cushions for pillows. Jodie slept like a log, cradling her attaché case in her arms. Lucy, however, didn't close an eye. Ruefully, she reflected that she had spent her first day of freedom being held hostage by a couple of desperados. Marcus would bust a gut laughing if he knew.

The phone rang and rang. Bosco ignored it. Jake, who had been asleep, stirred and got up automatically to answer it.

'Leave it!' Bosco barked. Jake came to his senses and halted in his tracks. After about twelve rings, the phone stopped. 'Who was that?' Bosco asked.

'How the hell do I know,' Jake replied. 'You wouldn't let me answer it.'

'Don't get smart,' Bosco threatened.

Undaunted, Jake said, 'I need to use the bathroom.'

Biddy and Jon-Joe came to at the mention of the bathroom, as did Monty. 'I need to go,' Monty said. 'And I think Biddy and Jon-Joe could use a visit.'

Bosco didn't know what to do. He couldn't cover them going to the bathroom with the sawn-off, and watch the others downstairs at the same time.

Jake sensed his predicament. 'There's a toilet and shower under the stairs. We could go one by one.'

Bosco, relieved that the problem was sorted, nodded in agreement, but added the proviso of no showers. Bearing that in mind, they began their pilgrimage one at a time.

When Bosco and Corky had hijacked the bus, the logistics of guarding six people had never crossed Bosco's mind. He regretted the loss of the replica pistol. Another weapon would make life a lot simpler for them.

'The dog needs to go out,' Lucy said.

'Yeh'll have t'wait till Cor – me friend comes down,' he said.

'But she's crossing her legs.' Lucy was indignant. 'It's cruel.' Fionn gave a little whine, right on cue. 'If you don't let her out, she'll explode.'

Thankfully, Corky put in an appearance at that point. He wandered downstairs, scratching his head and his armpits. His hair was standing on end and his eyes looked bleary. He had reached the bottom step before Bosco noticed that he had forgotten to put on his stocking mask. It was too late. Everyone, with the exception of Biddy, who wouldn't remember anyway, had seen his face. They were all staring at him.

'Wha'?'

'Yer bleedin' mask!' Bosco hissed.

Laid back after his sleep, Corky shrugged. 'Aw . . . fuck it.'

Bosco had no notion, however uncomfortable his Jolly Minstrel mask was, of showing his face. But if Corky wanted to risk it, it was up to him.

Fionn and Lucy got to go outside, accompanied by Corky who kept a close eye on them both. They walked towards the river and sat on a low wall while Fionn ran around and rolled in the grass. The rain had stopped and the storm had blown itself out. The day was bright if a little overcast. They both watched the dog enjoying the freedom after being cooped up in the house all night.

'I'm gettin' a dog,' Corky said, after a while. 'A greyhound. I want t'breed 'em. Yer man in there.' He indicated the mill-house with a jerk of his head. '. . . Yer man, Monty, was tellin' me he had a Greyhound Derby winner once.'

Lucy was surprised. She had never imagined that people like him would want such mundane things. But then she had never really thought about people like him before. 'Who is he?' she asked. 'Why did you kidnap him?'

'Fer the money a'course. It was me mate's idea. Yer man's filthy rich. He won't miss the cash.'

Corky had pushed the gruesome details of the deal to the back of his mind. He was in a sort of denial. He wanted the cash as much as Bosco but was still hoping his partner would deal with the obscene reality of the actual deed, and leave him out of that part. Jake's appraisal of his character was wholly inaccurate. He wasn't nearly as tough as he looked.

'He doesn't seem very upset about it,' Lucy observed, thinking of Monty munching chocolate and happily watching *EastEnders*. 'He doesn't strike me as a man afraid for his life.'

'Why d'yeh say that?' Corky snapped, at once suspicious. Did she know something?

Lucy, taken aback by his change of tone shrugged. 'Well – em – he just doesn't seem afraid, that's all.'

Corky relaxed. 'Oh, Righ'. I suppose he knows his missus'll pay up, no problem.' He stared down at the grass, unable to look Lucy in the eye, afraid that she would read in his face the appalling thing he and Bosco were going to do.

'We should get back.' He stood up. Fionn lolloped over, wagging her tail. She had a stick in her mouth, which she dropped at his feet, inviting him to throw it. She danced around him in excitement, wound up by the air and the run. Corky bent and picked up the stick, then tossed it towards the mill-house. 'It's nice here,' he said. 'I'd like a place like this.'

'For your dogs?'

Corky nodded. 'Yeah. Fer me dogs.'

They both watched as Fionn searched around for the stick. She was looking in entirely the wrong place. 'Not much of a tracker dog, is she?' Corky remarked.

Lucy noticed that he suddenly seemed subdued. 'No,' she said. 'She hasn't quite grasped the concept of *fetch* yet.'

'She knows well,' Corky said. 'She jus' doesn't feckin' feel like it. Smart dog, wha'?'

Following the directions the barman had given them, Cathy Grady and Micky Folan drove along the Boran road towards Kilkenny in the OB satellite truck.

The barman had called it the Boran road but, depending on which direction they were going, others sometimes referred to it as the Kilkenny road which made the journey a tad confusing. Fearing that they had passed the spot, Micky craned out of the window and asked directions from a man who was leaning against a gate, smoking a cigarette.

'You from the telly?' the man asked, surveying the RTE logo on the side of the truck.

'Yeah,' Micky responded. 'Well spotted. Is this the Boran road?'

The man caught sight of Cathy at this point. 'Is that yer woman from the news?' Cathy smiled in acknowledgement. At this, the man got quite excited. 'I seen yeh on the telly last night talkin' about the storms.' He pronounced the word *Shtor-ums*. 'And them wild animals.'

'That's right,' Cathy said pleasantly. 'Is this the Boran road?'

'Wait'll I tell the missus I seen yeh.' He was almost beside himself. 'What're ye doin' down this way?'

'Looking for the fucking Boran road,' Micky said testily. 'I don't suppose you could tell us if this is it – some time today maybe?' He'd had enough of this culchie eejit. He was tired and his back was sore. This was mostly due to the lumpy B&B mattress. He was also a bit under the weather after a few too many in the pub the night before.

'So yer lookin' for the Boran road?' the man said, picking up on Micky's tone. He had stopped smiling. 'Well, this is the Kilkenny road. Ye need t'go back the way ye came.'

'You shouldn't have been so stroppy with that farmer,' Cathy snapped when they eventually reached the site of the explosion which was, in effect, only thirty yards further down the road from the point at which Micky had insulted the farmer. They had travelled seven miles in the opposite direction before being directed back by a passing postman.

A Garda car and a lone cop stood guarding the entrance, which was taped off with blue and white police tape. There was no sign of any Garda technical team.

Micky pulled up on the opposite side of the road and they got out, toting their equipment.

Cathy saw the cop say something over his shoulder, then a second cop appeared. 'Leave the talking to me,' she hissed at Micky. She quickened her pace and reached the gate before her colleague. Micky started rolling.

'Hello,' she said to the two cops. 'Cathy Grady, RTE News. I wonder if you could tell us about the explosion? I heard in Boran that there's rumour of terrorist involvement.'

The cop gave her a half-smile. 'I'm afraid you'll have to get on to the Garda press office about that, Miss,' he said. 'I'm not at liberty to comment.'

'Well, we will,' Cathy said. 'We will do that. But off the record . . .'

'But they're missing, Sergeant. I know they set off, but they never arrived.' Jeannie Horan-Evans was getting hot under the collar. Sergeant Mulligan didn't seem to understand the seriousness of the situation.

When repeated calls through the night to her parents' house remained unanswered, Jeannie had got into the car and driven up to Boran. Jeremy's attitude had been as negative as the policeman's, though in his case he was just irritated that his schedule had been put out due to his having to stay home to mind the kids.

On arrival, Jeannie had gone straight to her family home, an isolated farmhouse about two miles from Boran town. It was with trepidation that she put the key in the front door and pushed it open. She was half expecting to find them both in a state of collapse on the living-room floor or lying helpless at the bottom of the stairs. Scraps of news items about the elderly being targets for robbers flashed across her consciousness. Awful stories about torture and worse. She was half relieved when she found the house empty, but the fact didn't allay her fears that something terrible had happened.

She was overcome by guilt. When she had first recognised that her mother was becoming a little vague, she should have insisted that they come and live with her. But Jeremy made little of it and told her she was over-reacting. She argued that it was too much for her father to cope with a sick woman, but Jeremy had pointed out that physically her mother was in the best of health and, anyway, he argued, 'They're independent people. They wouldn't want to give that up.'

Jeannie didn't really want her parents to live with her. She enjoyed her life-style and, if she were honest, she would have to admit her parents embarrassed her with their rural habits. The way her father left his top set of dentures out. Their countrified accents. It didn't fit in with the middle-class society she moved in. It was at her parents' insistence that they made the weekly pilgrimage to Cork, ostensibly to baby-sit. Jeremy was keen for them to get an au pair and Jeannie wasn't against the idea, but at the same time she baulked at the risk of making her parents feel redundant.

Sergeant Mulligan was tired. He was still smarting from having the face eaten off him the night before by a Dublin detective who looked as if he was only just out of short trousers, all because he had delayed calling for assistance by a couple of hours. Now they'd get all the glory, after he had done the leg work and identified the prime suspect. It wasn't every day you came across a crowd of Prod terrorists and a bomb factory this side of the border.

'What are you going to do, Sergeant?' Jeannie asked. She was verging on panic, but not yet quite there.

'When were you last talking to them?' Mulligan enquired.

'Yesterday,' Jeannie said. 'I talked to Dad yesterday, and he told me they were catching the bus at four o'clock.'

'I thought that bus left at two.'

'Normally. But Dad phoned and said there was some sort of problem and it wasn't leaving until four.'

'And how do you know that they caught the bus?'

'Where else could they be?' Jeannie countered. 'That was the plan.'

'Maybe they missed it,' Mulligan offered.

Jeannie was close to tears. She shook her head.

Mulligan suddenly felt sorry for her. 'Why don't you go and get a cup of tea somewhere and give me a chance to look into it,' he said.

Jeannie sniffed and pulled herself together. 'Thanks. Do you have a number for the bus driver?'

Mulligan reached under the counter, pulled out the local phone directory and flipped through the pages. 'Here we are,' he said triumphantly. 'Jake Devine.' There was a display ad for the brown bus and two phone numbers. One a mobile. 'No point in ringing the house, though. He won't be back till tomorrow.'

Jeannie wrote down the two numbers. When she had finished, Mulligan patted the back of her hand sympathetically. 'It'll be fine. Don't be worrying yourself,' he said. 'Go and get that cup of tea while I look into it. Drop back in about an hour.'

Grateful that someone was taking her seriously at last,

Jeannie thanked the cop and hurried off. Mulligan dialled Jake's mobile number.

Wesley was depressed. He couldn't get his bearings and he was still a touch groggy after his tumble down the embankment the previous night. He could hear traffic a good distance above him on the road, but the side of the hill was steep and his progress impeded by the thick undergrowth. The ground, muddy and slippery, made matters worse. He felt as if for every few feet he moved forward, he slipped a couple back.

He was exhausted, but he knew if he was to survive he would have to reach the road. He could smell the river. The river *must* be on the other side of the road. His instinct for survival was strong. Hadn't his species managed it when the dinosaurs had perished? Wesley blinked his beady eyes a couple of times and set off back up the hill.

At the mill-house the hostages were passing the time watching television. After Richard and Judy, Bosco switched channels to see the RTE News, just in case Cindy had double-crossed them and called the cops. He knew it was a stupid notion because there was nothing in it for her if she did any such thing. But, like a good general, Bosco was just covering every possibility.

There were a couple of items about the Peace Process. Gerry Adams giving one opinion and David Trimble the opposite view. There was more about the storm. A serious-faced Cathy Grady, who appeared to be having problems keeping her hair from blowing into her face, looked into the camera and stated that storm damage was estimated at over a million pounds. Lucy wondered how they worked it out so quickly. Did they just make up a figure and hope for the best?

'One of the circus animals is still loose,' she went on. Lucy gathered that the circus management were now admitting it was an amphibious reptile though the spokesman didn't seem too worried. Apparently, the geriatric tigers had given themselves up. 'The animal still at large is not said to be dangerous.'

With talk of a terrorist explosion, Cathy Grady had other fish to fry.

It just shows, Lucy thought. So much for *wild* animal acts. They should change the name to not-said-to-be-dangerous animal acts.

Aiden Nulty was more optimistic about the weather today. The storm, it seemed, had passed.

Lucy sidled over to where Jake was sitting. She regretted it immediately.

'Well, Edith. And how are you?' he asked.

Smartarse, she thought, and gave him a withering look. There was an uncomfortable silence.

He broke the ice. 'It's Lucy Spoon, isn't it?' His expression was open and friendly so she relented.

'You've blown my cover,' she said.

'God! It must be twenty years. What have you been doing with yourself, apart from getting hijacked on my bus?'

'Nothing much,' she replied. 'Apart from making shite life choices. How about you?'

To tell Lucy that he was completely happy with his life and most of his personal life choices seemed a little smug to Jake, so he just shrugged and said, 'Oh you know,' in a non-committal way.

The conversation was going nowhere. He patted her arm. 'Good to see you again,' he added warmly. 'We must get together after this is over. Talk about old times.'

He mustn't know I took his fifty quid, she thought, and heaved a sigh of relief. 'Yes, we must.'

A tinny tinkly version of the *William Tell* overture suddenly intruded on Richard and Judy's phone-in on hyperactive kids. Bosco jumped to his feet. 'Wha'?'

The sound was emanating from Jake. 'It's my mobile,' he said, retrieving it from his pocket.

'Switch the feckin' thing off.' Bosco was agitated. This

whole business was getting to him. Especially the extra hostages. He certainly hadn't planned on having five other people to deal with – and five loonies at that: a lippy hippie, Marianne bleedin' Faithful with a dog, two auld ones and a friggin' cowboy.

He was also beginning to regret taking Cindy up on her proposal. If he'd been straight with Corky about the money she had offered in the first place, they could have told Monty about it, and got more out of him. But he couldn't suggest that now. If he did, Corky would know he'd tried to cheat him out of his share of an extra hundred grand.

Jake switched off his phone and the tinny music ceased abruptly.

'Who was tha'?' Bosco asked, immediately feeling like a spa for asking. Jake smiled at him and gave an exaggerated shrug.

Bosco was becoming paranoid. 'Close the bleedin' curtains,' he snapped. When Jake didn't do it, he shoved the sawn-off in his face and screamed, 'I said, close the friggin' things. Now!'

Lucy jumped up and helped Jake to pull the heavy curtains across the windows. Gloom descended on the room.

'He's losing it,' she whispered to Jake. Taking everything into account, Jake was inclined to agree. It was a worrying development.

Bosco was pacing backwards and forwards. He looked very agitated. 'Why're people ringin' yeh?' he barked at Jake.

Jake tried to calm him down. 'I've a business. People ring me all the time. It's no big deal.'

Not strictly true. Jake only ran the bus as a hobby, and as Biddy and Jon-Joe were virtually his only customers, and they had the free travel which he didn't bother to collect from the relevant government department, it wasn't exactly a profit-making operation.

Bosco stopped pacing and stood with his back to the fireplace, covering everyone with the sawn-off. 'If anyone comes, ye're all t'keep quiet,' he roared. 'If there's a knock at the door, an any of yez makes a noise, I'll bleedin' blow yez away with this.'

He thrust the gun forward to emphasise the point. His face was scarlet and blue veins were standing out on his forehead. 'An' that goes fer the bleedin' dog too, Missus,' he added, throwing a mean look in Fionn's direction.

Fionn replied by baring her teeth and a low growling sound rumbled in her throat. Biddy, Jon-Joe and Monty froze where they sat, all staring at him open-mouthed. Jodie was dozing and missed the incident.

Corky looked bewildered and a little anxious. It wasn't like Bosco to bottle out and, in his view, it looked as if Bosco was seriously on the verge of bottling out.

He walked over to join his friend, and laid a reassuring arm across his shoulder. 'Hey, chill out, man. It'll be grand. Don't worry. It'll work out grand.'

The outburst and Corky's reassuring words seemed to calm Bosco down a bit. He lowered the gun and everyone relaxed again. Corky breathed a sigh of relief. He couldn't pull it off on his own. The last thing he needed was for Bosco to go off the deep end. 'You OK?' he asked. Gently.

Bosco nodded. 'I'm grand.' The moment of paranoia had passed. 'I'm grand,' he repeated. Things would work out fine. Didn't Corky say so?

Chapter Nineteen

Wednesday, 6 November, twelve thirty p.m.

Gnasher Gill pulled into an empty parking space and switched off the engine. He couldn't explain why, but he had a gut feeling that Jodie was still in the Boran area. Where else could she go? He knew she had no cash to speak of. And if the bus had turned back because of the storm, she was effectively stuck there until the next run. He tried Jake's mobile number again. He got the messaging service and hung up.

Emboldened by the rapport that he felt he had built up with Gnasher, Decco asked, 'Who's yer woman? What'd she do?'

Gnasher looked round at the young gurrier who was sitting in the passenger seat. Instinctively, he was about to bark some expletive at the boy, but he hesitated. Though he was loath to admit it, he quite liked the lad. There was something about him. Maybe it was his air of bravado. It gave Gnasher a faint echo of himself at that age. What was he? Fourteen? Fifteen?

Gnasher Gill had never had it easy. His mother was helplessly drug dependent and he was sexually and physically abused by his father. At the age of twelve, unable to stand it any longer, he had run away from home and lived on the streets. Awful as it was, it was better than home. He had had to learn very quickly how to look after himself. He was lucky that, unlike Decco, he had always been big for his age.

On the cold winter days he had taken to hanging around

a boxing gym, and Jimmy (The Gouger) Gough, the retired fighter who ran the place, took him under his wing. He taught him everything he knew about fighting. What Gnasher lacked in finesse, he more than made up for in tenacity. He had the killer instinct, for the most part because he had a deep well of suppressed anger to draw on, but also because he wouldn't satisfy his opponent by giving in.

When Jimmy discovered that Gnasher lived on the streets, he had allowed him to bed down in the gym at night and Gnasher became a sort of unofficial employee. Money had never changed hands but he swept out the place and kept it tidy, sparring with the contenders Gouger was bringing on. His paltry breadline life-style left him ripe for a career in crime. At first it had been just petty theft, shoplifting, the usual stuff. But soon, because of his size, he was recruited as muscle by Billy Bender, Hogan's predecessor. At first this was on a casual basis but Bender was quick to recognise Gnasher's talents and pretty soon he was on the payroll.

Hogan gladly kept him on when he took over Bender's turf after a power struggle. Hogan was twenty-six at the time and Gnasher a couple of years younger. Conscious of the need for security, Hogan employed Gnasher to be his driver/personal bodyguard. It was a sort of poacher-turned-gamekeeper strategy. It paid off. Shortly afterwards, Gnasher saved Hogan's life when a lone gunman on a motor cycle in Bender's pay attempted to shoot Hogan as they stopped at a set of traffic lights. Gnasher's lightning reflexes enabled him to grab the gun and yank it out of the assassin's hand before he had time to fire. Later, he tracked down Bender and the assassin, and held one while Hogan tortured the other. It was the stuff reputations are made of. The story, the reality of which was spine-chillingly gruesome, was exaggerated out of proportion and it was a reckless man who dared to cross Hogan or Gnasher Gill after that.

Decco was still looking at him, waiting for an answer. 'She knocked off some of his gear,' Gnasher said. 'Not very smart, wha'?'

Decco shook his head in agreement. 'Jeasus! Fuckin' headcase.'

They sat in silence, watching the comings and goings at the truck stop. After a couple of minutes Decco said, 'Why don't we find the feckin' bus driver. He'll know where yer wan got off.'

Gnasher had already made this decision, but he was trying to determine whether or not to call Hogan first. He decided not. He'd locate the girl first, then call his boss. He felt he needed the brownie points a result like that would give him. Gnasher wasn't exactly afraid of Hogan, in fact he wasn't afraid of another living soul, but he held Hogan in high esteem and took pleasure in the respect he enjoyed as a result of their association.

He restarted the engine and put the car into reverse gear. 'Righ'. Let's get this show on the road,' he said, as he pressed the accelerator. There was the sound of screeching brakes. Gnasher slammed on the anchors and Decco lurched forward as far as his seat-belt allowed.

The next moment, a woman appeared at the driver's side roaring and yelling. She was pale as a ghost. Gnasher opened the door and stepped out. The woman was still shouting the odds. Garbled hysterical ravings.

'Sorry, Missus,' Gnasher said. 'I didn't see yeh.'

Maybe it was Gnasher's size, or perhaps his reasonable tone, but whatever it was it brought Jeannie Horan-Evens back from the brink of hysteria.

Embarrassed by her over-reaction to the near incident, she pulled herself up short. 'Em . . . Sorry. I got a fright. I didn't expect . . . I'm sorry.'

''S OK, Missus.' Gnasher was all sweetness and light. 'No harm done.' It was low-profile time. He didn't want to draw attention to himself. Not with what he had in mind for Jodie fucking McDeal.

He got back into the car and backed out of the parking bay. Driving off he saw, in his rear-view mirror, the mad-woman moving into the vacated space. He pulled up in front of the café. 'Go in an' ask where the bus driver lives,' he ordered Decco.

Thrilled to be included in the operation, Decco swaggered into the café, confident in the notion that this was just the beginning. The woman inside told him to go and ask the petrol pump attendant.

The man was talking to the madwoman in the little kiosk between the pumps. Decco waited. His ears pricked up when he heard her mention the bus driver. He leaned in closer to hear what was being said.

'. . . in the mill-house about six miles down the road,' the pump guy said.

'Do you know if he'd be there now?' the madwoman asked.

The attendant shrugged. 'Dunno.'

Jeannie Horan-Evans filed the information away. 'I wonder if you'd know whether my parents got on the bus,' she asked. 'Jon-Joe and Biddy Horan? They usually get on here.'

The pump attendant, who was vaguely familiar, squinted at her. 'Are you Jeannie? Jeannie Horan?' he asked, cocking his head to one side.

'Em . . . yes. Do I know you?'

'Bunnie Ross.' He pointed at his chest. 'I sat next to you in third class, remember?'

Jeannie remembered all right. He was vile. He always smelled of turf smoke and ate with his mouth open. Conscious of the fact that she needed his co-operation, she smiled at him. 'Oh yes. Why wouldn't I remember you. How are you?'

'Grand. Grand.' He was grinning, nodding, and kept repeating, 'Jeannie Horan . . . well . . . Jeannie Horan,' the way you do when you meet someone after years and years, with whom you've nothing in common other than knowledge of each other's existence.

'Em . . . about my parents?'

'Oh, right,' he said, at once businesslike. 'Let me see.' He put on a thinking face. 'Well, there were the two hippies with the dog, and, yes, Mister and Missus Horan got on. I remember now.'

Having acquired all the information he needed, Decco didn't bother to wait to talk to the pump attendant, but headed back to the car.

Gnasher was on the phone when Decco slid into the passenger seat. 'Yes, Boss. I'm goin' t'see the bus driver. He'll be able t'tell me where yer woman got off. I've a feelin' she's still around,' he heard him say.

'Just have a sniff around. Don't do anything until I get there. She's mine, that one. I'll do what has to be done,' Hogan ordered.

Gnasher nodded a few times. 'OK, Boss. Whatever you say.'

'I should be in Boran around four. I'll call you then.'

'OK, Boss. See yeh then.' He put the phone back in his pocket. 'Well?'

'Yer man lives in a mill-house six miles down the road,' Decco said triumphantly. He hadn't a clue what a mill-house was, but repeated what he had heard.

Gnasher was pleased with the progress so far. Hogan's call had caught him on the hop. He had been hoping to have a result before he spoke to his boss again, but the man seemed happy with the way the situation was developing, so that was fine with Gnasher too. Hogan said he would meet him at the truck stop at four and that he was not to do anything until then, apart from keeping an eye on the situation. Gnasher was disappointed that Hogan wanted to see to the McDeal bitch himself, but cheered himself with the thought that at least she'd get what was coming to her, whoever it was who dealt with her.

The young-looking detective was polite but firm. Detective Inspector Gallagher, he introduced himself as. No sooner was Marcus home and in bed – the taxi had cost him eighteen quid – when he, Sergeant Mulligan and another uniformed cop had come banging on the door and dragged him down to the cop shop again.

Marcus had spent all night in a cell. It was freezing cold and they had only left him one skimpy blanket, but he was afraid to ask for another in case he antagonised them. If the cops had no intention of talking to him last night, why didn't they wait until morning to bring him in? They didn't have to use the strong-arm stuff. He would have come down willingly if they had asked. He was only too willing to help. Eager to show that he had nothing to do with Lucy's secret life.

After a breakfast of tea and toast, Marcus was taken to the same room in which Mulligan had interviewed him. They left him sitting there for a further hour before Gallagher put in an appearance. The questioning followed the same routine as the day before. Marcus repeated the same answers, embellishing a few points to damn Lucy further and make him look all the more innocent.

Gallagher was sitting across the table from him. He looked more like a librarian than a cop to Marcus. Grey trousers. Shirt and tie. Sports jacket neatly hung over the back of his chair. If they were playing the good cop/bad cop routine Marcus had watched countless times on TV shows, he would definitely be the good cop to Mulligan's bad cop.

Apart from the business of dragging him down there in the middle of the night, Gallagher had been polite and courteous. He had even sent out for coffee after the first hour, and allowed Marcus a toilet break.

Marcus was well and truly lulled into a false sense of security when, out of the blue, Gallagher asked, 'What can you tell me about the gun, Marcus?'

Marcus swallowed hard. 'Wha – what gun?'

'Come on, Marcus. You can tell me. You know she had a gun.'

'No, no. Really,' Marcus squeaked. His voice had suddenly risen by three octaves. 'I'd no idea. What gun?'

'We found a gun at the burned-out house.'

There was a tap on the door and Mulligan got up to answer it.

'How d'you know it was hers?' Marcus asked. He couldn't bring himself to mention her name. He was trying to distance himself as far as possible from his wife. Mulligan came back and muttered something to Gallagher, then left the room.

Eugene Mulligan was surprised to see Jeannie Horan-Evens standing in the public office. He'd forgotten about her and, despite his promise, hadn't had the time yet to make enquiries about her parents. He was just about to say as much, but he didn't get the chance.

'They definitely got on the bus, Sergeant.' She was out of breath as she had run from the car-park. 'I spoke to the petrol pump attendant at the truck stop where they normally get on, and he remembered. He was positive. He said they were the only ones on the bus except for two hippies and a dog. So you see, he couldn't have been mistaken.'

'Two hippies and a dog, did you say?'

'Yes, yes. Never mind that. What are you going to do? It's proof they – '

'Hold on a minute, Mrs, em – '

'Horan-Evens,' Jeannie assisted.

'Whatever,' Mulligan said, his mind on other things. 'Wait there, I'll be back in a minute.'

Jeannie had no choice, Mulligan left her standing and hurried from the office back to the interview room.

Marcus was sitting with his head in his hands when Mulligan re-entered. Gallagher had dropped the Mr Nice-Guy routine and gone in with all guns blazing. He accused Marcus of conspiring with Lucy and persons unknown to cause explosions; of membership of an illegal organisation. He even hinted they might have evidence that linked them to other crimes.

For 'might have evidence' read 'we'll fucking fit you up', Marcus thought grimly. He saw himself fifteen years down the line, locked in Portlaoise gaol. The only prisoner in the Protestant wing – did they even have a Protestant wing? The Boran One. *Free the Boran One* didn't have much of a ring to it. He couldn't see the public imagination being fired up to campaign on his behalf. In his mind's eye, he pictured *Free the Boran One* T-shirts gloomily. An image of his face with prison bars superimposed in front of it. Another victim of injustice; of a warped and corrupt judicial system.

Marcus brightened up slightly when the thought crossed his mind that perhaps he'd become an icon like Che Guevara. People were making a fortune out of posters and T-shirts and stuff with Che's image on them. Would he get a royalty for his picture on the *Boran One* posters? Marcus began to make plans for his next fortune.

He didn't notice that Mulligan had re-entered the room, and was only dragged back to the present when Gallagher tapped his arm.

'We'll leave it there for the moment, Marcus.' Gallagher stood up.

'Can I go?' Marcus was confused.

Gallagher shook his head. 'Oh no. Not yet a while. We'll want to talk to you again soon.'

Gallagher and Mulligan headed for the door.

Martyr Icon Marcus sat meekly where he was until he was taken back to his cell.

Gallagher was dubious, Mulligan frustrated. 'But the woman's parents are missing. Bunnie Ross saw them getting on the bus yesterday. He also said a woman answering Lucy Spoon's description, who had a dog, got on with another female, probably a second gang member. The detail of 'matching Lucy's description' was poetic licence, but Mulligan was desperate for Gallagher to take him seriously.

'The fact remains that the bus is missing. I can't get any reply from the driver's mobile or home number. I think the Spoon woman hijacked the bus and she's holding them hostage somewhere until her UVF friends get her out.'

'But how do you know the bus has actually disappeared? Has anyone reported it missing?'

'Well, no. But I told you, the driver's not answering his mobile or his home phone.'

Gallagher was standing with his hands in his pockets. It all seemed very far fetched to him. He wasn't altogether convinced by Mulligan's story about the UVF bomb factory, and if it hadn't been for the firearm they had found, he wouldn't have given the sergeant the time of day. Just as two swallows don't make a summer, two bags of fertiliser don't a bomb factory make. Still, if he didn't want to end up with egg on his face, he knew it was safer to reserve judgement until the forensic examination of the scene was complete. It was nearly time for lunch.

'All right,' he said, with an air of begrudgery. 'Go and show the petrol pump attendant the photo of the suspect. If he gives you a positive ID, we'll follow it up.'

On his way out, Mulligan bumped into Jeannie Horan-Evens. In his excitement he had forgotten about her again. As soon as she saw him she pounced. 'Well, Sergeant? Did you find anything out?'

Anxious to follow up his lead, and irritated that Jeannie Horan-Evens was delaying him, he attempted to hurry past, saying, 'I have to follow up a lead, Mrs . . . em – '

Jeannie's imagination ran riot. She grabbed his arm in such a way that it was impossible for him to shrug it off. 'There's something you're not telling me.' Her voice had a desperate edge. 'Something's happened to them, hasn't it?'

Mulligan shepherded her over to a bench seat by the wall and sat her down, prising her vice-like grip from his sleeve. 'Calm down. As far as we know, nothing's happened to your parents. I'm trying to trace the bus driver, that's all.'

'But you think something's happened, don't you? You're just as worried as I am.'

'We're a little concerned,' he conceded. 'It looks as if they might have got mixed up in another incident.' He didn't want to be any more specific. 'But so far, we don't think they're in any danger.' The last statement was rubbish, but Mulligan didn't want the woman to go completely off the deep end.

'What incident?' Jeannie persisted.

'I can't give you any more information at the moment. I'll be able to tell you more when I've spoken to the bus driver.' Mulligan eased towards the door.

'But if they're not in any danger, why are you concerned?'

Mulligan cringed. Communication wasn't one of his more obvious talents. He had the knack of painting himself into a corner. 'Well, maybe concerned's too strong a word,' he waffled. He made a break for the door. 'I'll talk to you later after I've followed up this lead.'

He heard her call after him but sped to the patrol car and made good his escape.

Chapter Twenty

Wednesday, 6 November, two p.m.

Mulligan entered the Garda station by the back entrance with the sole purpose of avoiding Jeannie Horan-Evens, should she still be in the public office. He didn't want to talk to her. He had more important things on his mind and he was excited. The petrol pump attendant had positively identified Lucy as the hippie he had seen the previous day getting on the bus in the company of a younger woman and a dog.

Gallagher wasn't back from his lunch, so Mulligan went straight to Marcus's cell. Through the spy hole he saw him sitting forlornly on the bed with his head in his hands. An empty burger box and a half-full carton of Cola lay discarded on the floor at his feet. He looked up when he heard the door open.

Mulligan swaggered in and leaned against the wall with his arms folded across his chest. 'We've had a sighting of your wife,' he said.

Marcus jumped to his feet. 'Where?'

'She was seen getting on to a private bus in the company of a woman.'

'A woman?'

Mulligan nodded. 'Any ideas who the woman could be?'

Marcus shook his head and sat down on the bed again. Suddenly it all made sense. A woman. That explained it. That explained her coldness towards him. Why she avoided sex. He should have seen it before. The way she waited for him to be asleep before she came to bed. The way she was always up before him in the mornings. Her constant whinges, on the odd occasion he made overtures, that she had a headache, or she had her period. Jesus! She was the only woman he knew who had twenty-eight-day periods, followed immediately by the next one. She should be in the flaming *Guinness Book of Records*.

Mulligan was talking but he wasn't listening. 'My wife's a lesbian,' he announced.

That stopped Mulligan in his tracks. 'What?'

'My wife's a lesbian. The woman on the bus must be her lesbian lover.'

It took a moment for Mulligan to get back on track. 'I'm sorry? What did you say?'

Marcus shook his head. 'I should have put two and two together long ago.'

'You're telling me your wife's a lesbian, Mister Pyle?'

Marcus nodded.

'So who's this woman, her lover? How long has she known her? Is she from the North?'

Marcus shrugged. He was trying to think back. How long since Lucy had started rejecting him. It was hard to recall because it had been a gradual process. That she might have been ever so slightly put off by his attitude towards her; that she could possibly have found it a turn-off to have him yelling and abusing her as a matter of form, didn't cross his mind. He couldn't understand why clumsily grabbing her breast and shoving his hand up her skirt didn't constitute foreplay as far as she was concerned. Lucy was a lesbian. She didn't want sex with him, therefore she *must* be a lesbian.

'Probably about a year. Eighteen months maybe.' Marcus was more certain by the minute. 'Nearer the eighteen months, I'd say.'

Mulligan wandered over and sat next to him on the bed. 'And the woman?'

Marcus shook his head. 'I don't know who she is. She could have met her at the market. She has a stall. Maybe she met her there.'

'So you don't know who she is. D'you know where she lives? Where she's from?'

Marcus didn't even know Lucy's mystery lesbian lover had existed until Mulligan mentioned this female. 'I've never seen her.'

'But you knew your wife had a lover?'

Marcus nodded enthusiastically. 'A man senses these things,' he said with an air of resignation. 'She was just using me. All these years she was just using me.'

Much as he disliked Marcus's sort, Mulligan couldn't help but feel sorry for him. Poor sod! His wife, not only a left footer, but also a fecking pervert.

The Garda press office didn't have a clue what Cathy Grady was talking about when she phoned them. They not only denied all knowledge of a terrorist-related incident, but also any knowledge of any explosion. This only strengthened her resolve that there was something big, and probably terrorist-related, going down. She called her anchor-man.

When Liam Goggin told her to follow it up, Cathy had an adrenalin rush. She left Micky in the pub and headed for the Garda station.

As she parked her car she saw a sergeant stride out of the building, making for the squad car. Hurriedly, she grabbed her bag off the passenger seat and ran over to waylay him before he drove away.

Unaware that there was need for a quick getaway, Mulligan sat behind the wheel and pondered the situation. If Lucy Spoon was holed up at the mill-house, how many other desperate, armed-to-the-teeth paramilitaries would she have with her? Should he call the Armed Response Unit before he checked it out? He dismissed the idea. Not through choice, but deep down he knew that Gallagher would never authorise it. Not yet, at any rate.

Just as he was coming to terms with the fact that he'd have to go it alone, he was startled by a loud rap on the window. He nearly had a seizure.

He half recognised the face peering in at him, but couldn't place her. He wound down the window.

The young woman smiled at him and held up an ID. 'Excuse me, Sergeant. My name's Cathy Grady. RTE News. I wonder if I could have a word?'

Mulligan knew her now. He'd seen her on the news many a time. 'A word?' he repeated. 'A word about what?'

'I understand that there's been an explosion just outside the town.' Mulligan stared at her. His expression didn't even flicker. Cathy gave up on the extended silence routine. 'A terrorist-related explosion?'

'Where did you hear that?' Mulligan sounded defensive.

'We have our sources,' Cathy replied non-committally. 'Do you have any suspects in custody? Have you made any arrests? Which organisation is involved?' She shot the questions at him one after the other.

'You know the form,' he said, getting rattled. 'You'll have to get on to the Garda press office.' He started the engine.

Cathy stood her ground on the assumption that he wouldn't drive away while her head was half in his window. 'I already did that. They knew nothing about it.'

Mulligan's hackles rose. That bastard Gallagher still wasn't taking him seriously. 'Is that so?' he barked. 'Is that so?'

Cathy couldn't fail to register his reaction. 'So come on, Sergeant, what's the story?' she cajoled. 'This is your patch. You must know the score far better than that crowd up in Dublin. What can you give me?'

Cathy's wheedling had no effect, mainly because Mulligan had stopped listening. He was seething inside. I'll show the bastards, he thought. Without further reply, he shoved the car into gear and, wheels spinning on the gravel, roared off.

Cathy Grady had to jump back out of the way to avoid being flattened. 'What the fuck was that about?' she asked a scraggy ginger cat who was lounging in a crevice on the wall.

But the cat ignored her too.

*

Bosco needed a chance to think. There were only two hours to go before he had to produce a dead body for Cindy George. Either that or he could kiss goodbye to the money.

He wasn't so much worried about the other five hostages. He planned to tie them up at the house and by the time they freed themselves he and Corky would be long gone. His plan to date involved taking Monty to the woods behind the mill-house, shooting him, showing the remains to Cindy, then burying the body deep in the woods where no one would ever locate it. Home free. The others would never even know that Monty was dead. It was the details of the actual killing that were causing him problems. Again and again he came back to the fact that the only foolproof way was to blow Monty's brains out with the shotgun. He was beginning to realise that he didn't have the stomach for it. He couldn't stand the sight of blood. Hadn't he fainted that time when Corky nearly sliced his finger off with his brother's fish-gutting knife?

He was sitting outside the chippy in Jake's jeep. Jake had taken the orders for food as on the previous night, but he volunteered to go instead of Corky, because he wanted a bit of time to himself.

The last of a crowd of schoolgirls burst out of the take-away door, all with grease-stained chip bags in their hands, open at the top. He watched as they barged noisily down the street, calling out to a group of boys on the other side. The boys shouted something back and made a run across the road towards the girls who scattered in different directions. One of the boys caught up with a small girl who didn't have the speed to evade him, and threw the liquid contents of a paper cup over her. As he ran off guffawing, she yelled after him, 'Yeh drownded me, yeh dickhead, yeh.'

Then it came to him. It was brilliant! No blood. No guts. All he had to do was take Monty to the river and hold his head under the water until he drowned. He wouldn't even have to dispose of the body. He could tip him in and Monty would be just another casualty of the storm. Bosco grinned.

He knew if he thought about it long enough he'd come up with the answer. With a spring in his step, he rooted the list and the twenty-pound note from his pocket and headed into the chipper.

As Bosco was ordering sundry junk food, Mulligan was driving in through the gates of the mill-house. Corky heard the car and at first thought that Bosco must have forgotten something. He peeked out through the side of the curtain and nearly wet his pants when he saw the cop car.

'Keep bleedin' quiet,' he barked, waving the gun menacingly. 'There's a cop outside. Not a sound or I'll feckin' kill yez.'

Mulligan drove right up to the front door. The place looked deserted, with no sign of Jake Devine's jeep. For a moment his confidence wavered and he wondered if he was making too many assumptions. Just because the woman was English that didn't mean to say she had Unionist sympathies. On the other hand if she was a lesbian like the husband said, and if anyone should know a thing like that it was the husband, there was no telling how she'd think. Mulligan didn't hold with that class of thing. It wasn't natural. What was it he'd heard the Mission priest say from the pulpit? Oh yes. 'God created Adam and Eve, not Adam and Steve.' So it didn't fit the situation in every sense, but it was the same thing. Man haters. Perverts, the lot of them.

Buoyed up by that thought, Mulligan rang the doorbell. When no one answered he tried again. After about half a minute the cop stood back and stared at the house. He had never really looked at it properly, having only ever caught a glimpse of it from the road. It was certainly grand. He remembered it vaguely from years back as a ruin, but now it was perfectly restored.

There had been talk about Jake Devine when he had first arrived in the village. Was it four or five years before? Mulligan couldn't quite remember. First there was speculation that he was a retired rock star. Someone else heard that he'd won six million on the English Lotto, but the English Lotto hadn't started then. Mulligan wondered if he could be a drug dealer, considering the look of him, but one day his son Hugh, who was computer mad, showed Mulligan a photo of Jake Devine in a computer magazine. He was standing with someone called Bill Gates. Hugh was disgusted that he had never heard of this Bill Gates character. He was not particularly impressed either that his father was equally ignorant about Jake Devine, the inventor of Treasures of the Labyrinth. The most advanced game of its time, it was the standard by which all other games were measured. Hugh told him that the Sony corporation – he'd heard of them – had bought the rights to all Jake's games for millions. Mulligan could never figure out why someone with that amount of money would ever bother to drive a bus.

As there was no sign of life, he wandered round the side of the house. A large two-storey stone barn stood about ten yards to the left of the mill-house. Both buildings backed on to the river. Mulligan leaned over the wall and peered at the swollen torrent rushing, hell for leather, over now submerged rocks. The sluice gates leading to the waterwheel were open because of the swell and pockets of foam, churned up by the rocks and the speed of the flow, had collected at the base of the huge wheel.

He'd heard that Jake Devine had restored the waterwheel and grinding mill to full working order. He wondered why anyone would bother to put a job like that on themselves, if they had no intention of using it. To the right of the waterwheel Mulligan noticed a wooden bridge across the river, leading from the back of the house to the woods. It looked new.

Corky watched the policeman from behind the kitchen blinds. He was standing by the wall looking into the river. What the fuck did the wanker want? The cop turned, and Corky flinched back against the wall. When he looked out again the cop was gone.

For an instant Mulligan sensed movement behind him. He

spun round but saw nothing. He headed back towards the barn.

The high double doors were locked, but he noticed that there was a three-inch gap at the bottom. Laboriously, he lowered himself on to his belly and peered underneath. In the gloom he could just make out the shape of the bus. The brown bus was inside all right. His heart quickened as he struggled to his feet again, as much from the physical effort of heaving fifteen stone into an upright position as from the excitement of finding the missing bus. He brushed the damp dead leaves from his tunic as he made his way back to the squad car.

Corky was relieved to see the cop getting back into his car. He hoped Bosco would not choose that moment to swing in through the gates.

There it was again – the sensation that someone was watching him. Mulligan shot a glance at the front window of the mill-house. Was it his imagination or did he see the curtain twitch? He started the engine and did a three-point turn in the driveway. As he drove towards the gates he glanced in the rear-view mirror. Yes, definitely. The curtain twitched. There was someone in there. Time to get back-up.

Bosco came round the corner just as Mulligan stopped in the gateway of the mill-house, waiting to turn right on to the Boran road. Bosco drove past, keeping a close eye on the cop car through the wing mirror. He slowed down and pulled into the verge about twenty yards further down the road. As soon as the cop had made off towards Boran, he turned Jake's jeep and sped back to base. Before he went into the house, he replaced his jolly minstrel mask. He had no intention of taking the risk of being identified should anything go wrong. If Corky was prepared to chance it, that was up to him.

'He was just nosin' around,' Corky said, making light of the cop's visit. 'No swea'.'

Bosco couldn't face another change of location. Chill out, he told himself. It was nothin'. He was just nosin' around, like Corky said. It'll be grand. Especially so as he had his new, no-blood-involved plan in place for the dispatch of Monty.

'Who ordered the Hawaiian burger an' onion rings?' he asked. Monty raised a podgy finger. Bosco felt a stab of regret. He was a harmless old prat. Hadn't given them a moment's bother. He quickly pushed such thoughts from his mind and handed Monty his junk food.

'Should really be cutting down on the old cholesterol,' Monty said, as he munched on a greasy batter-covered onion ring. 'My wife Cindy's always on at me. Says she doesn't want me dropping down dead on her, bless her heart.'

Corky blushed and looked uncomfortable.

Bosco gave Monty a strained smile as he picked out a polystyrene carton from the carrier bag. 'Whose was the cheeseburger?'

Fionn licked her lips and barked.

Gallagher met Mulligan on the way into the Garda station. He was not a happy man. He had just finished reading the forensic report. Mulligan was out of breath and flushed. He looks like a candidate for a heart attack, Gallagher thought.

'I found the missing bus, Sir,' Mulligan blurted. 'And I think the suspect's holed up in the mill-house.'

'Is that so?'

Mulligan was too wound up to notice Gallagher's jaded tone. 'Yes, Sir. The pump attendant gave a positive ID on the woman. I was talking to the husband, and he told me she's a lesbian. And she and her girlfriend are mixed up in all sorts.'

'Is that so,' Gallagher repeated. 'Can you be more specific?'

Mulligan still didn't notice that Gallagher was less than enthusiastic. 'Bombers, Sir. They're UVF bombers. They're holding the bus driver and two pensioners hostage in the – '

But Gallagher didn't wait for him to finish. 'Come into the office, Sergeant Mulligan.' He turned on his heel and marched down the corridor.

That was when Mulligan began to suspect that all was not

well. Inspector Gallagher held the door open for him, then closed it firmly behind him. He didn't beat about the bush. 'I got the forensic results back,' he said. 'Just what made you jump to the conclusion that the burned-out building was a UVF bomb factory, Sergeant?'

Mulligan was confused. 'Well, there was the fertiliser.' He counted out on his fingers. 'The firearm. The woman.'

'Ah yes. Two bags of fertiliser and a replica pistol.'

'A replica?'

'A replica, Sergeant.'

Mulligan shrugged. So what? It was nevertheless a firearm. It could still be used to coerce a victim.

'And the woman. Just what led you to believe she's a Protestant paramilitary – sorry a *lesbian* Protestant paramilitary, no less?' Gallagher's tone was condescending, verging on the sarcastic now.

Mulligan couldn't figure him out. What more did he need? 'Well, the husband said – '

Gallagher had a sheaf of papers in his hand. He waved them in front of Mulligan. 'Do you know how much it costs to bring the specialist anti-terrorist forensic team all the way down here from Dublin?' Mulligan swallowed and shook his head. 'More than you earn in a year, Sergeant. And it's up to me to justify the expense to my superintendent, so I'm not best pleased when a gobshite like you drags us down here to spend a night and half a day picking over a domestic-cooker explosion.' Gallagher didn't raise his voice, but Mulligan was no less intimidated for all that.

'But what about the firearm?' Mulligan said feebly. 'That crowd've been known to use replicas when they've nothing else. And what about the missing pensioners and the missing bus? What about the woman?'

'As far as I understand it, you've located the·bus, so it isn't missing, Sergeant. We've no evidence whatsoever that the woman is involved in anything illegal. And as for the pensioners, that's not my problem. I'm from the anti-terrorist squad, for God's sake. We've enough to deal with, with run-of-the-mill paramilitaries, without having to deal with geriatrics.'

Mulligan began to fume. Was this man thick or what?

'Unless, of course, you're going to tell me they're really trans-sexual Palestinian freedom fighters, cunningly disguised as pensioners.'

'But what about the hostages?' Mulligan started.

'Get a grip, Sergeant!' Gallagher lectured Mulligan for another five minutes about wasting valuable resources and jumping to half-cocked conclusions, but Mulligan wasn't listening. It was like being back at school with a Christian Brother ranting at him about his maths homework. The bastard! Only a couple of hours ago the jumped-up little shite was giving him a bollocking for the delay in calling out his fecking anti-terrorist crowd. Now he was at him because he called them out at all. He'd show the wanker what was what. As soon as the little shite was finished, he'd start round-the-clock surveillance in the mill-house. Even if he had to do it in his own time. He'd show them what good police work was.

Gallagher had stopped talking. He was staring at him as if he was waiting for a reply.

Mulligan cleared his throat. 'I'm sorry, Sir,' he said through gritted teeth.

Jeannie Horan-Evens couldn't stand the waiting any longer. No one seemed to be taking her seriously. The sergeant fobbed her off and the young Gard at the information desk kept telling her to go and get a cup of tea. What the hell difference could a cup of tea make? If she'd drunk the amount of tea that had been recommended since she got to Boran she'd be floating on the stuff. Jeremy wasn't a lot of support either.

She'd called him after Sergeant Mulligan had given her the brush-off earlier. He too had told her to go and get a bloody cup of tea. It was time to take matters into her own hands.

If the police wouldn't do anything about it, she'd just have to make her own enquiries.

She set off. The road was quiet and there wasn't much traffic. Her mind was in a turmoil. What if the bus driver wasn't there? What if he told her that he didn't remember them?

Wesley awoke from a doze in the shade of a rhododendron bush. The climb up the hill had exhausted him and he'd decided to take forty winks before proceeding on the final leg of his journey. His feet were sore and his legs ached from the effort. He sniffed the air again. The river was close now. Only another few yards and he'd be there. He picked himself up and meandered across the road. Half-way, he stopped. Tiredness overtook him again. Just rest my eyes for another minute, he thought and lay down again.

As Jeannie drove round a steep bend in the road she saw that the road was blocked by a hefty log about twelve feet long. Her heart sank. What else could happen to stop her finding her parents? Were God and everyone else conspiring against her? She slowed down and came to a halt. Just as she was about to get out of the car she thought she saw the log move. She blinked several times.

Shit! Wesley thought. A fucking human. Time to get out of here. He lifted himself off the ground, and scuttled away.

It took a minute for Jeannie's brain to engage think. It's all that caffeine, she scolded herself. Crocodiles are *not* indigenous to Ireland. Everyone knows that. But there it was. A twelve-foot crocodile, disappearing over the embankment towards the river.

She blinked again. Calm down. Deep breaths, she told herself. You're hallucinating. It must be the Valium. She had taken a fistful of pills to calm herself down when Mulligan was being so infuriating. That was it. She took the bottle from her bag and swallowed two more, then started the engine again and drove off.

The mill-house wasn't hard to find. Six miles down the road from the truck stop, the pump attendant had said. As soon as she passed the truck stop she'd tripped the mile counter. Six point one miles it turned out to be. Jeannie drove in through the gate and parked by the front door.

It was pretty impressive for a bus driver. Maybe it's his company, she speculated. Jeannie loved old houses. Her dream was to own a place like this one day. Nineteenth century she estimated. It was perfectly proportioned and in very good condition. The front of the house was covered in Virginia creeper, fading fast russet and yellow as autumn drew nearer to winter. Her feet crunched on the gravel drive. Was that someone at the window?

Bosco dropped the edge of the curtain. 'Shit! She saw me,' he hissed to Corky. Corky joined him and peeked out. The woman was striding towards the front door now.

'Who the fuck is she?' The doorbell rang. 'If she's seen yeh, ye'd better answer it,' Corky said.

Bosco wasn't into that suggestion. He looked over at Jake. 'You bleedin' answer it,' he ordered. 'Get rid of her.'

Jake stood up and walked towards the hall. Bosco followed closely with the sawn-off shoved in Jake's back, to leave him in no doubt that *get rid of her* meant just that. 'No funny stuff,' he hissed, standing out of view behind the door.

Jake opened the door.

'Would you be Jake Devine, the bus driver?' Jeannie asked.

'Yep.'

'I'm looking for my parents, Biddy and Jon-Joe Horan. They always travel with you. And they were supposed to be in Cork yesterday. I know they got on the bus – '

Before Jake could get rid of her, Biddy, on hearing her daughter's familiar voice, jumped up. 'Is that you, Jeannie?' she called.

Jeannie, Bosco and Jake froze. The next moment, Bosco came to his senses and leaped round the door, yanking Jeannie into the hall and slamming it closed.

Jeannie let out a yell.

Jon-Joe and Biddy raced into the hall shouting, 'What's up?' and 'Is that you Jeannie? What are you doing here?'

But Jeannie only had eyes for the sawn-off shotgun and was wailing, near to hysteria. It took at least half a minute for the cacophony to die down. Fionn was barking furiously and Monty, Lucy, Jodie and Corky crowded into the hall-way, adding to the commotion.

'Well tha' was smart!' Corky muttered sarcastically to Bosco when everyone was back in the sitting-room. 'Seven bleedin' hostages now. It's like ten green bottles on the feckin' wall, except we're gettin' more of them instead of feckin' less.'

'So wha' was I supposed t'bleedin' do?' Bosco demanded. 'She saw Biddy. I'd no feckin' choice.'

Corky sniffed. 'S'pose not.' He brightened up. 'Still, we'll be one less soon, wha'?'

Bosco looked at his watch. It was coming up three o'clock. Only an hour to go. Suddenly the thought of holding a struggling Monty's head under the water until he drowned didn't seem so attractive.

Corky took Bosco's arm and led him out of earshot of the assembled hostages. 'How're yeh goin' t' . . . yeh know.' He inclined his head in Monty's direction. 'How're yeh going t'do it?'

'I was thinking of drownding him in the river, but I don't know now.'

'Sounds good t'me.' Corky was relieved that there wouldn't be any blood. 'What's the problem?'

'D'you want t'do it?'

'No. I . . . em . . . I have t'watch this crowd.' He jerked his head towards the ever growing group of hostages. He knew there was no way he could kill Monty.

Bosco shuffled his feet. 'It's just . . . Well, I don't know if I can do it.' He felt a spa having to admit such a thing to Corky. They were supposed to be hard-men.

'Then we have t'tell him,' Corky said. 'Tell him wha' his missus wants us t'do.'

'D'yeh think?'

Corky shrugged. 'Can't see we've any choice, under the circumstances. You can't do it. I can't do it. If yer woman don't see no body, she won't cough up the cash. End of story.'

Bosco was relieved to hear Corky's admission. It made him feel less of a failure. 'OK. We'll tell 'im.'

Chapter Twenty-One

Blissfully ignorant that her assassins were about to drop her in it, Cindy was half-way on her journey to her appointment with destiny. This was the first day of the rest of her life, she told herself. Cindy was fond of clichés. When trying to impress, she had the habit of talking in clichés. She studied her *Oxford Dictionary of Quotations* every day. It was her way of educating herself. The odd judicious quote here and there and people were convinced that she was well read and educated.

Monty was no different. Her favourite, and in her mind wholly inaccurate, saying for him was, 'There's many a good tune played on an old fiddle.' Monty loved that one. Another was 'Size doesn't matter'. What eejit ever said *that*? She decided it had to be someone very gullible with a small willie.

She often reflected what a good job it was that she was an actress. Faking it in bed with Monty was second nature to her. If she thought about it she had never, in her whole life, done anything *but* fake it. Things would be different now, she'd told herself as she had put the case of cash into the boot of her BMW and set off for Boran, leaving herself plenty of time.

At about the same time as Cindy was leaving Sandycove, Rogan Hogan kissed Angelica Quinn goodbye and headed for the lift. He was in cracking form. He found it hard to keep the grin off his face. If Angelica thought she was the cause of his merriment, she was wrong. Rogan Hogan was elated at the prospect of giving Jodie McDeal just what was coming to her.

Gnasher, however, was not in good humour. When the pump attendant told Decco that Jake Devine's house was six miles down the road, he didn't make it clear in which direction.

On the first attempt he drove ten miles completely the wrong way, before giving up and turning round. Decco was keeping quiet in case Gnasher blamed him. As they passed the truck stop on the return trip, Decco watched the mile counter.

At six miles he sat forward in his seat. A few seconds later he pointed his skinny finger. 'There it is, Boss,' he said. He liked the notion of calling Gnasher boss. Gnasher liked it too, but didn't let on. In deference to Hogan, no one ever called him boss. This, and the fact that they had at last located the mill-house, improved Gnasher's humour. Sensing the lift in the atmosphere, Decco relaxed too.

Gnasher Gill drove on past the house. The perimeter wall, along with a garden full of mature shrubs, afforded him little view of the building so he carried on for about twenty yards until he came to a gateway leading into some woods. He turned in and parked out of sight of the road. 'Come on,' he said to Decco. 'Time for a little recce.'

Meanwhile Bosco and Corky were arguing among themselves as to who should tell Monty about his wife's wish for widowhood.

From the opposite side of the room Lucy and Jake were watching them. 'What do you think they're arguing about?' Lucy whispered.

Jake shook his head. 'I don't know. Maybe Monty's wife can't come up with the ransom money.'

'I wonder what they'll do if that's it,' Lucy said. 'You don't think they'll harm us, do you?' For the first time she was really anxious. Up until that point, it was as if the situation wasn't for real; as if they were in some sort of play or charade. It was difficult to take the two gurriers seriously. Despite the sawn-off shotgun they seemed like a couple of fairly harmless amateurs. It was something about the way the one called Bosco, despite trying on the hard-man act, was so respectful and nice to Biddy. How he stopped the tall one from hitting Jodie, and made sure everyone was fed and comfortable. OK, so he'd lost his rag a couple of times, but even then he hadn't raised a hand against any of them.

Lucy wondered once more if the whole thing had just got out of control. She didn't think for a minute that they had intended to hijack the bus. Even the dimmest kidnappers would make sure they had proper transport.

Biddy's and Jon-Joe's daughter hadn't said much. She looked pretty spaced-out, as if she was on something. Biddy was looking after her. She had an arm round Jeannie's shoulder and was rocking her gently, muttering comforting sounds.

Lucy leaned closer to Jake. 'Do you think we should try and escape?'

'The thought crossed my mind,' Jake said. 'But there hasn't been the opportunity. If Bosco loses it again and fires off that shotgun, everyone'll get hit. I don't want to risk it. That thing could blow a hole in a horse . . .'

'So what should we do? We can't just sit here.'

Jake shrugged. 'We don't have a lot of choice as it stands.'

'Well, we've got to do something. Why don't you call the cops on your mobile?' Lucy was becoming agitated.

'I tried that when I went to the toilet,' Jake hissed. 'But I can't get a signal under the stairs – bloody phone.'

'What are you two whispering about?' Jodie asked in a drowsy voice. She was lying with her head on a cushion, curled up on the floor at Lucy's feet. Lucy had thought she was asleep.

'The possibility of escape,' Lucy whispered.

Jodie's eyebrows shot up in alarm. 'Count me out of any

heroics,' she said, settling down again. 'I'm happy just to wait it out.'

Bosco drew the short straw. Monty looked as if he was dozing. He had moved from the sofa to enable Jeannie to sit by her mother, and was sitting in an armchair by the fireplace.

Bosco cleared his throat. 'Em . . . Monty?'

Monty opened his eyes. 'Yes?'

'There's somethin' we want t'tell yeh.' Monty sat up straight, an inquisitive expression on his face. Bosco cleared his throat again and looked at Corky for encouragement. Corky nodded. 'It's about yer wife,' Bosco began.

Monty looked alarmed. 'Nothing's happened to her, has it? Has there been an accident?' He was half out of the chair now.

'No, no, nothin' like that,' Bosco reassured him. 'She's fine.' Monty relaxed and sat down again. He exhaled and smiled, and patted his chest the way you do when you're relieved about something. Bosco felt terrible but he bit the bullet. 'It's just . . . well . . . When I asked her fer the hundred grand t'let yeh go, she offered us two-hundred an' fifty grand if we'd kill yeh.' He didn't know how else to put it. The silly grin froze on Monty's face.

'Yeh said it was a hundred an' fifty grand!' Corky was outraged.

Bosco made the save. 'She . . . she upped the offer last time I was talkin' t'her,' he said, hoping that Corky would buy it.

He did. 'Oh . . . righ'.' He sounded pleased.

Everyone's eyes, except Corky's, were on Monty. He hadn't moved a muscle. He still had the remains of the grin on his lips. Lucy, Jake and even Jodie were shocked to the core. Jon-Joe, who had missed the whole thing because he had been attending to a call of nature, walked in on the scene. He stopped in his tracks. 'What's happened?' he asked.

But everyone was still watching Monty.

His face was grey. He was rubbing his shoulder as if he

had a pain and shaking his head in disbelief. 'You're lying!' He made a lunge at Bosco. 'You're lying. My Cindy wouldn't – ' Suddenly he clutched his chest and gasped for breath.

Jodie was the first to react as he crumpled to the floor. She leaped up and rushed over to him. 'Quick! He's having some sort of attack,' she shouted.

Bosco and Jake helped Jodie as she loosened his collar. Monty was now in a state of unconsciousness. Jodie kneeled beside him. 'It must be the shock,' she said, as she put her ear to his chest, listening for a heartbeat.

'Yeah. He's got a dicky ticker,' Bosco said.

'He's not breathing,' Jodie sounded panicky. 'I can't hear his heart. What do we do? What do we do?'

'Kiss a'life,' Bosco said and kneeled down at Monty's head, pinching his nostrils closed, before leaning over and breathing into his mouth. He hoped he was doing it right. He had only ever seen it done on 999 *Lifesavers* a couple of times on the BBC.

'Who knows how to do CPR?' Jake asked.

'Aren't we supposed to thump his chest or something?' Jodie tried to remember what she had seen the doctors do on *ER.* 'Wait,' she said to Bosco. 'I don't think we're supposed to do the thumping and the breathing thing at the same time.'

Bosco stopped what he was doing. Monty still wasn't breathing. 'You have a go.' He turned to Jodie.

She placed her hands approximately where she thought Monty's heart was situated and applied pressure, releasing and repeating the procedure.

'Yer supposed t'count t'five,' Bosco said. 'Then I do the breathin' thing again.'

Jodie counted one, release. Two, release. Three, release. Four, release. Five. Everyone, including the spaced-out Jeannie, was standing in a circle round the recumbent Monty watching the operation, mentally counting with Jodie.

Bosco took over after five.

'Breathe,' Josie shouted. 'Breathe!' Everyone was willing Monty to draw breath. After about a minute, Bosco stopped and listened.

'He's breathin'. He's breathin',' he said excitedly.

'Does he have any pills?' Jake asked. 'Look in his pockets and see if he's any heart pills.'

Lucy bent down and slipped her hand inside Monty's jacket pocket. She produced a small plastic container.

Jake took it from her and read the label. 'Same as my old man's. Slip one under his tongue.'

'Are you sure that's OK?'

Jake nodded. 'Yeah, sure. That's what they're for.'

Lucy did as Jake asked. It wasn't easy getting it into Monty's mouth but Jodie helped her, and shortly afterwards Monty opened his eyes.

'What happened?'

'I think you had some sort of attack,' Jodie, who was still kneeling beside him, said. 'We put one of your tablets under your tongue. I hope that was right.' She felt for a pulse in his neck. 'Your pulse is stronger now, but take it easy for a minute.'

Monty smiled at her. This was the second time in just over a year that he had woken up with a crowd around him. 'Thanks,' he said. 'You saved my life.'

For the first time in living memory, Jodie blushed. 'It wasn't just me. Bosco got you breathing again.'

Monty struggled up into a sitting position, assisted by Jake and Bosco. Lucy pushed a cushion behind his head, which was resting against the front of the armchair.

'Do you want us to get you into the chair?' Jake asked.

Monty shook his head. 'Leave me for a minute.'

Jake and Lucy took Bosco and Corky to one side. 'Was that true about his wife?' Lucy asked.

Bosco nodded. 'Yeah, the hard bitch. She caught me on the hop. I didn't know what t'say t'her. I said I'd do it before I realised . . . It was the thought of all tha' money.' His voice had an apologetic quality. He sounded ashamed.

'But you couldn't do it,' Jake said gently. He didn't want the statement to sound like a criticism. 'And you saved his life.'

'We should get you to hospital, Monty,' Jodie said, brushing his hair back from his forehead. She looked up at Bosco and Corky. 'He should be in hospital.'

'No. I don't want to go to hospital. I want you to do something for me.' Monty looked at Bosco and Corky. 'When is my wife coming with the – I was going to say ransom money. I should say the blood money?' His voice was stronger now, and his colour better.

'You shouldn't excite yourself,' Lucy said. 'You should do as Jodie says, and go to hospital. That's right, isn't it, Bosco?'

Apart from being concerned for Monty, Lucy saw the opportunity for escape. A way of playing on Bosco's and his friend's guilt to diffuse the situation and bring it to a peaceful conclusion.

Bosco was uncertain. He was ashamed that he and Corky had considered killing Monty, but he wasn't willing to give up the ransom money either. He was about to say no to the hospital plan, when Monty saved him the trouble.

'I told you. I'm not going to hospital. What was the plan with my wife?'

'I'm meetin' her at the truck stop at four, an' she wants t'see yer body before she hands over the cash.' It all sounded very matter of fact. Like an arrangement for selling a car.

Monty nodded. Soft and harmless as he seemed, you didn't get to be worth forty-two point two million pounds without having certain strengths. And Monty had the strength and talent to make the best of every situation. That was why he'd sat tight and hadn't upset his kidnappers. He reasoned if they got what they wanted they'd let him go. They had no reason not to.

'OK. I'd like you to bring her here. I want to hear her say she wants me dead.'

'But – ' Lucy started.

Monty held up his hand. 'I know what you're all thinking.'

He shuffled into a more upright sitting position. 'I'm a pathetic middle-aged man, clinging on to some stupid illusion that a woman like my wife would love the likes of me for any reason other than the money.' No one commented. 'I'm not stupid. I know, at least I thought I knew, where I stood with Cindy. She's a beautiful woman. It was all a trade-off.' He shook his head sadly. 'I know love's the one thing money can't buy, but I kept my end of the deal.'

'So why do you want to see her, Monty?' Lucy asked. 'Why do you want to upset yourself?'

The whole company, even the totally insensitive Corky, felt a huge amount of compassion for Monty at that moment.

'I want to see her face when she sees I'm alive, and know what she's up to,' he said. 'I think I deserve that much.'

Who could argue?

Bosco thought about it. 'Wha' about the money?'

'You'll get your money if you do as I ask.'

'Wha'? All of it? The whole two hundred an' fifty grand?'

'The whole shebang. In a way, you'll have earned it.'

Lucy couldn't see the logic in Monty's thinking on that score. What did he mean, they'd earned it? None of this would have happened in the first place if they hadn't grabbed Monty. She said as much to Jake.

'That's true,' he replied. 'But at least he knows where he stands with his wife now. If it wasn't those two, she might have found a serious hit man. Who knows, maybe they did save his life in more ways than one.'

Corky was still clarifying the new deal with Monty. 'An' wha' about the cops? Will yeh go t'the cops?'

Monty shook his head. 'No, I won't go to the cops, if you do this for me.'

'No one else will go to the cops either, lads, if you let everyone go now. You don't need these people here any more,' Jake said.

There was a murmur of assent from the assembled hostages. Then Jeannie piped up. 'Well, I certainly will. The first thing I'll do when I get out of here is see that the two of you are locked up for what you've done to my parents.' She was standing away from the group around Monty with her feet planted apart and her arms folded across her chest.

'Shut up, Jeannie,' snapped Biddy. 'These nice young men didn't do us any harm.'

The effects of the Valium had worn off, leaving Jeannie very truculent. 'But Mother – '

'Don't you *but mother* me, my girl.' Even though Biddy was a full twelve inches shorter than her daughter, she looked intimidating. And, although on the road to senility, she was having a rare moment of perfect clarity. Jeannie opened her mouth to protest.

'Do as your mother says and shut up, Jeannie,' Jon-Joe instructed. 'There's a good girl.'

Jeannie shut up.

Bosco thought about it. 'Yez can all go except her.' He pointed at Jeannie. 'She has t'stay.'

Jon-Joe looked at his daughter and shook his head. She never knew when to keep her mouth shut. She always had to put her spoke in.

Lucy was gathering up her holdall and Jodie her precious attaché case. 'If no one minds,' Monty said, 'I'd like you all to stay with me till this is over. I could do with a bit of moral support when Cindy gets here. But if you'd rather not, I'll understand.'

What could they do? They dropped their stuff and sat down.

'Will I make tea?' Biddy said.

It was a weird situation. Seven hostages staying with their captors by choice; six willingly.

'It's the Stockholm syndrome,' Jake said to Lucy. Lucy had read about the phenomenon where captives develop an empathy with their captors. Though for her part, the reason she was staying was because of Monty, rather than Bosco and his friend. They'd all shared the experience so far, and somehow it didn't seem fair to run out on him at this stage. Particularly considering the circumstances.

Poor Monty.

Jodie agreed that she was staying for the same reasons. Jake conceded that maybe he was staying for Monty too. 'But you live here,' Jodie pointed out. 'Where the hell were you going to go anyway?'

Lucy asked if she could take the dog out. Corky agreed to the request and Jodie's, when she asked if she could get a bit of fresh air too.

Biddy made tea.

From their vantage point behind a large rhododendron bush, Gnasher and Decco watched as the two women walked across the grass and sat on the low wall near the river. A ginger dog was running around and rolling in the grass.

'That's her,' Gnasher said. 'The young wan with the blonde hair.'

She looked awful in the long skirt and scruffy sweater. Gnasher couldn't be sure, but were those yellow wellingtons on her feet? Feeling smug, he sniggered. Even from a distance it was obvious that her hair could do with a wash.

'Who's the other wan?' Decco asked.

'Someone she hooked up with after you knocked off the motor. She was drivin' Misther Hogan's car.'

Decco's mind was working overtime. 'So if I hadn't a'knocked off the car, yeh wouldn't a'found her?'

Gnasher hadn't looked at it like that, but there was a certain logic to what the boy was saying. He glanced at his watch. It was four o'clock.

He heard a car engine and a moment later a dark-blue Cherokee jeep drove down the drive towards the road. A young gurrier was behind the wheel. He looked back at the two women, who were still sitting on the wall. They briefly glanced at the jeep, then went back to their conversation. They didn't look as if they were going anywhere. He took out his mobile phone and dialled Hogan's number.

Chapter Twenty-Two

Mulligan was frustrated. He had been trying to get away from the Garda station for the last couple of hours to start surveillance on the mill-house. He knew if he didn't get there soon there wouldn't be any point. The birds, in all probability, would have flown.

Gallagher had ordered him to let Marcus Pyle go. 'I'd be very apologetic if I were you,' he said. 'Apart from the unauthorised search of his property, you'd no grounds to detain him. Let's hope, for your sake, he's not a bar-room lawyer, Sergeant.'

Mulligan didn't dare point out that it was Gallagher who had dragged Pyle out of bed in the middle of the night and thrown him in a cell.

'I want you to drive him home, Sergeant,' Gallagher continued. 'And I want you to be very, very nice to him.'

Mulligan cringed. The thought of sucking up to that sort made his flesh crawl.

Gallagher was merely winding Mulligan up. He knew Marcus Pyle would be only too relieved about being released to kick up any kind of fuss. And, in the unlikely event that he should complain, Gallagher was making sure that Pyle would be in no doubt about who was really responsible for the whole sorry cock-up.

Mulligan couldn't bring himself to be even civil to Marcus on the twenty-mile drive home and he certainly didn't enlighten him about his superior's opinion of the case.

Marcus was a bag of nerves. He chattered away about

how hard-done-by he was; how he had no idea his wife was a Protestant paramilitary, or even a lesbian; how everything made sense now; how, if he'd even suspected she was mixed up in anything of that nature, he would have turned her in.

Mulligan was tired of listening to him. He stopped the car on the main road at the bottom of the mud track that wound its way up the mountain to Marcus's house. The mountain was shrouded in mist. Marcus considered asking Mulligan to drive him all the way, but thought better of it. The sooner he was away from the cops the better.

He climbed out of the car. The air was cold and damp, and he shivered. In the panic of the previous night he had only grabbed a light jacket to take with him. Mulligan drove off at speed without looking back. Marcus set off up the track towards home. He knew the cottage would be cold and damp. There was no Lucy to keep the stove stoked up and he was shit at lighting the bloody thing. He felt a slight pang of regret that he would probably never see her again, then remembered all the trouble she had caused him, and that she was a lesbian Protestant terrorist bomber. He'd miss the dog, though.

As soon as Mulligan arrived back at the Garda station he was called into the Superintendent's office. He got a further bollocking from him, on account of the bollocking the Superintendent had received from the Assistant Commissioner, about the waste of resources. The entire incident seemed to have the properties of a radioactive hot potato with anyone even remotely connected tossing the buck back down the line, and the line ended with Mulligan. He knew they were all wrong. He felt it in his water. When they're handing out medals after I crack this, they'll all be lining up claiming the credit, he thought cynically. He knew it. As sure as eggs were eggs.

After the lecture, the Super sent him to do a neighbourhood-watch talk at an old people's home, as if he hadn't been humiliated enough.

*

Cindy George was agitated for she was late. She was also rather shaken because not long before she had witnessed a traffic pile-up on the motorway through her rear-view mirror. If she had left the house thirty seconds later she might have been involved herself. It agitated her so much she had to stop for a brandy to steady her nerves. Why did you always get held up when you were running late? Calm down, she told herself. He'll wait. Why wouldn't he, with the promise of quarter of a million at the end of it?

Three minutes afterwards she drove her silver BMW into the truck stop. It was ten past four. She was only ten minutes late. She looked around to get her bearings, then drove over and parked in an empty space near the woods. She pulled down the sun visor and fixed her lipstick in the vanity mirror. She had butterflies in her stomach. Not long now, she thought.

Rogan Hogan was stuck in a traffic jam fifty miles away from his destination. He was fifteen minutes behind Cindy and so had been caught up in the aftermath of the pile-up. He was talking to Gnasher on the phone.

'Don't worry, Boss,' Gnasher said. 'I've things under control. The girl's here all right. I seen 'er with me own two eyes.'

'That's good.' Hogan wasn't unduly bothered about the delay. Jodie wasn't going anywhere. Gnasher Gill was on to it. He did wonder just a tad why Jodie hadn't called him since the day before. Maybe she thinks she's making me sweat, he thought, smiling to himself. As if! She'd pay for trying that one, the slapper. 'Keep an eye. If she looks like she's any thoughts of moving on, nab her.'

'OK, Boss,' Gnasher gave Hogan directions to the mill-house, then hung up. He was elated. Hogan's instruction to take action, should he think it necessary, was licence to give the slut the hammering she deserved.

Bosco saw Cindy George as soon as he drove in to the truck stop. She had parked exactly where he had asked her to. He put the jeep in an empty bay a couple of spaces down from her BMW.

Cindy was looking in the vanity mirror as he slid into the back seat. She gave a little girlie gasp when she heard the rear door open and she caught sight of his reflection in the mirror.

'Yeh righ'?' he asked.

She turned round in her seat. 'Did you do your end of the deal?' she asked.

'Yeah,' he said. 'All done. D'yeh want t'see?'

Cindy nodded. 'How do you want to do this? Will I drive you, or what?'

Bosco opened the door again. 'No. Folla me.' He ambled back to the jeep and got in. He wondered where she had hidden the cash. Prob'ly in the boot, he thought, despite her story about not having it with her, or handing it over till she'd seen the body. He drove off. He saw her in his rear-view mirror following closely.

Back at the mill-house Monty was organising everyone. He had recovered remarkably quickly from his attack. Perhaps it was the incentive of repaying Cindy for her betrayal.

Plan A was that Jodie, Lucy, Jake, and the others would stay out of sight in the kitchen when Cindy arrived. Monty was to play dead until Cindy had admitted that she was glad that Monty was gone, or words to that effect.

Jodie didn't think Monty looked dead enough, so she suggested a bit of judicious make-up. With the aid of a dab of her Lancôme pale and interesting liquid foundation to his face and lips she transformed Monty into a cadaver. A touch of smudged eye pencil to create shadows under the eyes and she was satisfied.

'There's no blood,' Corky observed. 'How'd we feckin' kill him?'

'I'd say you probably shot me,' Monty said. 'Have you any red sauce?'

Jake didn't possess anything as mundane as ketchup but

he did have a jar of fresh organic Italian *pomodoro* sauce. Between them, Lucy and Jake splattered Monty's shirt-front with Italian tomatoes.

Lucy examined the results. 'It doesn't look red enough for blood.'

Jake suggested they switch off the overhead light and just leave a couple of lamps on. That did the trick. In the dimmed light Monty lay back on the floor and looked remarkably dead. Even Jeannie said as much.

Gnasher got a little edgy when he saw the jeep returning with a silver Beemer close behind. A good-looking blonde was at the wheel of the second vehicle. What the hell was the McDeal slut up to? Who were these people? Then he had it. She was dealing the Smack. She'd got greedy. She had no intention of selling it back to Hogan. She wanted all the profit for herself. Stupid cow! Surely she didn't expect to get away with it.

He and Decco drove back up the road, closer to the gate, to have a better view of the house. He wanted to be ready.

Cindy parked right behind the jeep. Bosco waited for her by the front door. She was nervous as hell, but hid the fact by acting in a casual and laid-back manner. She took her time getting out of the car, and she smoothed her skirt carefully before locking up and strolling over. Bosco waited patiently, then led her inside.

Monty was lying on his back on the rug in front of the fireplace with his arms by his sides. His eyes were closed. Bosco was as shocked as Cindy when he saw, in the dim light, what looked like blood all over Monty's chest.

Cindy gave a little squeak. 'You shot him!'

'What did yeh think we'd feckin' do?' Bosco said.

'But there's blood,' Cindy said. 'Couldn't you have done it some other way less – ' She searched for a word, but could only come up with 'bloody?'.

'Yeh only said yeh wanted us t'feckin' kill him. Yeh didn't specify how.'

The initial shock had worn off. Cindy got down to the practicalities. 'OK, OK,' she said impatiently. 'So what about the body? How are you going to get rid of it?'

'Aw come on,' Bosco said, warming to the part. 'Yeh never said nothin' abou' gettin' rid a'no body.'

Cindy wasn't having any of that. 'Of course you've got to get rid of the bloody body. You can't leave it here. It's in your interests as well as mine to get rid of the evidence.'

The evidence! That's all I am to her now, Monty thought. Just the evidence.

'Anyway, I won't pay up unless you're going to dispose of it,' Cindy said with an air of finality. She folded her arms and planted her right foot firmly in front of her.

Monty cringed. Dispose of it. She was referring to him as if he were a bag of garbage.

'OK,' Bosco conceded. 'I'll bury him in the woods. No one'll find him there.'

Monty lay still listening to them talking. His initial anger had passed and now he felt an overwhelming sadness. He couldn't figure out what he'd done to Cindy to deserve this. As far as she was concerned, he was lying dead on the mat in front of her, and she didn't give a damn about him. 'Wha' about the cash?' he heard Bosco say.

Cindy was satisfied. 'It's in the car boot.' She handed him the keys.

Monty chose that moment to come back to life. He sat up.

Cindy passed out.

Gnasher became more worried when he saw, from his viewpoint at the gate, a tall thin gurrier walking out to the Beemer and opening the boot. He lifted out a case and carried it back into the house. It must be the cash. It looked as if the deal was closed. He felt he should get in there before the Smack left the premises. He dialled Hogan's

umber to keep him abreast of the situation and to get some
dvice.

Cindy woke up with a crowd round her. On Monty's say-so,
hey had left her where she had fallen on the floor. The first
hing she saw when she opened her eyes was Monty's pale,
hostly face looking down at her.

'Hello, Cindy,' he said. 'Sorry to disappoint you.'

Cindy curled up into a ball and started to cry.

Corky dumped the case of cash on the floor. Together, he
nd Bosco snapped the catches and looked inside. It was like
omething out of a movie: rows of neat bundles of bank
notes. Bosco closed it and shoved it behind the sofa in case
Monty had second thoughts. Out of sight, out of mind. He
needn't have bothered. The last thing Monty had on his mind
was the money.

Lucy gathered her stuff together once again.

'So what are you going to do now?' Jake asked her.

She shrugged. 'I hadn't any real plans. I suppose I'll go
down to Cork.'

'Are you still painting?'

Lucy shook her head. 'No. Not for a while. My husband
discouraged it.'

'That's a pity. You were good. Is your husband in Cork?'

'No. I walked out on him last Monday after twenty years.
Marcus was one of the shit life choices I was talking about.'

'Marcus? The weird guy you brought back from Glastonbury that time?'

'The same,' Lucy said. 'When I screw up, I don't do it by
halves.'

'It didn't work out, then?'

Lucy laughed. 'You could say that. But it took me some
time to figure it out.'

Jodie sidled over to them. 'Are our tickets still good for
Cork?' she asked.

'Sure,' Jake replied. 'How about when everyone leaves, I
cook us something to eat, then we'll set off?'

'Sounds good to me,' Jodie replied.

Cindy was sitting on the edge of the sofa next to Monty. They were talking quietly together. 'What are you going to do?' She sniffed. 'Are you going to call the cops?'

Monty shook his head. 'No,' he said. 'But I'll expect you out of the house by tonight.'

She didn't bother to apologise or even attempt to concoct a story to get herself off the hook. How could she? She had been caught with the proverbial smoking gun in her hand. Instead, she went for the sympathy vote. 'But where'll I go, Monty?' She had put on her little-girl-lost voice. 'I've nowhere to go.'

But Monty wasn't buying it. Hearing her discussing plans for the disposal of his body with Bosco had rendered him immune. 'I'll give you ten thousand and the car,' he told her. 'And I never want to see you again. You're to leave the country. Is that clear?'

Cindy was smart enough to realise when she was well off, and didn't argue.

Jeannie was advising her father on the merits of reporting the incident to the guards as soon as they were out of the place, but Jon-Joe wouldn't hear of it. Apart from his promise to Bosco, he knew Biddy would never stand up to a trial. Even now she was slipping back into her own twilight world. The lucid intervals were getting less and less. He worried about how long he would be able to care for her. He was conscious that he was becoming forgetful himself. He said as much to his daughter.

'You could come and live with me,' Jeannie offered, her guilt returning. 'I could look after you.'

Jon-Joe patted her hand. He knew she meant it but, equally, he knew it would never work. He was aware that he was an embarrassment to his daughter and her husband, but felt no resentment about it. Anyway, he couldn't bear to live in the city. He loved to walk the land and to tend to his few sheep.

The atmosphere was like that of a party that was at an

end. People standing or sitting in groups, not sure how to leave.

Bosco and Corky made the first move. They walked over to where Monty was sitting with Cindy. 'We'll be off, then,' Bosco said.

Monty looked up at them. 'OK, lads. And thanks.'

'Could we have a borra of yer woman's Beemer?' Corky asked, holding up Cindy's car keys.

'No, you cannot!' Cindy snapped, indignant.

'Of course you can,' Monty said. He looked at Cindy. 'In fact, lads, why don't you keep it? If you call in to me at home later in the week, I'll give you the log book.' Cindy looked horrified. Monty took her hand. 'Don't worry, Precious. I'll let you keep the Fiesta. You can pick it up from the office.'

Cindy gritted her teeth and nodded. 'Thanks a bunch.' A flaming ten-year-old Fiesta the office messenger used to run around in. The cheek of it! She glared at Bosco and Corky, with murder in her heart. She hadn't thought Monty had it in him to be so spiteful. Ironically, she felt a sort of grudging respect for him.

As the two desperados turned to leave, Monty called after them, 'Hey – ' They stopped and turned back. ' – Don't give up the day job.'

'What did he mean?' Corky asked as they reached the door.

Bosco put down the case. 'He means we're crap at bleedin' kidnappin',' he replied, a little affronted.

At the same moment that Bosco reached up to open the door, it flew inwards whacking him in the face. He staggered backwards and fell over the case of cash, knocking Corky off his feet. The domino effect. They were left in a heap on the floor looking up at Gnasher Gill brandishing an Uzi automatic machine pistol.

Chapter Twenty-Three

Wednesday, 5 November, four forty-five p.m.

He was officially off duty so he couldn't take the patrol car. Probably all for luck, he thought. Better to be inconspicuous for now. Eugene Mulligan climbed into his five-year-old VW Golf. He had no plan other than keeping an eye on the house, watching for anything suspicious enough to merit calling for back-up. The woman was in there. He knew it. Something was going on, and if it took his last breath, he'd prove it. The humiliation he had suffered earlier in the day was still burning in his guts. Every time he thought about that jumped-up little shite, Gallagher, he felt the anger rise again.

As he started the engine, Garda Joe Flynn, who was manning the public office, called out to him, 'Someone to see you, Eugene.'

He closed his eyes, resigned to the fact that everything was conspiring against him.

Cathy Grady and Micky Folan sat in the OB truck, about twenty metres back along the road from the Garda station, and waited. The sergeant was up to something, of that she was sure. But why all the secrecy? Usually, on sensitive issues, particularly terrorist-related issues, there was an official press embargo issued by the Garda press office, but they were still denying all knowledge. Why?

'Are you sure that gobshite knows what's what?' Micky said. 'He looks pretty thick if you ask me.'

'I wasn't,' Cathy snapped. 'He's not as thick as he looks. He knows something all right.'

A neatly dressed man of about thirty-five was standing in the public office. Mulligan didn't recognise him. He was of medium height and build, with just the suspicion of a paunch.

He offered a limp hand. 'Jeremy Evens,' he said. He had a hesitant voice, light hair, rimless glasses and a skimpy ginger beard. He looked like an accountant. Good call. Jeremy Evens was an accountant, working for a large dairy company.

Jeremy was ambitious, and at night he laboured over ledgers and shoe boxes full of receipts, massaging the accounts of his private clients in the hope of setting up on his own one day soon. Jeremy and Jeannie had been married for ten years and had three children, twin boys aged eight and a girl of five. To call Jeremy reserved would be understating the situation. He had great difficulty sharing his feelings with anyone. Even with Jeannie, he found it hard. Over the years she had brought him out of his shell to a certain extent, but she was fighting against the baggage of his upbringing. Jeremy's parents belonged to a strict break-away fundamentalist Welsh Methodist church, and had raised their only son to be as strait-laced and repressed as they were.

Jeannie had been a secretary at the accountancy firm where Jeremy worked. It was love at first sight for him, but it took him six months to pluck up the courage to ask her out. Even after ten years of marriage, due to his deficiency in the shared-feelings department, Jeannie was not aware of how deeply Jeremy loved her, but she never doubted that in his own undemonstrative way he cared. He was good to her and was a commendable provider for the family. Jeannie loved Jeremy dearly, but sometimes she found him a little boring.

'I believe you were talking to my wife this morning.' Jeremy had a nervous habit of pushing his glasses up the bridge of his nose repeatedly.

Mulligan stared at him, until it registered. 'Oh, yes. Yes,

of course. She reported her parents missing,' he said. Then he realised that he hadn't seen Jeannie Horan-Evens since lunch-time. 'Where is your wife?'

'That's just it, Sergeant,' Jeremy said. 'She – she seems to have disappeared too.'

Mulligan couldn't stop the wide grin from spreading across his face. At last! Someone who would take him seriously.

Jeremy Evens looked confused. 'She hasn't called since this morning. She said she'd ring me at lunch-time and – I'm sorry, but I don't happen to think this is funny, Officer.'

'I'm sorry, Mr Evens, neither do I.' Mulligan forced a suitably solemn expression to take up residence on his face. He took Jeremy Evens by the arm. 'I think we'd better go outside.' He cast a meaningful glance towards Joe Flynn and lowered his voice. 'I must talk to you in private. There's something I need your help with.'

'Here he comes,' Cathy said. 'Let him get a good way ahead, but for fuck's sake, keep him in sight.' They watched as Mulligan and another man stood in a huddle by the door of the Garda station. They were in deep conversation.

'Yer man must be plain-clothes,' Micky said. 'Could be anti-terrorist.'

'You're probably right.' Cathy nodded. She was getting excited now. If things panned out, this would be an exclusive.

After talking earnestly for a couple of minutes, the two men got into their respective cars. Mulligan drove off first and turned right out of the gate. It was no surprise to Cathy when the other man followed him. After a few seconds Micky started the engine of the truck and joined the procession.

Jodie's heart sank when she saw Gnasher. Where he was, Rogan Hogan wouldn't be far behind. Instinctively, she hugged the attaché case close to her chest. Gill was yelling at everyone to stick their hands in the air, and to keep quiet.

Decco spotted the sawn-off on the floor where Corky had dropped it when Bosco fell over him and grabbed it. He pointed it menacingly at the two ex-kidnappers lying in a tangled heap.

Monty was still sitting on the sofa, a confused look on his face. Cindy had jumped up and was screaming. Jeannie, hyper after the effects of the Valium had worn off, was screaming too. Jon-Joe was in the toilet – his prostate was giving him trouble – so missed the excitement again. Lucy and Jake just stared at the scene open-mouthed. Gnasher's bellow to 'Shut the fuck up!' achieved just that.

The room fell silent. Biddy popped her head out of the kitchen. 'Will I make the tea?' she asked.

Even Gnasher couldn't yell at Biddy. He stood uncomfortably for a moment. Bosco jumped to his feet, hurried over to her, put his arm round her shoulder and led her over to Jeannie. 'Not jus' yet, Biddy. Sit here for the minute,' he said gently.

Jeannie gave him a weak smile of thanks. They all heard the sound of a toilet flushing, and a moment later Jon-Joe walked back into the room. Everyone, with the exception of Jodie and Biddy, was wondering what the hell was happening.

Gnasher assumed control again. Ignoring the others, he looked straight at Jodie and reached out his huge paw. 'Gimme that!' he barked. For a moment, Jodie held on more tightly to the attaché case, then reluctantly handed it over. 'I think it's time yeh told me just what the hell's goin' on here.'

'Nothing's going on.'

Gnasher looked at Decco and smirked. 'She expects us t'believe nothin's goin' on.' Decco took his cue and gave a loud guffaw. 'She thinks we're both spas.' Decco guffawed louder. 'She thinks she can bleedin' go inta business fer herself an' get away with it.' Decco was almost helpless with mirth by this stage.

Gnasher turned his gaze on Cindy. 'You,' he said. Cindy,

who was trying for invisibility, mutely pointed at her chest and mouthed *me?* 'Yeah, you. Who're yeh bleedin' dealin' for?'

Cindy hadn't a clue what he was talking about.

'No one's dealing, Gnasher,' Jodie pointed out. 'I was waiting for Rogan. We've an agreement.'

'That's not what he told me,' said Gnasher.

Lucy eyed Gnasher. 'Look, this is nothing to do with us. Why don't you just sort it out among yourselves and let the rest of us go?'

Thanks a bunch, Jodie thought.

'No chance,' Gnasher barked, with such ferocity that Lucy flinched. 'We'll all wait here 'til I find out what's bleedin' goin' on.'

'He's your psycho boyfriend, I assume,' Lucy muttered to Jodie.

'No. He's the monkey, not the organ grinder,' Jodie said, loudly enough for Gnasher to hear. 'I've more taste than to let an ape like that lay a hand on me.'

With lightning speed, Gnasher lashed out and punched her full in the face with his fist. The force of the blow lifted her off the ground. There was a crunching sound as her nose broke and blood splattered everywhere. Jodie didn't make a sound. She was out cold. Lucy and Jake darted forward to help her. Gnasher was smirking. Decco was rendered silent. He had never seen anything like that before. Suddenly he was afraid of Gnasher Gill all over again.

Mulligan peered out at the mill-house from behind the gate pillar. Jeremy Evens was standing beside him. 'That's my wife's car!' he said, striding forward.

Mulligan caught his arm and pulled him back. 'Wait, Mr Evens. We don't want to put your wife's life in danger by going off half-cocked, do we?'

Jeremy pushed his glasses back on his nose. 'You think she's really in danger, Sergeant?'

'Haven't you been listening to me?' Mulligan said, perhaps

a tad too sharply. Evens was getting right up his nose. Hadn't he explained the situation? Hadn't he told the eejit that he suspected that Jeannie Horan-Evens and her parents were being held hostage by a couple of lesbian terrorists? He'd only brought him along because there was no one else. He thought the man would be a help. A witness if all else failed. Why would no one take him seriously?

Jeremy *had* been paying attention but he thought that Mulligan was crazy, one preliminary payment short of a self-assessment tax return.

Mulligan's attitude, when he first approached him, was suspect to say the least. The way he almost cracked up laughing when he had reported Jeannie missing. To begin with, as the cop was laying out the facts to Jeremy, he misheard him and thought he was talking about *Libyan* Protestant paramilitaries. That version was just about credible – Jeremy knew little enough about Libya, in fact he always confused it with the Lebanon and thought that Beirut was its capital. He was aware that there were numerous factions involved in the conflict in Beirut, and it was just possible that apart from the Shia Muslims, Sunni Muslims and Christian militia, there could well be a Protestant militia too. But would two *lesbian* Protestant paramilitary terrorists abduct Jeannie and her parents, for God's sake? Who'd ever heard of such a group anyway? He was a good God-fearing Methodist and he couldn't imagine the Orange hierarchy embracing, if that was the word, any of that class of deviant feminist behaviour. It would be more plausible if Mulligan had said that aliens had come down in a spacecraft and whisked them all off to the planet Zerphon for the purposes of experimentation. And no doubt, were Marcus to be asked for his opinion on the matter he would heartily agree with that, except perhaps the bit about the planet Zerphon. Everyone who mattered knew the proper destination was the Dog Star, Sirius.

Mulligan still had a tight hold of Jeremy's arm. 'Your wife and her parents are in that house, Mr Evens,' he said through gritted teeth. 'I have reason to believe that your parents-in-law were on a bus that was probably hijacked by these lesbian terrorists, and that your wife was detained by the same terrorists when she called at the house looking for them.'

Jeremy Evens, thoroughly intimidated by both Mulligan's bulk and manic attitude, only blinked behind his glasses in reply.

'I suggest you sit in your car and wait until I have thoroughly assessed the situation,' the cop continued.

Jeremy swallowed hard. Good grief! He was serious.

Glaring at him, Mulligan let go of his arm. His vicelike grip had cut off the circulation. Half-heartedly, Jeremy rubbed the life back into it as he walked to his car, which was parked behind Mulligan's. In a daze, he sat in the driver's seat.

They heard the sound of an engine and, a moment later, an RTE satellite truck drove round the corner at speed, almost ploughing into the back of Jeremy Evens's car.

Micky jammed on the brakes and the truck skidded to a halt only inches from the bumper.

'Bollocks!' he roared as they were thrown forward, he against the steering wheel, Cathy against the dashboard. 'I thought I'd lost them.'

'Well, you fucking found them again, didn't you, you wanker,' Cathy snapped. So much for covert surveillance.

Mulligan was equally upset. The last thing he needed right now was the TV news sniffing around.

He left Jeremy and ran over to the truck. 'What the hell do you think you're doing?' he raged.

Cathy was picking the remains of Micky's packet of popcorn out of her hair, while still trying to look professional. 'We're just following up a lead, Sergeant. Would you care to comment on the situation?' She was hoping that this statement would infer that she actually *knew* something about what was going on.

Mulligan wasn't having any of it. 'What situation?' he barked. 'I told you to get on to the Garda press office.' He looked anxiously towards the mill-house. 'You'll have to move on. You can't stay here.'

Cathy climbed out of the truck.

'I said you can't stay here.' Mulligan was visibly jittery. 'You'll have to move along.'

Cathy was standing in the road now, with Micky beside her. 'But if there's no situation, if there's no terrorist incident, what's the harm?'

Jeremy walked up at this point. 'Please do as the sergeant says. My wife's in there. She's a hostage.'

Mulligan groaned.

'A hostage?' Cathy said.

'Yes. Yes, she is.' Jeremy was very agitated. 'By a crowd of lesbian Protestant paramilitaries.'

Cathy had the same problem with the concept of lesbian Protestant paramilitaries as Jeremy had initially. '*Lesbian* paramilitaries? Are you winding me up?'

'Lesbian *Protestant* para –' Jeremy emphasised, but Mulligan cut him off.

'For God's sake. We have a hostage situation here,' he snapped. He took hold of Cathy's arm in order to steer her back towards the truck. 'You'll have to move on or I'll be obliged to arrest you.'

As far as Cathy could see, Mulligan was on his own. You and whose army, she thought.

Micky broke the stalemate. 'Come on. There's no need to get heavy.' He walked a few yards down the road and hunkered down by the wall, leaning the camera on top and pointing it in the general direction of the mill-house. 'Come on, Cathy. We'll just stay out of the way over here.'

Cathy hesitated, but Micky's frantic gesticulating behind Mulligan's back persuaded her to back down.

'OK, Sergeant.' She relented. 'We'll just stay out of sight over here.'

Mulligan knew when he was beaten. It was Catch 22. The only way he could get rid of the TV people was to arrest them, and if he did that, he couldn't watch the house.

After further hasty negotiations, Cathy and Micky agreed to pull the truck out of sight further down the road, and only film when Mulligan said it was OK. Micky agreed to this, but Cathy noticed that the red *record* light was blinking away as he said it.

With that taken care of, Mulligan's mind was now firmly back on the matter in hand. He was concentrating on the windows of the house, straining to catch any movement.

The situation was changing by the minute. Jake Devine's jeep was parked in front now, along with Jeannie Horan-Evens's blue Fiesta. Who did the two BMWs belong to? A silver two-door coupé and a bigger series seven job? He made a note of the registrations and called Joe Flynn on his radio.

Hogan put his foot down. It was a relief after the stop-start driving of the previous forty minutes. Brünnhilde and her Valkyries were blaring from all six speakers. He adored Wagner. Now that was music to make you high, and he was certainly feeling high at the prospect of catching up with Jodie McDeal. He'd popped a couple of amphetamines after he had last spoken with Gnasher, and now he was invincible. The signpost for Boran said forty kilometres. Not long now, he thought. Not long now.

Gnasher was reclining in the armchair where Bosco had been sitting. It was obviously the command chair. He was pointing the Uzi in the general direction of the hostages who were assembled together at the other end of the room. He counted. Nine of them. He didn't have a clue or care about who most of them were. Hogan would sort that out. He was certain that the blonde in the Beemer was a dealer, and the cowboy looked suspect too. But why were the two gurriers taking the money away? They had to be mixed up with the McDeal bitch. That was the only answer.

Decco had taken up position behind Gnasher, armed with the sawn-off. He had got over the shock of Gnasher's violence towards the girl. The incident only served to reinforce his respect for the man.

Bosco was looking over longingly at the case of ransom money, which Gnasher had confiscated and was now using as a footstool. He had no idea of Gnasher's dangerous assumptions concerning him, the money and his association with Jodie, or the even more hazardous-to-health matter of Hogan's Smack.

Jodie was lying, her upper body supported by Lucy, near the sofa. She had only been unconscious for a few minutes but she felt lousy. Her head was throbbing, her nose felt as if it was on fire and she wanted to puke. The front of her jumper was caked in blood, as was Lucy's skirt. She was holding a blood-soaked towel to her face in an effort to stem the bleeding. She eased it away and gingerly touched her nose. The bleeding appeared to have stopped. It was hugely swollen so she was obliged to breathe through her mouth. She could taste the blood at the back of her throat. It was fortunate that there were no mirrors handy. If she had caught sight of her reflection she would have passed out again. She looked hideous. Her eyes had already blackened, and the whites had turned bright red from the tiny burst blood vessels. It gave her the look of some pugilist vampire, as her beautifully neat, straight nose was swollen to the size of a medium salad tomato and angled to the left. It was now similar in colour to an aubergine. Had not the pain been so excruciating and had she investigated further, she would have discovered that Gnasher had fragmented the delicate bridge into a large number of irreparable pieces.

Jake was sitting on the sofa close by. He had figured out that the gangster with the machine pistol was after Jodie and that he was now waiting for his boss to make an appearance. He had, however, no idea of Gnasher's complicated scenario involving Bosco, Corky, Cindy and, to a lesser extent, himself.

Lucy was equally ignorant of Gnasher's machinations and hoped that there was safety in numbers: i.e. that Gnasher and Hogan wouldn't dare to kill nine hostages. Nine dead bodies would amount to carnage – a veritable blood bath.

Jeannie, who had surreptitiously quaffed half a dozen happy pills, was only semi-unconscious.

Monty was, for the first time in the last couple of days, afraid. He had never witnessed anything like the way Gnasher Gill walloped Jodie full in the face with his closed fist. He seemed to take pleasure in it too. Monty had heard the bones crunch as the fist made contact and it made him feel sick. The incident shocked him to the core. More so, even, than Cindy's betrayal. It was frightening stuff. The way he was casually holding the machine pistol was also disturbing. Unlike Lucy, Monty had no doubts that Gnasher would happily blow them all to kingdom come without a second thought.

Jon-Joe was worried about Biddy and Jeannie. And Biddy was happily rocking backwards and forwards where she sat, humming the national anthem and thinking about making the tea.

Fionn was standing guard on Lucy and Jodie, while keeping a weather eye on Gnasher. She would have preferred it if Lucy weren't clinging on to her collar as if her life depended on it. She would have been delighted to sink her teeth into Gnasher's leg. Instead, she made do with throwing the occasional threatening growl in his direction. That would suffice for now.

Gnasher dialled Hogan's mobile.

'Should be there in about half an hour, give or take,' Hogan told him. He was stuck behind a slow-moving tractor and trailer, and because of the narrow, twisty road, couldn't overtake. He didn't mind. The bitch would keep. All the longer for her to think about what she had done and, more to the point, what he would do to her.

Chapter Twenty-Four

Wednesday, 6 November, five thirty p.m.

It was dark on top of the mountain. Marcus was attending to his daily ritual of lighting the lamps on the landing pad. He had revived the practice a couple of months before after reading about a number of UFO sightings in the Wicklow area. A couple of the lamps wouldn't light. He tried shaking the offending torches, in the hope that maybe it was just a loose connection. No joy. The batteries had gone. He wasn't sure what to do about it. Lucy usually took care of that sort of thing.

He sat down despondently on a rock. He was cold and hungry. The old iron range was resolutely refusing to burn properly – he wasn't aware that the ashes had to be emptied – so the hotplate was only lukewarm. Consequently there was no hot water and he couldn't boil the kettle because the fuse in the plug had gone and he didn't know how to change it. Wasn't that just typical of Lucy. Never around when he needed her. He got up and spaced the torches further apart, then he cheered up. Maybe he'd have a sighting this evening. Perhaps they'd come tonight and whisk him off to a better place.

Mulligan was elated. Joe Flynn had just got back to him with the registration details of the BMWs. The smaller coupé belonged to a Mr Monty George of Sandycove and the larger, series seven job, to one Gabriel Gill, aka Gnasher, who was known to the Gardai as being an associate of Rogan Hogan, aka the Untouchable, aka the Grim Reaper, aka the Rogue.

'See if you can rustle up some back-up, Joe. I know I'm on to something. Something's going down. Something big.' Mulligan was an avid watcher of *NYPD Blue* and usually slipped into the vernacular when excited. He tried to keep the whinging tone out of his voice, but he was desperate. Although Gill only had a couple of convictions as a juvenile, Garda intelligence was well aware that he was a dangerous man, who was mixed up in Hogan's drug trade and prostitution empire as well as being Hogan's enforcer. If he was on the spot, something big had to be afoot. Joe promised to do his best.

That was the moment that Rogan Hogan chose to come round the corner. The sight of the uniformed Garda standing, surreptitiously watching what could only be the mill-house and talking into his radio, caused him to change his plans. Driving on, he registered that there were two cars, one with a plain-clothes cop at the wheel. As he sped on by, he caught a glimpse of two more figures, a woman and a man, crouching by the wall. Before he had time to wonder who they were, he flashed past an RTE outside-broadcast truck, complete with satellite dish.

'Jesus, fucking Christ!'

He drove round a sharp bend in the road, then pulled into the grass verge and dialled Gnasher's mobile. 'What's the story?' he barked.

'Everythin's under control, Boss.' Gnasher was relaxed and happy after the pleasurable experience of giving Jodie a slap.

'The hell it is!' Hogan snapped. 'There are two cops and half of bloody RTE sitting right outside the gate watching the bloody place. What's that about?'

Gnasher bounded out of his seat across to the window and squinted out from behind the curtain. In the darkness he couldn't see anything. Then, by the headlamps from a passing vehicle, he saw a bulky figure and the front end of a car at the gate. 'Dunno, Boss,' he said. 'Nothin' t'do with me.'

'Of course it's to bloody do with you. You're in there. My

stuff is in there. That bitch McDeal is in there and half the local plod and the national media are at the bloody gate.'

Not renowned for his quickness of thinking, Gnasher surprised both himself and Hogan. 'There's a back way in, Boss. Where are yeh?'

'About twenty yards down the road, why?'

Gnasher dropped the curtain and sauntered back to his seat. 'There's a road through the woods a bit further on. If yeh folla that for a bit, yeh come to a bridge across the river at the back a'the house, here. Yeh can't be seen from the road.'

The one-sided conversation gave the hostages no clue that possible rescue in the form of Sergeant Mulligan and Jeremy Evens was so close at hand. Jodie realised that Gnasher must be talking to Hogan, and from the way Gnasher's end of the discussion was going that he couldn't be far away. 'I tik Hobads ouptide,' she muttered to Lucy.

'What?'

'Robad Hobad. He'd ouptide.'

'What the hell are you talking about?' Lucy hissed.

'I think she's trying to tell us her boyfriend's outside,' Jake offered.

Jodie nodded, immediately regretting it as her brains seemed to rattle round inside her skull, causing her further severe discomfort.

The sky was pitch black. Not a single star due to the heavy, high cloud cover. Eight thin beams of light radiated upwards in a circle from Marcus's landing pad. He was still sitting on the same rock, looking up at the sky. He was more relaxed now, due to the narcotic benefits of the huge joint he had rolled, sacrificing the last of his stash in order to relieve his depression. He was dreaming of Nirvana.

Suddenly a swirling wind almost knocked him off the rock, then came a deafening noise and a bright beam of light cut through the darkness, completely engulfing him. Dazzled, he shielded his eyes from the glare. His heart was pounding. This was it. He was dizzy with anticipation and from the effects of the pot. 'I knew I was right. I knew I was right,' he kept repeating.

They had come for him at last.

Marcus stood up and raised his arms above his head in an open gesture of welcome. Through the wind and the deafening noise, he lifted his face to the light and closed his eyes. 'Beam me up,' he murmured. 'Beam me up.' Tears of relief and joy were running down his cheeks.

Rogan Hogan hurried along the forest path by the river. His eyes were accustomed to the darkness now but he also had the aid of a small lightweight flashlight. He pointed the beam down to avoid being seen from the road. Very soon he came upon the bridge across the river at the back of the mill-house.

Mulligan crept up the drive, being careful not to crunch the gravel. When he reached the lawn he darted from one shrub to the next, pausing to get his breath between dashes. A well-matured rhododendron five yards from the house gave him sanctuary after the final dash. His lungs felt as if they would burst and he could hear the blood pumping around in his brain. He made a mental note to pack up the fags. The noise in his head and the buzzing in his ears left him unaware that he had company. Micky and Cathy were darting from shrub to shrub not five yards behind him.

Micky tracked him with the camera. 'Light's shite,' he muttered to Cathy. He considered switching on the integral halogen spot mounted on the side of his camera, but deferred it until there was something actually to shoot other than the fat arse of a culchie cop.

Mulligan poked his head round the bush and peered at the house. Close up, he was conscious of a chink of light at the edge of the window to the right of the front door. He crept forward, aware of the sound of his laboured breathing. When he reached the corner of the house he stopped and listened. Everything was quiet. Then, in the still night air, in the distance, he picked up the sound of – was it a mobile phone? A few yards behind, Cathy heard it too. The noise ceased abruptly.

'I'm outside the back, you moron!' Hogan hissed into his new, top-of-the-range, teeny-tiny, state-of-the-art mobile phone with fifty different ringing tones. 'Open the frigging door.'

Gnasher sent Decco to do the honours.

Jodie was frantically trying to formulate a strategy. She was confident Hogan wouldn't do anything to her in front of witnesses. Would he be satisfied once he got the Smack back? Being realistic, she doubted it. Jodie was afraid.

Lucy wasn't madly happy either. If Gnasher Gill was only the monkey, what did that say about Rogan Hogan? She was also beginning to have nagging doubts about her earlier certainty that Hogan wouldn't dare to harm all nine of them.

At this point, the organ grinder made his entrance.

Mulligan sidled along with his back against the wall until he was right beside the window. The view through the crack in the curtain was strictly limited so he could only see Gnasher brandishing the Uzi machine pistol. He wondered what connection Lucy Spoon had – she of the lesbian wing of the UVF – with Gnasher Gill and, by association, with Rogan Hogan. Then it came to him. Drugs! It had to be drugs. Everyone knew that that crowd dealt drugs to finance their gun running, and explosive buying, and the like. The Uzi machine pistol was all the reason he needed to get back-up.

He edged round towards the grass, keeping his eyes on the window. Then, as he reached the first shrub, he turned to make a run for the gate. As he did so, he crashed into Micky. The two of them stumbled to the ground and, in the resulting mêlée, the halogen lamp on the camera was accidentally switched on, almost blinding Mulligan. The camera was still rolling.

'What the fuck – ?'

Hogan had Jodie by the wrist and was dragging her towards the kitchen. In his other hand, he was holding a 9mm Glock automatic, fitted with a silencer. It was sufficient incentive to deter any heroics on the part of Jake, or indeed Monty who had taken quite a shine to Jodie, particularly after she saved his life.

The attaché case was lying on the floor beside Gnasher's chair.

'Pick that up,' Hogan barked at Jodie.

'Jut tape ip,' she said. 'Tape ip ad lep be go.'

'What?'

'She said, "just take it and let me go",' Jake assisted.

Hogan glared at the cowboy. 'Who asked you?' He gave Jodie a shove towards the attaché case. 'Pick it up!' Motivated by fear, Jodie did as she was told and grabbed the case. Hogan dragged her nearer the kitchen.

'Bot dow?' she asked. 'Bare are be goig?'

'She wants to know where you're taking her?' Jake said, without being asked.

Hogan ignored him. 'Keep an eye on this lot until I get back,' he said to Gnasher, before yanking Jodie after him in the direction of the back door. Gnasher picked up the case of cash and slid it behind the sofa before returning to his armchair. He was seriously considering keeping it. He hadn't mentioned the money to Hogan, only his suspicion of the drug deal. With luck, Hogan would be so pleased to have both the McDeal bitch and the Smack, it was possible he would forget about it. He decided to play it by ear.

'What are you going to do with us?' Lucy asked. 'Are you going to let us go?'

'Maybe,' Gnasher said. 'But first I want yeh t'tell me what happened here.'

It took a moment for Lucy to cop on. 'Oh . . . What happened here? Nothing. Nothing happened here. No one saw anything happen here, did you, guys?' Her tone, as she looked around the room at her fellow hostages, took on a pleading quality.

Jake helped her out. 'Sure. No one saw anything. No one saw you or the other guy. Nothing happened.'

'Right,' Monty echoed. 'Nothing.'

Bosco and Corky were nodding like dogs on a rear window, repeating 'Nothin' nothin' ' with utter sincerity.

Jon-Joe gave Jeannie a warning look, in case she decided to come over all belligerent, but she was still half out of it on her Valium sandwich.

Biddy woke up. 'Will I make the tea?'

Hogan shoved Jodie viciously in the back. She stumbled over her long skirt and only just managed to keep her balance. She considered making a break for it, but didn't fancy having a hole the size of Gnasher's fist blown in her back. Even had she had any idea that Sergeant Mulligan was at the front gate, screaming was out of the question. The state her nose was in made breathing almost impossible, let alone yelling.

They were at the bridge now. Ahead of them was the forest. Jodie stopped in her tracks and turned to face Hogan. To hell with it, she thought. She had no intention of meekly going to her certain death. If he was going to kill her she wasn't going to make it easy for him. She held the attaché case over the side of the bridge.

'Top dare, Robad!' she said.

Hogan was catching on to her mutilated lingo. 'What are you doing, you mad bitch?'

'Top bite dare,' she said taking a step backwards. 'Pup de gud dowb ad bove bap.' Hogan took a step towards her. 'I'b baordig du!' she said, shoving the case further out over the fast-flowing river.

Hogan got the message. He stopped. 'Come on, Jodie.

Don't do anything silly,' he said in a friendly but firm voice. 'Let's talk about this.'

Jodie moved nearer to the side of the bridge. 'D' gud,' she said. 'Pup de gud dowb, Robad.'

Hogan hesitated, then gently placed the 9mm Gluck on the ground about a foot in front of him. Jodie walked backwards across the bridge, keeping the Smack suspended over the river. Hogan watched her. As she reached the other side he lunged for the gun. At the same instant he saw Jodie swing the case and then let go. It flew high into the air in an arc.

Wesley was in crocodile heaven. On reaching the river he had found the swollen and rotting carcass of a fox and had feasted well. The cadaver had reached the perfect state of putrefaction to allow the meat almost to fall off the bones with little or no encouragement. He settled down for a doze.

Hogan, half on his knees, reaching for the gun, froze as he followed the flight path of his precious Smack. He heard a thump as it landed on the bank on his side of the river. Forgetting about Jodie, he darted towards the wall and jumped over to the bank below.

Jodie didn't wait for a second chance. She hitched up her skirt and ran like hell down the forest path towards the road. She didn't look back, just kept her eyes fixed firmly ahead. She couldn't hear any footsteps behind her. She forgot about the pains in her face and her head, and ran for her life. She could see a gateway ahead of her. 'Please, please be the road,' she said aloud. (It came out as, 'Pleebe, pleeb be de roab.') Her chest felt as if it was about to burst. She looked over her shoulder, expecting to see Hogan, but the path was empty. The gate was only a couple of yards ahead now. With superhuman effort, she picked up speed and ran through it into the road.

There was the screech of brakes.

*

Hogan was on his hands and knees searching the river bank for the case of Smack. He was angry beyond belief. The knees of his Georgio Armani pants were wet and his hands covered in mud. Frantically, he rooted around in the long grass. Then relief. He found the attaché case. It was lying on a rock and had burst open. One packet of drugs was lying nearby, but he couldn't see the other. He felt around some more.

Suddenly the rock moved.

Chapter Twenty-Five

Wednesday, 6 November, six p.m.

Micky was rolling. Rocking and rolling. A few minutes earlier, a van had driven up and disgorged eight or nine armed cops, all done up in riot gear. Cathy, never one to let an opportunity pass, had called the news room on her mobile and was busy organising the live feed to the studios. She was truly exhilarated. How lucky can you get, she thought. And all in time for the Six-One News. Eat your heart out, Kate Adie!

The cops were taking up position, a couple crouching in the lee of the wall, others scuttling up towards the mill-house, covering each other as they used shrubs and trees for cover. They looked a lot more expert at it than Mulligan had.

Cathy Grady looked around for Mulligan but he was nowhere in sight. Maybe his camouflage capabilities had improved. Instead, she collared the hunky ARU Inspector who was talking into his radio.

Hogan had been gone for more than half an hour. Gnasher was getting tired. He was suffering from the lack of sleep of the previous night. He yawned. How long did it take to put a hole in the back of the bitch's head? He wasn't worried about the culchie cops at the gate or the TV people. As soon as the Boss got back they'd leg it through the forest before the stupid bastards knew they were even there. With his already feeble brain further dulled by fatigue, it didn't occur to him to wonder what they were doing there in the first place.

Lucy, unaware that the Boran constabulary was skulking at the gate, was feeling guilty that she hadn't made any attempt to help Jodie, even though it would have been suicide. She strained her ears, listening for a shot, then remembered the silencer. Would he really shoot her in cold blood? Probably, she told herself. And the rest of them too.

She looked over at Jake. He was sitting on the stairs to the left of Gnasher. She realised that he had moved and was gradually working his way out of Gnasher's line of vision. Did he have something in mind? He caught her staring and put his finger to his lips. Lucy took his cue and looked away. Maybe if she created a diversion and grabbed Gnasher's attention, Jake would be able to jump him and take the gun. On the other hand, he looked as if he was half asleep. If he dropped off, that would be a safer option.

Monty stood up and said, 'I have to use the bathroom.'

Gnasher snapped awake. 'Siddown,' he barked.

'But – '

'Siddown!'

Monty sat down. Lucy groaned inwardly. She looked over at Jake again. He shrugged and shook his head.

'Can't you let us go now?' Lucy said. 'We won't say a word, really.'

'The Boss said t'wait till he gets back,' Gnasher answered. 'So we wait.'

Without any warning, they heard a loud distorted megaphone voice. 'Armed Police! Come out one at a time with your hands in the air.' Then they made out the distinct *whap whap whap* of a helicopter, increasing in volume as it drew closer. The voice kept repeating the message.

Everyone froze, then Gnasher leaped to his feet and ran to the window. The front of the house was bathed with spotlights. The helicopter was hovering about twenty feet from the ground and one of the lights was making wide circular sweeps of the driveway and lawn. At the gate he could clearly see the flashing lights of at least half a dozen police vehicles. 'Holy shit!'

'Wha'?' Decco was right behind him at the window. 'Are yeh goin' t'fight, Boss?' he asked, ready for anything.

Gnasher, despite his reputation as a hard-man, knew when the odds were stacked against him. He was no Butch Cassidy. 'No fuckin' way!' he said. 'I'm fuckin' outta here.'

Decco was disgusted.

'Keep 'em covered with the sawn-off,' Gnasher told him as he hurried towards the back door.

Fionn grasped the opportunity. With a blood-curdling growl, which built into a cacophony of savage barking, she launched herself at Gnasher's retreating bulk. She landed on his back and sunk her teeth into his shoulder.

He didn't know what had hit him. He howled and tried to shake her off. But Fionn was having none of it and clung on with her teeth and claws. There was a tearing sound as the fabric of Gnasher's Italian suit was shredded by her flailing claws. The Uzi clattered to the floor and skimmed across the tiles.

Jake made a lunge for it, swiping Decco out of the way. Decco lay in a heap, pointing the sawn-off at the floor. Lucy relieved him of his weapon.

The whole episode only took a matter of seconds. Grudgingly Fionn let go of Gnasher, but only after considerable coaxing from Lucy.

The hostages gave Fionn a round of spontaneous applause.

The ARU officer in charge, crouching among the bushes, spoke into his radio. 'Someone's fucking clapping.'

It was fortunate that the Garda helicopter was in the area. The drug squad had called it and the Armed Response Unit after a tip-off warned them that a large quantity of drugs were due to be flown in from France by light aircraft and dropped by parachute. Persistent sightings of a circle of lights on the Wicklow mountains led them to believe that this was the landing point.

Joe Flynn had managed to persuade the powers that be,

merely by mentioning the names of Rogan Hogan and Gnasher Gill, to divert to the mill-house. The drug squad and the ARU never liked to be sent on a fool's errand and Flynn's call gave them a good chance of a result.

Marcus was under sedation in a psychiatric hospital. For reasons known only to themselves, the drug squad didn't buy his story about the landing pad. And when he went on to explain that his wife was a lesbian Protestant paramilitary bomber, and he was waiting on top of the mountain for the alien beings to transport him home to the Dog Star Sirius, they called the men in white coats.

Jodie had run into Mulligan as she hit the road. Or, more accurately, Mulligan had almost run Jodie down as she had emerged from the forest gate. Aware of the forest path, he had decided to take a look around at the back of the mill-house.

She managed, despite her temporary speech impediment and the fact that she was almost hysterical, to tell him about Hogan and Gnasher Gill. Mulligan could have kissed her, except for the fact that she looked hideous.

The drug squad were equally pleased to see Gnasher Gill arrested under section thirty of the Offences Against the State Act. They did him for possession of a firearm with intent to cause grievous bodily harm, for starters.

There was no trace of either Hogan or of the Smack.

The Armed Response Unit called everyone from the house. They came out one at a time with their hands in the air, except for Jon-Joe, who led Biddy with a protective arm round her shoulder.

Decco adopted a *victim* expression. Bosco and Corky the same, except in their case they actually *were* victims. When asked later, none of the hostages could remember seeing Decco after that, or had any idea where he went. He had disappeared into thin air.

Jeremy, overcome with relief that Jeannie was unharmed, hugged her in full view of everyone. It was an unprecedented public show of affection on his part, never to be repeated.

Lucy wasn't so lucky. Because of Jodie's communication problem, Mulligan was still under the impression that she was a lesbian Protestant paramilitary bomber. She was cuffed and whisked off to Boran Garda station under armed guard. Fionn stayed reluctantly with Jake.

It took a couple of hours for the cops to check out Lucy's alibi. She was extremely glad that she had reported the Hiace stolen when she did, and that she and Jodie had spent the relevant time together in the full view of numerous witnesses at the truck stop café, waiting for Jake's bus.

Funnily enough, maybe in deference to Monty's agreement with Bosco and Corky, or perhaps because of the Stockholm syndrome, no one mentioned the hijacking. After a hurried discussion while they were all waiting in front of the mill-house for a van to take them to the Garda station to give their statements, they got the story straight. The definitive version of events was that Jake had to turn the bus back because of bad weather. Monty told the cops that Cindy had come down to pick him up. No one bothered to ask what a man reputedly worth a small fortune was doing on a Mickey Mouse bus to Cork in the first place.

Jodie blamed everything on Gnasher and Hogan. She said that they burst into the mill-house and Gnasher beat her up because, having discovered how Rogan Hogan earned a crust, she was so horrified that she had decided to leave him.

Cathy got her moment of glory as events at the mill-house unfolded live on the Six-One News. The bulletin was extended until the operation was concluded, and Micky got great footage. Fortunately, she got her facts straight and didn't blather to the nation on live TV about a Protestant lesbian paramilitary bomb factory. She gave up on her interview with Jodie because of the obvious communication problem but managed to get good sound bites from the ARU officer in charge of the operation, and an invitation to dinner the following week. She also got a curt couple of words from a drug squad officer, elated by Gnasher's arrest.

Jeremy obliged with an account of his ordeal, as did

Jeannie. Her 'out of it' appearance was put down to shock rather than to the amount of pharmaceutical products she had quaffed in the previous twenty-four hours.

Mulligan was the hero of the hour. Gnasher Gill was a catch. After thirteen hours of interrogation, to avoid a charge of grievous bodily harm, firearms offences and attempted murder, he asked to be placed on the Witness Protection Programme and turned super-grass.

When Lucy left the Garda station very late that night, Jake was waiting outside for her in his jeep with an over-excited Fionn. He was grinning.

'It's not funny,' Lucy said, referring to the fact that she'd been questioned for hours about her involvement with some loony lesbian Protestant liberation movement.

'Yes, it is,' he said, as they made off.

He drove her back to the scene of the crime. Only Gnasher's BMW was still parked in front of the house. Jake told her the cops were coming to pick it up the next day. As he set about making toasted sandwiches and strong coffee, he informed her that Monty had ordered an air ambulance to whisk Jodie up to the Blackrock clinic for corrective facial surgery.

Bosco and Corky had dropped by to collect Cindy's BMW and the bag of cash. He said that Bosco had handed him a brown paper bag full of used notes – Jake estimated it to be about twenty grand – and asked him to pass it on to Jon-Joe and Biddy. Jake said Jon-Joe was reluctant to take it until he pointed out that it would be useful if he ever needed a bit of help with Biddy, and that Monty had given it to Bosco and Corky willingly.

They talked about old times and Lucy went into more detail about her shit life choices. Jake told her about his good fortune.

There was a lull in the conversation just as the sun was coming up. Lucy had her eyes closed and was resting her head against his shoulder on the back of the sofa.

'Why *did* you give up painting?' Jake asked. 'You were very talented.'

Lucy shrugged. 'I sort of didn't have the time,' she said.

'That's a cop-out!'

She revised her answer. 'OK, then. I suppose, because Marcus said I was crap.'

'Not true,' Jake said, taking her by the hand. He led her up the stairs. Lucy was curious, but followed him. He stopped at the top and pointed to a large abstract canvas hanging near the door of his bedroom.

Lucy immediately recognised it as one of hers. 'Where the fuck did you get that?'

'You left it behind when you baled out with the hippie. I figured it more than covered the fifty quid you nicked.' Lucy was mortified, until she saw that Jake was smiling. 'I think that makes us even,' he said.

Lucy smiled back and shook her head. 'No way. That canvas is probably worth a fortune now.'

'Oh yeah?'

'Yeah. In East Belfast I'm a folk hero!'

Chapter Twenty-Six

Towards the middle of the Six-One TV news bulletin, Cathy Grady filed the following report:

'The missing circus crocodile that escaped after the container transporting it and other animals to Kilkenny crashed, was found dead today, on the banks of the Nore river near Boran. Preliminary reports suggest that it died of a drugs overdose. A forensic veterinary pathologist at the Dublin Veterinary school stated that up to two kilos of heroin and a man's lower limb were found in the stomach of the reptile. As yet, the limb remains unidentified. When questioned, the reptile trainer said he couldn't understand why the creature had ripped off the limb, as he is usually very docile. He thought perhaps that the heroin must have had something to do with it. The Garda Siochana are interviewing members of the circus staff.'

The following day, Cathy Grady filed a further report from Boran:

'The body of a man was found by fishermen last night in shallow water at the edge of the River Nore in Boran. The pathologist's preliminary findings state that the man died as a result of drowning. He has been identified as Mr Rogan Hogan, the Dublin man whom the Gardai were anxious to interview in connection with a firearms incident and other matters.

'Gardai were called to the scene when it was discovered that half of one of Mr Hogan's lower legs was missing.

Comparing the deceased man's shoe with that found in the stomach of the dead circus reptile, Gardai are confident that the severed limb belongs to the body of Mr Hogan. An unidentified source told RTE that the Gardai suspect that while fleeing from them, Mr Hogan must have disturbed the crocodile, possibly by standing on it. It is not yet known how the creature came to ingest the heroin. Gardai are still questioning circus staff.

'Cathy Grady, RTE News, Boran.'

Epilogue

Lucy only intended to stay for a couple of days with Jake, but the days drifted on. It was a new and enjoyable experience for her to have a decent conversation with a sane adult person. He eventually persuaded her to start painting again and now Lucy Spoon canvasses are much sought after. They are now officially an item. The irony of the situation hasn't dawned on Lucy: her mother would be proud of her.

Fionn lives happily in the mill-house and fills her days chasing the ducks and being tormented by Jake's big ginger tom cat.

After surgery restored Jodie's nose to it's former glory, she recuperated in Monty's Sandycove mansion. The exit of Cindy left a vacancy for a presenter on his new TV channel so he gave the job to her. Against all her best efforts she fell for Monty in a big way. She tried her hardest to avoid it, but in the end his sweetness and kindness won her over. No one was more surprised than Jodie, except perhaps Monty. After Cindy, he was naturally wary, but it was as if they had been infected by some virus.

Cindy moved to London and is at present working in a topless bar in Soho.

Cathy Grady now works for CNN, and is based in Atlanta. Micky still works for RTE News.

Corky bought his greyhounds. He also sent his ma and two of his sisters on a cruise, which coincided with his da's next shore leave.

Bosco bought his ma a rocking chair and told her she

could retire. He also bought Natasha a pair of size 38d bazookas. He spread the story around that he had won the Lotto. Two weeks after he returned from Boran he really did win the Lotto. He chose to remain anonymous, as who would believe anyone could win the jackpot twice in as many weeks. He bought a house in Glasnevin which he shares with his ma and Natasha, and lives off the income from his jackpot win. He is regularly seen at the GPO posting mysterious padded envelopes.

Jon-Joe got a nurse in to help him with Biddy. Mysterious padded envelopes containing used bank notes periodically arrive at his house through the post.

After obtaining immunity on a number of counts, Gnasher Gill is at present serving a three year term of imprisonment in Arbour Hill. As a part of the Witness Protection Programme he is in solitary confinement and under twenty-four hour protection. At the end of his sentence he will be given a new identity and has been advised to leave the country.

Decco's whereabouts are unknown.

Jeremy started his own accountancy firm and Jeannie got an au pair. They never speak about the incident.

Sergeant Eugene Mulligan remains stationed at Boran Garda station. He is still convinced that, despite her cast iron alibi, Lucy Spoon is a covert lesbian Protestant paramilitary bomber. He watches her closely, convinced that one day he will get the proof.

Wesley is now a matching set of luggage.

Marcus Pyle thinks he is Jesus Christ . . . So what's new?

If you have enjoyed
The Flight of Lucy Spoon
don't miss
Maggie Gibson's latest novel

FIRST HOLY CHAMELEON

Available from Orion
ISBN: 0 57540 323 3
Price: £5.99

Chapter One

'I think you're overreacting, Mizz Ryan.'

He was a pompous bastard, and Cash Ryan hated pompous bastards. Tall, with patrician features and the regulation dark three-piece suit, he stood beside his car, a shiny, new, low-slung, pseudo sports jobby with metallic paint. A regular mid-life-crisis-mobile. He peered at her over his glasses, which had slid halfway down the bridge of his nose.

'And what would you know about my life that would enable you to be the judge of that?' Cash's dander was up.

Pompous Bastard gave her a patronising smile, well, more of a sneer really. 'Mizz Ryan, as you are well aware, Donovan Development purchased this property at public auction over six months ago. I think, under the circumstances, Mr Donovan has been more than reasonable. You've had ample time to relocate your little project.'

'You know we can't afford anywhere else.' Cash was hoping to appeal to his better nature. Vain hope.

Pompous Bastard shuffled his papers. 'You have until next Tuesday, the end of the month, to remove all your belongings.'

'Or?'

Weary sigh. '*Or* they will be removed. Please, Mizz Ryan, don't make this any more difficult than it already is.'

'I'm not making it difficult. Niall bloody Donovan's the one who's making it difficult. The Theatre Workshop's a public amenity, for God's sake. You can't just close us down.'

'And Donovan Development intend to build housing here. Twenty families will live on this site, Mizz Ryan. Twenty families. Surely housing is more important than an amateur theatre school in this day and age?'

'Twenty apartments? You're building twenty bloody apartments here?'

Cash was flabbergasted. Twenty apartments at around two hundred and eighty grand a throw hardly qualified in her book as *housing*. Housing implied *public* housing, not the luxury end of the market.

There was no doubt about it, Templebar was going to the dogs. Since the early nineties, when the developers had moved in, rents had gone sky high. The spin that Templebar was full of trendy Bohemian arty types was a crock. All the Bohemian types were moving out because of the spiralling rents, to be replaced by upmarket galleries, restaurants and high-cost apartments.

What would happen to the Workshop now?

Cash Ryan couldn't take credit for the Strolling Players Theatre Workshop. That credit went to a formidable woman by the name of Verity Gregory.

Miss Gregory, a woman of good family and charitable by nature, at the age of fifty had founded the Strolling Players Theatre Workshop in an old grain store owned by her family, in Templebar, in 1958. The history of the Gregory family brewing business stretched well back into the seventeen hundreds, preceding Arthur Guinness by at least twenty years.

As an actress, despite her enthusiasm, Verity was no better than average. She did, however, have a substantial trust fund, so put it to good use by founding the

Workshop. The idea behind it was to give children, for a nominal fee, all day Saturdays and on Tuesday evenings, training in all the skills of speech, stagecraft, dance and drama.

Many of the great and the good of Ireland's Thespian community had had their first smell of the greasepaint in Miss Gregory's academy, as had Cash Ryan. She, and a number of her peers, repaid Miss Gregory by giving the Saturday and Tuesday evening drama and dance classes when otherwise unemployed.

Verity Gregory had succumbed to cancer the previous January at the age of ninety, and the executors of her estate had put her entire property portfolio up for auction not long afterwards.

Cash was surprised that Miss Gregory hadn't made provision for the Workshop as she had promised all those involved that she would make sure that it would carry on after her death.

It was said that Verity Gregory had died intestate. Cash found that hard to believe, too. Dotty though Miss Gregory had been, where money was concerned she was sharp as a needle. But the sad fact remained that no will was produced. And an even sadder fact was that the Strolling Players Theatre Workshop was homeless.

As was Cash.

Three years before, after vandals had broken in and trashed the place, Miss Gregory had suggested that Cash should move into the top floor to act as a sort of unpaid caretaker. This had suited Cash fine, as work had been thin on the ground at the time. It was only ever meant to be a temporary arrangement but, three years on, Cash Ryan was still enjoying the benefits of a rent-free loft in the centre of Dublin. At least she was until Pompous Bastard put his spoke in.

Pompous Bastard unlocked his car and crammed

himself behind the wheel. Cash stood on the pavement and stared down at him. For someone who looked so ridiculous, it was ironic that he should have the last laugh, so to speak.

'One week, Mizz Ryan,' he said, before gunning the engine and screeching away on the wet cobbles.

It was raining but Cash didn't care. She stood and watched as PB turned the corner into Fleet Street.

It had not been a good couple of weeks for Catherine Ann Ryan, thirty-one, resting actress and spinster of this parish. Her big break had fizzled out like a damp squib.

Maurice Foley, her agent, had been certain, despite the fact that she had been contracted for only six episodes, that her character, Fifi Mulligan (the cynical hooker whose hard exterior concealed beneath it a heart of gold), would become a regular in the Dublin-based TV soap, *Liffey Town*. And it would have. Cash played a blinder, but circumstances beyond her control came to bear.

Jimmy Hatton, the actor playing Fifi's pimp, had a disagreement with the producers and was written out.

When Cash heard this through the grapevine she wasn't unduly worried. Fifi had plenty of mileage left in her, with or without her brutish pimp.

Then she read her lines. Every soap actor's nightmare. The dreaded word 'dies' glared at her at the bottom of the last page of her thinner-than-usual script.

Fifi, it transpired, was to be a victim of Jimmy's falling-out with management. She was to be brutally murdered by the mild-mannered schoolteacher, Sean, acting completely out of character due to a brain tumour. She hadn't even made it to the ad break.

'Those are the fractures, kid.' (Maurice continually made these little plays on words. He thought they were

4

amusing.) He softened the blow. 'But you never know what's round the next corner.'

'How true. Who would have thought, as well as having the thrill of being dumped by the national TV station, I'd be evicted, too.'

She moaned about it to Mort that afternoon. Mort Higgins was the sole proprietor of M&J Investigations. The 'J' of the company name belonged to his estranged wife, Janet.

Mort, an ex-Garda sergeant, had resigned from the force six years before, on health grounds (alcoholism), and after a spell of drying out he went into business for himself. Mort worked mainly alone, but employed off-duty cops on a freelance basis when the workload demanded.

Cash worked for him, also on a part-time basis, taking care of the secretarial work. It was a convenient arrangement all round. It allowed Cash to take any acting work, voice-overs, and so on that came along, and, as Mort didn't need a permanent secretary, it saved him having to put up with a never-ending line of uninterested temps.

'I don't know where the hell I'm going to live. Everywhere's so expensive now,' Cash whinged.

'Why can't you move in with Simon?' Mort asked.

Simon Moore was Cash's partner of three years. He was also an actor, and was at present out of the country filming a biblical TV mini-series in the Gobi desert, playing Judas Iscariot. He had been away for the past two months and, due to the remoteness of the location, she had heard little from him.

'He sublet his place when he went away,' Cash said forlornly. 'He's supposed to be moving in with me when he comes back.'

'You could always go home.'

Cash gave Mort a withering look.

'Why not? Your mother'd be only too pleased to have you.'

Cash's reluctance to run home in her present predicament was nothing to do with whether or not her mother would put out the welcoming mat – it was more to do with the fact that she held the strong conviction that anyone over twenty-five who lived at home was a sa-a-ad person.

She was also well aware that spending more than six consecutive hours in her mother's company would lead to homicide – or, more accurately, matricide.

This wasn't due to any lack of love she felt for her mother. In theory she loved her mother dearly. It was down to the two things that annoyed her most about Yvonne Ryan. Everything she said, and everything she did.

It was a two-way street.

Yvonne was acutely embarrassed and disappointed that Cash hadn't been more successful in her chosen profession. Famous even. In her youth, Yvonne's aspirations had leaned towards the theatre. In the beginning, when Cash had showed an interest in drama, Yvonne had hoped to fulfil those aspirations vicariously, but sadly Cash wasn't obliging in the fame department. Yvonne had had a rush of hope when her middle daughter landed a part in *Liffey Town*, only to have it dashed with Fifi's last on-screen gasp.

Cash hadn't had the courage to warn her mother about the demise of Fifi. Like everything else, including the problem of the grain-store sale, she hoped if she ignored the problem it would go away. Her only saving grace in her mother's eyes was Simon. It gave her heart that her middle daughter wasn't a complete failure. At least she had a man.

Mort's phone rang before he could offer any better suggestions, so Cash left him to it, and got on with transcribing the Dictaphone tapes that were lying on her in-tray.

When Cash had first started working for Mort she had been fascinated by the stuff on the dictation tapes. Illicit affairs, companies checking up on prospective executive employees, insider theft, bogus personal injury claims – a current trend was career-women checking into the background of prospective husbands. But now she hardly took any notice, and tapped out the information on her word processor, without even taking it in.

It took her most of the afternoon to catch up with the backlog, and by the end of the day she had typed up case notes and made hard-copy files for three cases Mort was currently working on. She also took care of half a dozen letters.

Just as she was putting her coat on to leave, the outer door of the office opened and a smartly dressed middle-aged woman walked in. Cash thought she looked familiar, but couldn't place her. The woman smiled uncertainly. She looked embarrassed to be there, and kept glancing over her shoulder as if afraid that someone was following her.

'Can I help you?' Cash asked.

The woman gave her a nervous smile. 'I'm here to see Mr Higgins. I have an appointment.'

Another philandering husband?

The inner office door opened at that point and Mort stuck his head out. 'Mrs Porter?'

Cash had it. She was Eileen Porter. Cash had been in the same class as her daughter Holly in the Loretto College on St Stephen's Green. They'd been quite friendly and only lost touch when Holly went on to study medicine at UCG.

The woman nodded. 'Mr Higgins?'

Mort opened his office door wide. 'Please, don't be nervous, come in.' Then to Cash he mouthed the word 'coffee' and raised his eyebrows in a question. Cash nodded and filled the kettle. Mort and Mrs Porter disappeared into the inner office.

After she had brought in the coffee, Cash finished work for the day and went home, leaving Mort and Eileen Porter discussing whatever problem it was that Eileen had brought along.

She was tempted to stop in at the Palace for some strong drink to lift her spirits, but in the end couldn't be bothered. There were bound to be people there she knew, and she didn't feel like being sociable. Instead she went straight on home to Templebar and veg'd out on the sofa, watching TV, eating chocolate and generally ignoring her problems in the hope that they would go away.

Chapter Two

Due to a strike by the maintenance men, the lift was still out of order. Sister Jude sighed. It had been six weeks now and repeated calls to Dublin Corporation had proved futile.

Phrases such as 'out of our hands' and 'beyond our control' and 'if it were only up to me' were no consolation. The fact remained that a number of less mobile residents had been marooned in their homes since the second lift had broken down four weeks previously. It was all too bad.

She rearranged the shopping carriers so that the thin plastic handles cut a little less into the palms of her hands and headed for the stairs, mentally girding her loins for the climb.

By the time she reached the fifth floor her breathing was laboured. She stopped and put down her bags, giving herself time to catch her breath.

At the age of fifty-one, Sister Jude was becoming increasingly irritated by her body and the way it failed to co-operate with her these days. She had never had any problem with the stairs before this. In fact, the twice-daily climb over the past six weeks should have resulted in an improved state of fitness, not the opposite. Maybe I'm just tired, she thought. Maybe that's it.

She sighed impatiently, picked up her bags and offered it up for the holy souls. It occurred to her, as she stood back against the wall to avoid three kids who were tearing down the stairs full pelt, that maybe there was no such thing as a holy soul any more. Had purgatory been abolished at the same time as limbo? On second thoughts, what did it matter anyway?

A voice bellowed down the stairs. 'Get back up here, ye little fuckers!'

Sister Jude continued to climb.

'I said get back here, ye little bastards, or I'll beat the shite outta ye . . . Oh . . . sorry, Sister.'

'Don't worry about it, Mrs McKenna.'

On the eighth landing, Sister Jude sagged with relief and gratefully covered the last couple of metres to her door. The flat was in darkness. The girls weren't back yet.

She unpacked the shopping and filled the kettle. That's what she needed. A caffeine shot. That would liven her up.

Those not personally acquainted with Sister Jude would have difficulty in putting an age on her, but they would be in no doubt of her calling. She was tall, but carried the extra half-stone that middle age had slapped on her hips well. Statuesque some might describe her, if she didn't look so dowdy. But, then, nuns were hardly expected to be fashionable.

She wore her grey hair straight and short, and usually favoured the same navy polyester trousers or pleated skirt, with a white polo-neck and navy cardigan or V-necked sweater. Her only adornment was a chunky silver cross on the long chair she always wore around her neck.

Hard to imagine that she was once a child of the sixties. Had done the sex, drugs and rock and roll thing. Had slept with Brian Jones. She had never been a holy Joe. A cruel twist of fate had given her a late vocation.

The kettle boiled and she made a pot of strong coffee, one of her few indulgences – along with one secret pack of Benson & Hedges a week – and sat down at the kitchen table.

She *was* tired. Weary. Not surprising. Since Omagh she'd been having the dreams again and she was sleeping badly because of it. Almost afraid to close her eyes. After twenty-five years the images were as vivid as ever. Broken bodies, torn limbs. Scorched air, burning flesh. And the screaming. The moaning.

Unconsciously she rubbed her arm where the shrapnel had torn a small chunk of flesh away from the bone. The flesh had healed long ago. She had thought she was over it until Omagh had brought it all back.

She heard the front door open and a moment later Sandra strolled into the kitchen.

'What's for the tea?'

'I'm fine, thanks, Sandra. And how was your day?'

Sandra leaned against the door frame. 'Okay, I s'pose. Except for tha' spa Mr Moran. He hasn't a clue, wha'?'

Sandra was thirteen going on thirty. She had been placed in Sister Jude's care by the Eastern Health Board. It was felt that, as Sandra had repeatedly absconded from children's homes, a less structured place of care was preferable. After a difficult and traumatic start, it seemed to be working out.

Sister Jude had been caring for troubled youngsters for the past eight years. It had started by accident when she took in one of her pupils, Paula, who had turned up on her doorstep one night soaking wet and distressed, having been badly beaten by her stepfather and thrown out into the street in her nightdress.

Paula had stayed three years. Others followed. Some more successfully than others.

At the present time, as well as Sandra, she had the

care of Tiffany, fourteen, and seven and a half months pregnant as the result of sexual abuse by her uncle.

Of the two, Sandra was the easier. Although she could be sullen and at times cheeky, at heart she was a good-natured kid.

Tiffany, on the other hand, was unpredictable and prone to temper tantrums. Not surprising under the circumstances. Allowances had to be made to a degree. Time would tell.

Sister Jude tried as far as it was possible to run a domestic democracy. She felt it was good training for the youngsters, all of whom had come from dysfunctional backgrounds and had no understanding of any alternative way of solving problems other than by means of confrontation and violence.

Sometimes, when there would be an incident, she wondered if she was kidding herself that she could make a difference. But on balance she'd had more successes than failures. She felt, on her better days, that she *had* made a difference. On her not-so-better days she just hoped so.

Sandra slumped down at the table. She was a lumpy ungainly girl, prone to greasy hair and spots. 'Where's Tiff?'

'She had an appointment with her social worker.' Sister Jude refilled her coffee mug. 'She should be back soon. Have you homework to finish?'

Sandra nodded. 'A bit. I can do it tomorra.'

Sister Jude smiled. 'Don't forget my essay. It's supposed to be in by Monday. Why don't you go and get started while I get the tea ready, then you'll be free for the day tomorrow?'

Sandra gave an exaggerated sigh and heaved herself up from the table. It was all show, of course. She was exceptionally gifted at English, despite coming from a family whose vocabulary barely included anything other than the most basic of Anglo-Saxon expletives. 'Can I watch *Home an' Away*?'

'I'll call you when it's time.'

By seven-thirty, when *Coronation Street* came on and Tiffany still hadn't put in an appearance, Sister Jude began to get anxious.

'Chill ou', Sister.' Sandra tried to make light of it. 'She'll be back. Where else has she t' go?'

'Did she say anything to you? Did she say she had plans?'

Sandra shrugged. 'Dunno.'

The next moment the door flew open and Tiffany breezed in. Sister Jude's first instinct was to demand an explanation. She opened her mouth to speak, but something stopped her. Later, on reflection, she realised it was the look of utter joy on the young girl's face. She was glowing.

'Sorry I'm late. I met these really cool people. Is there any tea left?'